Lake

of

Three

Sorrows

Clifton LaBree

Published by
Fading Shadows Imprint
New Boston, New Hampshire

PAPERBACK ISBN-10: 0-9746450-2-8
EBOOK ISBN: 978-1-943329-11-3

Cover Design by Vivian LaBree

FORWARD

When American soldiers arrived in France in 1918 the war against Germany was going badly for the Allies. After four years of bloodshed, the Allied and German soldiers were on the verge of exhaustion and collapse. A generation of young men had already been sacrificed on the killing fields of France and the end was not yet in sight. The cocky Yanks were determined to show the world that they were not so consumed with soft living that they could not fight. They were innocent and had a lot to learn, but they were also eager to do their part. Shortly after entering combat, their over-confidence quickly turned to respect for their Allied comrades who had been fighting the Germans for so long.

By mid-1918 the powerful German Army was poised for an assault on Paris. If successful, the attack would mean the end of the war. The Allied command worried that they could not stop a determined German effort to capture Paris. The future looked grim! After years of painful attrition, despair and defeatism were commonplace.

At this low point in morale, the intrepid Americans were given a decisive section of their own at the front that was most threatened by the German advance toward Paris. Within days the inexperienced American Divisions had challenged the enemy with a ferocity and determination that brought the German momentum to a halt. The Allies witnessed the Yanks defeat one of the strongest European armies ever put into the field, and they did it with an élan and valor that won the admiration of nations around the world.

The American citizen-soldiers even surprised themselves. It had taken them a while to adjust to combat, for they were inexperienced and poorly equipped for war. Likewise, the casualties they suffered during their first few days had shattered any preconceived notions of warfare. A difficult emotional adjustment was required of them as well. However, the American doughboy was famous for his resourcefulness, and adapted to various military situations quicker and more effectively than the European troops, because they were not hindered by inflexible traditions. He never failed to rise to the occasion at every level of command each time that extra bit of effort was needed.

Despite the phenomenal odds against them, they marched to the front with an air of invincibility in stark contrast to the French and British soldiers, whose units had suffered untold brutalities in frontal assaults that had accomplished nothing for the Allied cause. Consequently, the Allied soldiers no longer believed that their cause could be won; they had simply seen and been through too much. Despite their deeply entrenched cynicism, they were encouraged by the determination and willingness of the Yanks to close with the Germans. Morale was quickly boosted and the Allied cause seemed reborn with a new sense of nobility and honor. When the French high command warned the American forces that they wouldn't be able to stop the Germans, the Yanks collectively shrugged their shoulders and proceeded to stop the enemy everywhere the lines were held by American soldiers. They saved Paris for future generations, and rekindled the prospect of victory when it had seemed unattainable just a short time before.

The United States entered the conflict because it was a just and righteous cause. The untried Yanks had crossed the cold Atlantic to fight a type of war they knew little about for a people they hardly knew. American citizen-soldiers had marched to war in defense of liberty and freedom for all of mankind, asking nothing for their heavy sacrifices. They were like a breath of fresh air to the war weary peoples of France and Belgium, bringing hope where there was despair, and victory where there was stalemate and defeat. It was a selfless act of charity by the American people unequaled by any other nation in the world, and their contribution was decisive.

Chapter One

First Lieutenant Dale Cooper was one of the first Americans sent to France. He was a tall, slender man with unruly sandy hair and an easy grace to the way he moved. He was not particularly muscular, but he had endurance and stamina and the men in his command admired his ability to take long marches with ease. The characteristic most people liked about him was his indomitable spirit and cheerfulness even when things were not going well. However, it was his loyalty to and affection for the men under his command that sealed their respect and trust for the Lieutenant.

The lowly infantrymen, who had the unenviable job of facing the enemy's rifle and bayonet, were quick to spot sincerity or deception in their officers. They took note of Lieutenant Cooper's consistent and unwavering concern for their welfare. They saw how he badgered the quartermasters for adequate foods and supplies and his constant efforts to obtain hot food and coffee for the troops.

Lieutenant Cooper never shirked or degraded the importance of orders given his platoon, fulfilling any mission conceived by higher authority was their only reason for being. Nevertheless, Dale made certain to examine every aspect of every assignment, in order to minimize the cost to his men. He was a soldier from the top of his unruly sandy hair to the tip of his steel-toed shoes and carried himself with pride and dignity. He was always up front with his men leading by example rather than issuing commands from a safe rear area. It was a world of violence, chaos, and extreme exhaustion unlike anything Dale had ever experienced. The sound of the guns, and the mournful cries of wounded men during the intermittent lulls between explosions, would haunt him for the rest of his life.

Everyone was afraid, and the physical environment seemed to embody that fear, especially when the Germans started to shell the sector for days without relief. For as far as the eye could see, the landscape was plowed into grotesque shapes from the merciless artillery. Black soil was pulverized into a fine powder-like consistency that clung to everything when it was moistened. Gaping craters and loose debris littered the once productive farmland.

There wasn't a living tree or shrub visible for miles. Majestic oaks which had once lined the roadways, were now stark shreds of tree trunks dotting the landscape like silent sentinels beseeching an uncaring God for an end to the turmoil and destruction. Gone, also, were the gentle birds that had inhabited the once lush canopies. The desolation and unrelenting destruction of the landscape contributed to the mens' worst fears that the violence would never end. Death and the threat of death were constant companions. Those who experienced the trench fighting in France would never again look upon life the same way. Most found relief in letters from loved ones and recollections of a happier time in their lives. It was a direct link to pleasant memories that helped maintain their sanity.

Lieutenant Cooper was singularly moved by the young soldiers killed in action. He took their losses personally, and spent a good deal of time in his dimly-lit underground bunker, trying to explain their deaths to the mothers, wives, and sweethearts. Yet, try as he might, Dale never found a satisfactory way to describe the deaths of his men without inflicting additional pain and suffering on their loved ones. This was the part of his job as a leader that he most hated. He was painfully aware that anything he might write after imparting the brutal news of their death was insignificant and probably never read at all. Additionally, the news of a soldier's death invariably raised the unspoken question as to whether the loss was the result of incompetent preparation and leadership on the lieutenant's part. He was overcome with a sense of inadequacy each time he reached for a clean sheet of paper and pen to announce the death of still another comrade-in-arms.

Dale had graduated from the University of Maine with a degree in forestry and military science. A short time after he graduated from college he was commissioned as an infantry platoon leader in the Maine National Guard. It was activated into the Regular Army that same year, as a part of the expeditionary forces being sent to France. By the time Dale's regiment arrived in France it had been so altered by the addition of specialty units and replacement troops that it lost its identity as a Maine National Guard organization.

One of the original members from Maine was Staff Sergeant Bernie Johnson, a tall, muscular, raw-boned Swede with blond hair, blue eyes, and a brusque no-nonsense manner. Like Dale, Bernie was also from Monson. He had graduated from Monson Academy and immediately went to work in the Monson slate quarries where he soon became well-known as a man completely impervious to heights. Bernie's job at the quarry included the erection and maintenance of large swinging booms used to hoist slate from the deep open pits, and to transport workmen to and from the cavernous openings that extended several hundred feet below ground-level. The booms were positioned at the edge of a reinforced platform beside the pit, and were anchored by thick steel cables. The workmen were hoisted to the lower depths of the pit in small boxes suspended at the end of the steel cables, where they blasted and cut large chunks of slate that were lifted to the surface.

The pulleys at the top of the wooden booms required daily lubrication for safe operation. The agile Bernie Johnson was proud of his responsibility. He made the ascent to the top of the booms with precise deliberate movements, firmly planting each foot on one evenly spaced steel rod before moving on to the next. It was difficult for some of the workers to watch Bernie make the climb. Every once in awhile, after he had greased the pulleys and carefully inspected their fastenings, he would effortlessly pull his full length to the top of the boom and do a headstand by grasping two of the guy cables and stretching his two legs into a "v" position.

His fellow workers below held their breath at Bernie's fearlessness. The derrick was over one hundred feet above the ground, and positioned several hundred feet above the dark hole below. Any miscalculation on his part meant certain death, but the risk did not seem to bother the burly Swede. Whenever he was asked about it, he would shrug his shoulders and answer: "It's a job and pays the bills."

Dale Cooper and Bernie Johnson had known each other long before the war. They grew up together attending the same school. Dale was two years younger than Bernie, but they shared many fond memories of the small rural community. Bernie's and Dale's families lived on the outskirts of town on the southern shore of Lake Hebron, on the same road. The Coopers passed the Johnson homestead whenever they went to or from the village. As such they were well acquainted.

The Johnson family had four children, three boys and one girl. Bernie was the oldest. The girl, Lenore, was the same age as Dale. With her long blonde curls and laughing blue eyes, Lenore had been the prettiest girl in Dale's class. Her good looks and easy-going personality had made her very popular. Every young man in town competed for her attention. Dale was no exception. He had loved her ever since the first grade. By the time they graduated from Monson Academy high school, Dale and Lenore were a frequent twosome at school and town events.

Dale had lost touch with many of his friends after he left for college at Orono. Going away to school was a big step for him and he was extremely homesick his first semester. Lenore faithfully wrote to him all the four years he was at college, and they spent as much time together as possible when he returned home for vacations and holiday breaks. Overall, it was a happy time in their lives. Their love for each other grew with each ensuing parting, for they knew that their future held a promise of still greater happiness and fulfillment. With visions of a lifetime with Lenore ahead of him, Dale threw himself into his studies with intense dedication. He wanted nothing more than to have Lenore at his side. Each completed semester brought him closer to the realization of that dream. When America entered the war, everything changed. Dreams and plans for the future were postponed.

Just about everyone in the small town of Monson thought Dale and Lenore were a perfect match. The statuesque Lenore and tall slender Dale made an attractive couple and everyone who know them simply assumed that one day they would marry. After all, they had the knack of being able to read each others' thoughts and were tolerant of the areas in which they disagreed. Dale was the more serious of the two, but he enjoyed Lenore's zest for life, and she loved his unique blend of seriousness and humor. They were truly a couple in love.

Located in the north central portion of Maine between the organized townships and the vast spruce-fir forests of the north, the little town of Monson was comprised of hardworking families who rarely had much in the way of financial wealth. Money was scarce and everyone worked hard just to provide for the essentials of daily living. The townspeople never thought of themselves as poor, because everyone was struggling the same way. Support for those in need came from neighbors and families, for everybody at one time or another had needed a helping hand.

Hard times in Monson had created a community spirit that pulled people together to function as a group rather than as isolated individuals. For instance, each year virtually everyone participated in the annual winter ice-cutting project on Lake Hebron. When the ice on the lake was ready for "harvest", a large circular saw powered by a gasoline engine mounted on a sled was pulled along the surface cutting large slabs of ice, each about two feet by eight feet long. Strong men wrenched the slabs out of the water and packed them on horse drawn sleds, which then carried them to several ice houses conveniently scattered around town. The ice slabs were packed tightly in the center of these temporarily built structures and insulated with a layer of sawdust a foot or more thick on the sides and top of the ice pack. The ice kept all summer until it was used in the iceboxes to preserve food. Dale and his friends used to lay on the top of the pack during hot humid days.

Dale's assignment as a platoon leader in the first battalion of the regiment was a fortunate coincidence: Bernie was to be his platoon sergeant. Ironically the two became better acquainted than they ever had been growing up, as they underwent extensive training prior to and after being shipped to France. Even though Dale was Bernie's commanding officer, their relationship was warm and friendly. Dale relied heavily on Bernie's knowledge and experience. Bernie watched Dale handle the responsibilities of command and was impressed with his dedication to the men in the platoon. In fact Bernie thought his baby sister was making an excellent choice in her husband-to-be and told Dale so. Bernie's simple declaration meant a great deal to Dale, for he knew that Bernie was never one to make rash statements.

During an intense battle on the road leading from Metz to Paris, the regiment was ordered to maintain a blocking position to stop the main German advance toward Paris. It was a heavily contested fight. The Americans held their ground. Not only did they stop the Germans all along the attacking front, they slowly began to push them back. The losses were horrendous on both sides. The dead and wounded outnumbered those surviving physically unscathed, and nobody escaped the emotional trauma of the ordeal. One of the many casualties of the battle was Sergeant Bernie Johnson. A machine gun had caught him in the open, nearly slicing him in two. He died instantly. Bernie's death gave Dale a nauseous feeling that he had failed Lenore's family. Sleepless nights filled with guilt and visions of unspeakable horror weakened him.

Several days later, Dale's regiment was relieved. They pulled back to a relatively calm sector where they could receive replacements and take some well earned rest. Dale did not welcome the respite period, for now he was faced with the daunting task of writing letters of notification to the families of his deceased men. He had lost seventy-five percent of his platoon during the two-day blocking maneuver. The battalion Chaplain helped him draft a statement that could be incorporated into each letter. Given the sheer number of men killed in action, Dale reluctantly used the form letter for most of his notifications.

His first letter after being pulled from the line was to Bernie's family. Artillery barrages beyond the distant hills continued to light the sky with flashes of fire, and explosions ripped through the stillness of the night:

> Somewhere in France
> September 30, 1918

Dear Mr. and Mrs. Johnson and Family;

I write you tonight with great reluctance and a heavy heart. I am obliged to inform you that your son Bernie was killed in action two days ago when the regiment was holding the Metz - Paris road. We successfully stopped the Germans but it cost us dearly. One of our losses was Bernie who performed heroically. I share the sadness and despair this letter brings to your family. I loved him like a brother and have been tormented by his death. I'm thankful to know that he welcomed me as a future brother-in-law with an open heart.

Bernie's men also loved him and they share our sorrow. I hate the fact that I have to be the bearer of such horrible news. I can imagine the pain that you're all feeling as you read these lines because I feel the same pain. I pray that you can find some consolation in the fact that Bernie's death was instantaneous. He did not suffer. He was killed by a German machine gun when he exposed himself to the enemy while searching for one of his wounded men. You know how he was. He was immune to danger and in many ways he seemed to live a charmed life. His exploits at the Kineo Quarry will be remembered for as long as we live.

I'm thankful I had a chance to get to know Bernie better after we shipped out for France. In many ways he was the same carefree Bernie that I'd known in Monson, but I also saw a more sober and serious side to his disposition that I'd never seen before. He was determined to make his family proud. He certainly loved you, Lenore, and enjoyed being the big brother who watched out for you.

My thoughts and prayers are with you in this time of great sorrow. I share your loss, for Bernie was my responsibility, and I lost him for all of us.

Respectfully,
Dale Johnson

When he had finished, Dale folded the letter and carefully sealed it. He was exhausted, and couldn't remember when he had last had a full night's rest. He stretched out on the folding army cot and instantly fell asleep.

Later that night gunfire woke him from a deep slumber. Lying there in the darkness, unable to sleep, Dale's thoughts turned to Lenore. It was comforting to escape from the horrors of the battlefield to a time that was soft and warm, when life had been sweet. Tonight, though, Dale was troubled by Bernie's death, and he had not heard from Lenore for the past two weeks. Mail call had not been consistent, but the higher command did their best to make sure that mail got to the men on the front lines, at least every other day. Letters from home were the men's most treasured items, and served as the main source of morale during prolonged periods of combat. No mail opened the doors to depression and uncertainty. Though Dale had been sick about the lack of news, he hadn't said anything to anyone. He was worried that something had happened.

His regiment participated in some of the heaviest fighting of the war around the Argonne sector, and was no longer an effective fighting unit. Casualties were over sixty percent, so they were once again rotated out of the line and transported by four-wheel-drive trucks to a safe area near Paris. It was a weary group of soldiers who climbed out of the fetid trenches to the waiting trucks. No one talked much, merriment seemed out of place. Each man thanked his God that he had survived the ferocious battles, and looked forward to the hot food and real beds that awaited them.

The soldiers in Dale's platoon were housed in several French homes located in a small village. The French people were anxious to show their appreciation to the weary Yanks, and treated them generously. Strong bonds of friendship were formed between them.

By this time, however, Dale was desperate for word from Lenore. At each mail call he prayed for a letter, and day after day was disappointed. Then, one day his heart leaped when he spied Lenore's handwriting on a letter placed on his field desk by the platoon sergeant. His hands shook with relief, so much so that he had trouble opening the envelope. He scanned the first page quickly for news and the cruel words struck him with the force of a physical blow. He sat in order to steady himself. Dale reread the first page, again and again, desperately hoping that he had somehow misread Lenore's words. He had not:

My Dearest Dale,

I've put off writing this letter for several weeks now, but the time has come when I cannot keep it a secret any longer. You deserve the truth, no matter how difficult it may be for you to understand. By the time you receive this letter, I'll be married to Stanley Moore. I'm pregnant with his child. Please forgive me.

Since you went away, I've been lonely and worried. Stan has been most attentive to me and there's no other way but for us to get married. I think highly of Stan, but I do still love you. All the dreams and plans we shared for the future are still dear to me, but this child that I am carrying has changed all of that. Please don't hate me, Dale. I've prayed for guidance, and the marriage to Stan seems to be the best for all concerned.

Please believe me when I told you I loved you. I meant it with all my heart and still mean it. You'll always carry a part of me with you, Dale. I cannot deny those feelings, but Providence has dictated that I cannot be your wife.

Forgive me dearest, Dale. You'll always be in my thoughts. I pray for your safe return home.

Lenore

Chapter Two

Dale suffered the bitter pains of rejection and loss in silence, shaking his head in disbelief. Lenore had failed him at a time when he most needed her support.

Over the next few days, Dale directed his anger and frustration towards the only place he could, the enemy, displaying a reckless disregard for his own safety. The men noticed the change in him and correctly guessed the root cause to be his sweetheart back home. His company commander, Captain Lyle Barrett, was one of the first to notice that Dale was tempting fate at the front lines, so he paid a visit to Dale's platoon command post one evening.

"What's wrong with you, Dale?" Captain Barrett asked bluntly, puffing his pipe. "To be perfectly frank, I'm worried about you. You're beginning to act like a one-man-army and I won't tolerate that kind of behavior in my command. Either you pull yourself together and start taking better care of yourself and your platoon, or I'll find someone to replace you. The choice is yours. If you continue the way you're going, you'll get yourself killed and the platoon will suffer for your foolhardiness."

"I don't want to be relieved, Captain Barrett," declared Dale, stunned to learn how close he was to losing his platoon. "I admit I haven't been myself lately, but I promise to correct the deficiency."

Captain Barrett was a small dark-haired man with a reputation of a perfectionist. He had his finger on the pulse of the company and was very perceptive when something was not running routinely. He meticulously calculated everything he did. Dale and Captain Barrett had worked well together since they had left the United States.

"Is there anything I can do to help, Lieutenant?" inquired the captain.

"No, Sir," answered Dale hesitantly. "My problems are personal. To be real honest about it, I'm having trouble accepting something I never dreamed could happen to me."

"Well, I can understand personal problems, but you know as well as I that we're dealing with men's lives here. If personal problems interfere with your responsibility to the men, then I have no other alternative but to relieve you at once."

"I understand that, Sir," said Dale. "If I was in your position, I'd do the same thing, but I promise to do better."

"My reason for coming to see you is twofold. First, I wanted to speak with you about your erratic behavior, then I wanted to talk to you about an opening for a company commander in the regiment." The captain studied Dale's reaction. "If I recommend you for the opening can you assure me that you'll get back to work and perform to your usual high standards?"

"Yes, Sir. I realize that I've handled a personal problem very badly by letting it interfere with the welfare of my men. I'd be grateful for the opportunity to lead a company."

"Well, Lieutenant," said Captain Barrett with a decisive nod, knocking the ashes from his pipe. "I've already recommended you for the opening and it's been approved by regiment. Your promotion to captain is also part of the package."

"Thank you, Sir," Dale replied, offering his hand to his superior. "I appreciate your confidence in me and won't let you down."

"Report to regiment first thing in the morning, Lieutenant. Your new company is part of the second battalion which is holding the line adjacent to the Canadian Division on our left flank. You'll be working closely with them. I've admired your instinctive concern for the men and the way you've been able to rally them and execute difficult missions. I'm glad I don't have to relieve you on the basis of your behavior these past few days. You've always been a man of your word and I'll hold you to it. Good luck, Dale."

"Thank you, Sir. You won't be sorry."

The added duties of running a company of infantrymen helped Dale to get his mind off Lenore. An Army company is comprised of three platoons and is the basic organization unit of the Army where personal records and files were maintained. Now Dale had three platoons to be concerned with instead of just one. He worked tirelessly getting to know his new men. The new position of increased responsibility demanded an adjustment. He would have to be a little less personal in the way he handled the company than he had a platoon. After Dale's arrival at the company command post, the abutting Canadian Division's Chief of Staff, Colonel Gerard Clough, visited the headquarters, to introduce himself to Dale and to size up the new company commander.

"Captain Cooper, I'm your Canadian neighbor and I just wanted to say congratulations and hello," said Colonel Clough in a booming voice. He was a tall, broad-shouldered officer with blond hair and an authoritative air which belied his easy-going nature. He displayed a unique aptitude for liaison with nearby forces and evaluating tactical situations. In addition, Colonel Clough's extensive experience in police work made him an expert at assessing the officers in the units he visited.

Dale met the towering Colonel Clough with a salute. "Welcome to our command post, Colonel. I'm new at this job so I'm glad to learn that your experienced Canadian Division is on my flank. May I offer you some coffee, Sir?" asked Dale, holding up a fresh pot.

Colonel Clough accepted the offer. "There's a nip in the air today, Captain. I'd be delighted to join you."

"The mess sergeant just sent this pot to me along with a tray of warm bread," Dale said, pouring each a cup of hot coffee. "Commanding a company has its advantages, at least we control the mess facilities."

"Ah yes, rank does have its privileges," agreed Colonel Clough, helping himself to the tray of fresh bread taking a seat beside Dale. "Where are you from, Captain?"

"I was born and raised in central Maine. I attended the University of Maine where I studied Forestry and went through four years of the Reserve Officers Training Corps. The Maine National Guard offered me a commission after graduation, so I joined and was activated to regular status. We became part of the first United States echelons to land in France. What about you, Sir?"

Colonel Clough told Dale that he had functioned in several different positions since the war started, but none of them had involved direct command of troops. In fact the Colonel was, by profession, a Royal Canadian Mounted Policeman, who had joined the Army with a Mounted Police battalion when the war started. There was an air of invincibility and strength about the man that was reassuring.

"I can tell you that I'll be glad for this blooming war to be finished so that I can return home to my wife, and get on with my police work," remarked the colonel.

"You echo our sentiments, Sir. How long do you think it will be?" Dale asked curiously.

"That's a big question, Yank," answered Colonel Clough thoughtfully. "But I think we're near the end. Before you Yanks entered the lines this past summer, it was my impression that the war wouldn't continue another month before everyone just collapsed from exhaustion and we'd have a stalemate. But when the United States finally organized its formations into the superb fighting force you have become, you rallied all of us with your spirit and courage. Now, we've stopped the Huns cold in their tracks and even started pushing them back toward Germany. They're a formidable foe, and I think we've got them on the run, this time for good."

"The fighting is much worse than I ever expected it to be," Dale told him, thinking of all the American lives that had already been lost. "It's hard to prepare for the actualities of war until you experience it first hand."

"That's the main argument for exhaustive training beforehand, so that routines that can save lives and secure missions become instinctive, without need for second thought or contemplation. War affects everybody differently. Its long-range impact on the life of a participant depends on the person. Nobody's exempt from the trauma."

"Have you been in combat very long, Colonel?"

"I've seen enough to last me for a lifetime. I yearn for the peace of mind and solitude of the Canadian forests back home. Just to watch the sun set behind the snow-capped western mountains and to watch the fiery symphony of the aurora borealis will be an answer to my prayers."

"We have the same prayers, Sir," Dale added.

By September and October the Allies had begun to gain momentum against the German forces in the Argonne Forest region when, the entire line was abruptly ordered to hold in place pending further orders. It was November 10, 1918, a date that Dale would remember the rest of his life. Neither side fired a shot. In fact the silence along the line was the most memorable part of the day. For the first time in months the men could talk without shouting and they could hear their watches ticking without holding them to their ears. The Canadian Division on Dale's left flank sent a message by runner with the following announcement:

> Dear Captain Cooper:
> All units of the Canadian 44th Division have been ordered to cease fire and remain alert in position until further notice. I'm assuming that you've received similar orders. If not, please inform the messenger. Let's hope this means peace!
> Respectfully,

Colonel Gerard Clough
Chief of Staff,
Canadian 44th Division

Dale stared at the young Canadian dispatch-runner for a second after reading the message and thought about his Canadian neighbors. They were good soldiers, and they had borne the heaviest of the fighting for the past four years. Their reputation for tenacity and valor was well deserved. While they operated under the same rules of engagement and from the same tactical manual as the British Army, the Canadians possessed an independent streak atypical of the British Isles troops. In that respect, the Canadians resembled the Americans more than the British Commonwealth forces. Dale only hoped that Colonel Clough's prophecy was correct.

At eleven o'clock on the eleventh day of the eleventh month the battlefield was filled with cheers from soldiers on both sides of the line, a welcome alternative to gunfire. The fighting was over! The men of Dale's company embraced each other amidst spontaneous yells and cries of thanksgiving. The previously contested "no-man's-land" between the opposing forces was now filled with tearfully relieved soldiers from both armies. The euphoria of surviving the cataclysmic conflict was felt just as deeply, by the Germans.

For the first time since the war started, open fires burned bright and welcoming across the silent battlefields. And the coffee! Coffee, that life-sustaining brew that cold soldiers constantly dreamed about and seldom obtained, was being brewed at every bonfire where a suitable pot could be found. Company kitchens worked feverishly keeping up with the demand. Here and there a few German soldiers hesitantly approached the fire-lit circles of the Americans to warm themselves and to share the warming brew now offered them by their former enemy.

It quickly became clear to the Yanks that, near the war's end the Germans had been poorly served by their supply companies. Despite the jubilance of the German soldiers on this occasion of peace, they had suffered greatly from the lack of food and medical supplies. Their uniforms were tattered and they staggered from physical and emotional exhaustion. The Yanks looked upon their former foes and realized that they were just like themselves... frightened, hungry, and thankful to be alive. The soldier who risks death at any moment shares a universal bond of fraternity and brotherhood with every other soldier; they are kindred spirits, regardless of the uniform they wear or the language they speak. The Americans could not help but welcome them.

Dale ordered his company mess attendants and cooks to wind up their field kitchens to run at capacity with no restrictions. One of the bakers even managed to turn out several chocolate cakes with white frosting to celebrate the armistice. The ensuing celebration would be etched forever in Dale's memory.

The evening was cool with a harsh tinge of winter in the air. Bright fires burned joyfully as far as the eye could see. The company's mess attendants set up makeshift tables filled with cakes, sandwiches, and coffee between two of the roaring bonfires. A spontaneous call went out to the German soldiers across the devastated battlefield to help themselves for as long as the food lasted. Only a few men came, hesitantly, at first, then more and more wandered over as they saw that the Americans' invitation was sincere.

A small group of four German soldiers entered the lighted circle of the bonfires carrying a small litter holding a very young and obviously severely wounded soldier. The Germans carefully placed the litter on the ground near the food tables and propped the young soldier into a sitting position. His blond hair was matted with dried blood, and a white blood-stained bandage encircled his head, covering his eyes. The soldier's legs were wrapped in soiled blankets still wet from the blood. Most conspicuous, however, was the empty shirtsleeve that hung limp from his right elbow. Touched by the Germans' trust and by the young soldier's obvious pain, Dale's mess attendants hurried to serve the young soldier's friends. One of his

17

comrades accepted a cup of coffee, placing the handle into the shaking hand of the injured soldier. The Americans watched as the wounded soldier slowly lifted the cup to his trembling lips and tasted the warm, sweet liquid. A slow smile came over his face.

"Thank you," he said in hesitant, understandable English.

A young American soldier from Pennsylvania, moved by the scene, took a large piece of chocolate cake from the table, knelt beside the wounded German and held a piece of cake to his lips. The German took a bite and chewed slowly as if to savor the taste. Soon tears started to flow from beneath the bandage covering his eyes. The American noted the tears and gently wiped them from the wounded man's grimy face, continuing to feed his former enemy the chocolate cake.

Someone in the group, no one could remember exactly who it was, began to sing the forlorn and beautiful ballad, "Lily Marlene". Its plaintive refrain, known to friend and foe alike, echoed across the stillness of the night:

> "…Your sweet face seems to haunt my dreams,
> "My Lilly of the lamplight,
> My own Lilly Marlene, My own Lilly Marlene…"

All five stanzas were sung in that hauntingly sad tempo familiar to all. The music and its message touched everyone's heart transcending language and nationality. The longing of a loved one and the sweet recollection of precious memories were a daily companion of the soldier's harsh life.

After the young soldier had eaten, Dale called for two stretcher bearers and an ambulance to transport him to the nearest hospital. As he was carried from the field, the young soldier raised his good arm in salute. His comrades watched sadly knowing that even proper medicine might not be sufficient to save their young comrade, given the severity of his wounds. One could not contain his emotions any longer, and wept openly as he said good-bye.

For a while the mood lightened and everyone forgot the war, allowing themselves the luxury of dreaming about the loved ones they would soon be returning to. Surviving the cauldron they had just experienced would prove to be their greatest achievement. No longer must they suffer the fear of being wounded, the hopeless longing for loved ones far away, or the disappointment of rations that failed to arrive. These and countless other hardships were also shared by their enemy counterparts. The exultation of being spared from the crucibles of war was a glorious feeling common to all. They had looked death in the eye and survived the ordeal, and that made them a part of a select and lucky fraternity. It had left a permanent mark on all of their lives. The men would return to their homes and loved ones, but things would never be the same.

That night Dale had the best night's sleep since he arrived in France, despite the fact that he dreamed of Lenore and awoke with a feeling of loss and rejection. However, by the time he circulated among his platoon leaders the next morning his depression had passed. He joined with every man in his company in rejoicing over the order they had just received. They had been ordered to Paris where they were billeted in some French Army barracks for rest and relaxation. It was a boisterous bunch of Yanks who climbed aboard the four-wheel-drive Nash trucks for the trip to Paris.

Soon into the journey, a dispatch rider on a motorcycle pulled alongside the truck in which Dale was riding. The rider passed him a leather satchel. Upon opening it, Dale found several copies of records for some of his men and his current orders for the billeting of the men in Paris. There was also a letter addressed to him from Mr. Fred Olman, the soft spoken bespectacled principal of the high school in Monson. Curious as to why Mr. Olman was writing him, Dale tore the envelope open and read the enclosed letter:

October 10, 1918
Monson, Maine

Dear Dale,

I have the unfortunate obligation to inform you that both your mother and your father have fallen victim to the Asian flu epidemic, a horrible scourge that has wiped out ten percent of our Town. I promised your parents that I would write to tell you if they succumbed to the deadly disease. I'm so sorry to spring such terrible news on you without any preparation or warning. May God be with you and help you find the strength to accept that which God has done.

I was with your mother to the end. Her passing was peaceful and quick. The high fever made her unconscious towards the end, and she just slipped to another world where I'm sure she's at peace in the arms of Jesus Christ.

Your father was ill at the time and he took it very badly. It was after your mother's death that he made me promise to contact you. I honestly believe that he was ready to follow your mother, and he did so within a couple of days. They were two of the dearest friends I've ever had and I'm horrified that both passed in such a short period of time. My wife, Charlene, and I did all we could to make them comfortable, but the outcome was beyond our ability to change. Over thirty-five people have died in Monson so far. It's a tragedy that hasn't been fully comprehended yet, but when its magnitude sinks into our consciousness, we'll be in mourning for a long, long time.

I'm sorry, Dale, to be the messenger of such devastating news. You've certainly seen enough death on the battlefield. Have Linda, young man! Our prayers and thoughts are with you.

Fred and Charlene Olman

Color slowly drained from Dale's face as he folded the letter and placed it in his tunic pocket. Then he placed his head between his knees and wept, as his men sang merrily in the rear of the truck.

Chapter Three

Dale struggled to accept the news of his parents' death. He was an only child, and his world had evolved around his mother and father. Though he continued to maintain firm control of his company, Dale wondered what the future held for him. Lenore had married another man and his family was gone. Now, the prospect of returning home was uninviting. He only hoped that, in time, he would be better able to accept the changes that awaited him at the scene of his childhood.

Though the Armistice ended the primary mission of the Allied armies, a short period of occupational duty in Germany was required to ensure Germany's adherence to the Armistice agreement. A small American force was selected to take part in the occupation mission and Dale volunteered to stay for at least one year. Given the circumstances, time to sort out his life without the stress of combat would be welcome. In fact, Dale thought seriously of making a full-time career in the Army. An extended tour of duty in Europe would help him make up his mind.

And so, for the next year and a half Dale commanded an infantry company doing security work. The company was housed in Berlin, at what had once been a dormitory for a fashionable junior college. The job was much less demanding of his time and energy than what he had been accustomed to, and he was able to enjoy occasional leave days visiting several working forests in the Black Forest region of northern Germany.

Dale found that European forests were much more intensely managed than those in Canada or the United States. There was a neatness and a level of utilization of dead branches and smaller diameter sections of trees that would never be economically feasible with current North American forest harvesting methods. In Europe the local population of farmers and peasants were permitted to gather the residue of logging operations. These were known as "faggot rights". The local peasants used the smaller pieces as fuel to heat their homes. Observing the beautiful and productive park-like forests of Germany helped to re-ignite the passion that Dale always had for forests and their management. Once he had completed his current tour of duty, he was ready to return to Maine and become involved in forestry once again.

Despite his recent losses, this decision enabled Dale to arrive at an acceptable level of peace. He also used some of his leave time to visit Paris. He knew that the French were in the process of building a national monument to honor the thousands of unidentified patriots that had lost their lives in the service to their country. The "Tomb of the Unknown Soldier" was being constructed in the heart of Paris beneath the towering Arch de Triumph. An eternal flame burned within the tomb, a symbol of the unquenchable spirit of the dead young warriors who would remain unknown for eternity.

In the late Fall of 1919, Dale took several days leave to tour some of the battlefields in France where his company had served. It still sickened him to see the gaunt black stubs of broken trees standing as silent witnesses, giving their mute salute to the end of the savage struggle that had reduced them to shattered shreds of decaying wood, devoid of life.

Large cemeteries were being improved by the construction of memorials to the men buried in the hallowed ground. As far as the eye could see there were row upon row of graves marked with white crosses or Stars of David. It was a place of beauty and serenity which is a sad contradiction to the circumstances and environment that caused the death of so many young men. When Dale closed his eyes and listened to the heartbeat of the land, he could almost hear the rumble of gunfire beyond the distant horizon and feel the earth reverberate from their deadly discharge, but he knew that these were figments of his imagination. Soon the memory of ear-splitting artillery barrages would fade and disappear, and the memory of the valor and selflessness that also took place on this hallow ground, on both sides of the battlefield, would eventually fade away to the pages of history.

For every broken body buried beneath the blood drenched soil, there was a corresponding broken heart in the breast of a mother and father and possibly a wife or sweetheart. The value of the future is measured by the silent tears of the nation's mothers, who buried a part of their heart and soul with the mangled bones of their warrior sons.

Dale searched up and down the rows of graves looking for one grave in particular. He found it in the St. Mihiel Cemetery at Thiaucourt where a large stone sundial had been carved in the form of an American eagle with the following inscription: "Time Will Not Dim the Glory of Their Deeds." One of the American heroes of the vicious battle of St. Mihiel was Sergeant Bernie Johnson. The simple stone seemed such an inadequate reminder of the man he had admired and respected. His grave was surrounded by the graves of several officers who had been killed at the same time. Dale reflected on the aspect of equality and democracy that existed within the large cemetery, and was content that the contributions of all its occupants were equally important. The battlefield was the great equalizer of men.

These visits to the burial places of so many of the men Dale had known rekindled the pain and anger over the losses he himself had suffered. As a matter of fact, he had been in a sort of denial for the past year. It wasn't just the combat losses that troubled him deeply. He still found himself unable to fully face the fact that his mother and father were not alive back home in Maine waiting for him. In addition, Lenore still weighed heavily on his mind. Her betrayal and rejection, without just cause, still hurt, and Dale continued to struggle with acceptance.

A year and a half had passed since the death of his parents and loss of Lenore, and Dale still felt a deep yearning to return to some part of his past, to orient himself and to seek direction for the future. His searching heart was like a restless river urgently winding its way through the mountains on its journey to the sea. He felt, like that river, as if he was plummeting through the path of least resistance to some predetermined destination, praying that he would eventually find calmer waters and a safe harbor for his soul. His mental search for peace of mind always ended with a vision of his beloved Lake of Three Sorrows.

There were scenes from Dale's childhood that could still make him smile. They were the vivid memories of a small log cabin located on an isolated lake in the Maine wilderness known as the Lake of Three Sorrows. It was a calming place of beauty from which Dale had always drawn sustenance and renewal. The lake's crystal blue waters, and the stately cone-shaped spruce trees lining its shores, were the scene of some of Dale's most precious childhood memories.

The lake derived its name from the tragic death of an Indian mother and her young daughter and son. Dale first heard the story when he was very young from an elderly woodsman from Greenville who claimed to have witnessed the tragedy. As the old man told it, the Indian maiden had been paddling her canoe, with the two young children, along the northwesterly shore of the lake where raspberries and low bush blueberries grew in abundance. After they had filled several baskets to the brim with berries and placed them in the bottom of the canoe, they began paddling back towards their campsite on the south shore.

As they approached the center of the lake, however, a violent storm suddenly arose. The wind whipped the water into large waves which easily swamped the fragile birch bark canoe. The three occupants were thrown overboard into the surging water. The lake's outlet was on the western shore where large rock formations had been worn smooth by the water. The current at the outlet was swift and dangerous. When the terrified mother saw that her two children were being drawn by the strong current, she swam towards them to no avail; she simply was not strong enough to combat the force of the outlet current. Their three bodies were recovered later downstream where the river ran into a catchment basin of still water.

The lake's sobering history was incompatible with the pleasant memories the lake held for Dale. The small cabin on the north shore had been built on large rock formations towering twenty feet above the water by Dale's father and his uncles when Dale was a very young boy. A path led from the cabin down over the rocks to the water's edge, where a sturdy boat dock had been constructed from cedar pilings. The water at the end of the wharf was over ten feet deep. Dale had learned to swim by jumping off the wharf into the cool water with his father and uncles close by in case he needed assistance. He had become a strong swimmer, enjoying the lake's clear water.

The stream that entered the body of the Lake of Three Sorrows flowed over a four foot waterfall created from a broken piece of granite outcropping, then traveled rapidly along the rocky northern shore in an arc to the outlet. The most turbulent portion of the river was located at the lake's northern bank, where the rushing water flung itself against the rocky shore. At that point the churning water had undercut the granite outcrop so that a portion of the ledge hung ten feet over the turbulent water. The overhang was relatively flat and included a round tunnel-like hole about four feet in diameter through which one could see the water below. When the moon was visible on a clear evening, a bright ray of moonlight penetrated the opening, illuminating the cavern of churning waters below. Dale especially remembered those mornings when the water was colder than the surrounding air and the mist arising from the surface of the lake diffused the sunlight, creating a scene so magical that he could not look away.

For Dale, the Lake of Three Sorrows was as much an emotional experience as it was a physical body of water. Those experiencing its beauty found that the lake had the capacity to generate a wide range of sentiment and passion, from hope and enlightenment, to despair and stagnation. He and his family had found it inspiring.

The main trail to the cabin started in Greenville on the southeastern shore of Moosehead Lake. Located on land owned by the Great Northern Paper Company, his father paid easement rights of a dollar a year for ninety-nine years to the Company. The Maine Game Warden Service had occasionally sought its shelter.

The cabin and the lake seemed a long way from France. One day, in the spring of 1920, Dale received a notice from his regimental commander, Colonel Gregory Nelson, to report to headquarters as soon as possible. When Dale reported to Colonel Nelson's office, three company commanders were also present.

"I got here as fast as I could, Sir," Dale explained.

"I called this meeting to let you company commanders know that I just received orders from Division to close down our security operations in Germany," announced Colonel Nelson, walking to the map behind his desk. He was a heavyset man with broad shoulders who moved gracefully, projecting an air of authority and great strength. He also had the somewhat disconcerting habit of glaring at his subordinates for a fraction of a second before speaking. Many, including Dale, found the famous stare unnerving. "Right now Congress and the people who hold the purse strings want to demobilize the Army even more than they already have. Hence the elimination of our security patrols."

"How soon can we expect to be phased out?" Dale asked.

"You know how it is, Captain Cooper, we hurry up and wait until the politicians are satisfied, but I think we can expect mission termination within a couple of weeks. I've been asked to reduce manpower immediately."

This conference was not entirely unexpected by the company commanders. They knew that it was a temporary assignment, and only a question of time before demobilization orders arrived. On his part, Dale was still uncertain as to whether he would continue in the Army or resign his commission to pursue a career in forestry.

Colonel Nelson helped him make his mind up. "Captain Cooper, you're the only Reserve officer in the regiment, except for myself. Reserve officers will be allowed to retain their present rank if they transfer to inactive reserve status. Now I'm not asking you to resign, Captain Cooper, just pointing out an alternative for your consideration. Those desiring to remain in service will do so at a reduced rank to be determined by command billets available in the Army. As for myself, I'm ready to take early transfer. I came into the war with the New York National Guard and I'm ready to return home to my old job as a banker."

"This is kind of sudden," Dale replied.

"You should realize, Cooper, that with your combat experience, you'll be able to remain in service if you choose to do so," said Colonel Nelson, observing him carefully.

Dale had functioned well in the structured environment of the Army. Emotionally, he felt safe within the military's clear boundaries. Nevertheless, lately, he had been thinking more and more about returning home to Maine. He knew that sometime he had to face the reality of his parent's demise and he was more prepared to accept it now than he had been a year ago. The Lake of Three Sorrows also held a strong attraction for him. Finally, he informed the Colonel that he was selecting the Reserves, and thus he would retain his captain commission without any regrets.

A week later, Dale was relieved of his duties and immediately boarded a train for Cherbourg, where he had reserved berth space on an Army transport bound for New York City. Things happened so rapidly that he didn't have time to think about the chain of events that were sending him back home.

The ocean had always been a fascination for Dale who had lived all of his life many miles from the coast. The endless body of water filled his imagination with dreams and wonder about the people and places beyond the distant horizon. The constant turmoil and movement of the water had awakened within him a vitality and energy that he had not realized was missing from his life. The ocean's unlimited power and inherent dangers gave him the same feeling of awe as a panorama of unbroken green forest.

On the second day of the voyage, Dale was wakened by an urgent knocking at his cabin door. He sprang to open it and saw a troubled Colonel Gregory Nelson leaning against the door jamb in an advanced state of inebriation.

"I was hoping that you'd be on the ship, Dale. I apologize for my condition but I have something very important to ask of you…" Before he could finish the sentence, Colonel Nelson slid down the door jamb and passed out!

Chapter Four

Dale reacted quickly, dragging Colonel Nelson into the room, placing him on a sofa before anyone noticed his condition. This was an extraordinarily out-of-character performance for the colonel. He had a reputation among his fellow officers as a light drinker and meticulously circumspect in his behavior.

Later that evening, Dale learned a lot about his former commander. Colonel Nelson awoke from his alcohol-induced sleep with a headache and a desire to discuss a private matter with Dale. The New York City bank where Colonel Nelson was employed had financed a large section of land in the northern part of Canada. He was the agent responsible for approving the transaction, prior to his departure with the Army for Europe. Now, however, the person who borrowed the money had suddenly disappeared, and the bank was foreclosing on the property. The bank officials were holding Colonel Nelson responsible for approving the unpaid loan, leaving the Colonel's position with the bank in serious jeopardy.

The prospect of being fired had been too much for the proud officer. At the height of his inebriation and the depth of his indiscretion, Colonel Nelson remembered that Dale was a professional forester and was on the same ship. Maybe if Dale evaluated the situation and reported back to him, they could find an acceptable solution. Colonel Nelson understood that the tract was heavily forested, so Dale Cooper would be ideal for the project!

By the time the Army transport docked in New York City Dale and Gregg were on a first-name basis. Dale informed

Gregg that he would be staying at his parent's place for a while, and then, he planned to travel to an isolated location at the Lake of Three Sorrows for an undetermined period of time. Dale left Gregory the name and address of Fred Olman, the local high school principal, who would be able to get a message to Dale at either place and assured the Colonel that he would give any proposal regarding the Canadian land tract due consideration. The men said good-bye and shook hands warmly, both anxious to get home.

Dale took a taxi from the ship to Grand Central Station, where he boarded an overnight train to Maine. He was back in the United States at last. He had a satisfying feeling about the prospect of a temporary job. Gregory's project was a tangible opportunity to be productive and useful while Dale made up his mind about permanent employment as a forester. It seemed like a perfect answer to his concerns. However, his pleasant glow of anticipation soon faded. The closer to home Dale drew, the more troubled he became. The Colonel's project might occupy him for a while, but Dale knew that he could not think rationally about the future until he had dealt with the death of his parents, and the betrayal of Lenore. For months he had been denying the painful facts. He had to return to his roots to find himself again.

The train left Dale in Newport, Maine early the following morning just as the sun was beginning to rise. This was the same station from which he had departed for the war. It seemed a lifetime ago. He had a cup of coffee at the small restaurant next door to the station and inquired as to where he could rent an automobile. A railroad worker directed him to a local garage, where Dale rented a Model T Ford, and headed north for Monson.

Try as Dale might to focus on the landscape and the familiar roads, thoughts of Lenore dominated his mind. Of course he still had feelings for her, it was impossible for him to turn them on and off as if his love had never had any basis for being. The fact that she was able to erase what they had shared for so many years angered him. Despite her betrayal and all the unanswered questions, the intensity of his love for her had not faded.

Two hours later, Dale turned the Model T on to the road following the south shore of Lake Hebron. His senses were dulled and oddly disassociated, as if a stranger were returning to the scene of his childhood. When he passed by Lenore Johnson's home his hands tightly gripped the steering wheel until the knuckles turned white. He slowed a bit, relieved that no one was in sight. For the most part, the place looked the same. The small barn behind the cedar shingled house had recently been painted red and several cords of firewood were piled beside the house drying for the long, cold winter season ahead.

Next door, the sight of his family's home brought a lump to his throat and an ache in his heart. The familiar bungalow style house seemed to be waiting for his return. Echoes from the past ran through his consciousness. He could almost hear his father calling him from the small barn behind the house, and half expected to see his mother open the kitchen door and run across the porch to greet him. But, alas, he was alone with only his memories. Leaving the car beside the white screened porch he searched in his pocket for the key to the door leading to the parlor. The house had been closed up for so long that it had a musty smell when he first entered. Leaving the door open, he got as far as the living room and sat down in the large chair that had been his father's favorite. The flood of tears could no longer be denied. His body was wracked by convulsive cries.

Dale anticipated that it was going to be difficult, but he was unprepared for the intensity of pain he now felt. The reality that his beloved parents were gone could not be dismissed. He never had a chance to say good-bye or to thank them for being the best friends he had ever had. The rooms were filled with their presence, he felt it as acutely as if they were sitting on the couch across from him. Was it the voices of the past reverberating from the walls that he heard? He wasn't sure. He wasn't sure about anything!

He had suppressed his sorrow so effectively that it took a long time for it to be purged from his soul. Finally, what seemed like hours later, he dried his eyes. Then, Dale turned his head to find Lenore's mother quietly watching him from the doorway. She spoke first.

"I knew it had to be you, Dale. I saw the car go by the house," she said, reaching out to hold him in her arms. She had loved her neighbor's son as if he was one of her own. "It's been a long time, young man, and it's nice to have you home where you'll be safe." Mrs. Johnson's eyes filled with tears. He had survived the war that took her son. She was so proud of the two soldiers.

"I guess I overreacted to the emptiness and stillness in the house, but I'm all right now. How have you and the rest of the family been?" asked Dale sincerely. Wilma Johnson was a heavy set woman with piercing blue eyes that never seemed to miss anything around her. She wore her long blonde hair wrapped in a braided bun at the back of her head. She was a kind-hearted person who gave freely of herself. Dale had always loved her for her kindness to him and his family.

"Your letter about Bernie's death arrived two days before we were officially notified," she said, still holding him close to her. The top of her head came up to his chin and he could feel her tenseness. "It was thoughtful of you to write, Dale. In all honesty, it was not as much of a surprise as you might have imagined. It still hurts something terrible, but in our hearts we had a premonition of his passing. He had a talent for tempting fate, and this time he lost. We pray that he has found peace and comfort with our Lord. Sometimes when I hear steps on the porch, I turn and expect to see him. Then I realize that he's never coming home again, and the hurt returns."

"He was a good soldier, Mrs. Johnson. The men in his unit looked up to Bernie. I was proud to call him my friend."

"Bernie thought a lot of you too, Dale. He mentioned you in every one of his letters from France. Your mother and father were so proud of you and we shared their pride. If they could only see you now, in your uniform with Captain bars on your shoulders, they'd be doubly proud. I miss your mother and father terribly. They were such good neighbors. I've nothing but sadness in my heart when I think of how you and Lenore were with each other."

"How is she?" asked Dale, avoiding her searching eyes.

"She's a good mother. The baby is healthy and happy. I can't say the same for Lenore. I don't think it's working very well between her and Stanley."

"I would have expected her to be a good mother."

"Can you forgive her, Dale?" cried Mrs. Johnson.

"I'm not sure, Mrs. Johnson. How can a person erase a lifetime of memories? I was hurt and angry at what she did to me, and the way she did it. I almost lost my sanity."

"Of course it was a cruel thing to have happened when you were away from home fighting in the war. I've wished so often that it could have been you."

"In time, my forgiveness will come. That's not the same thing as not wishing her happiness, for I hope that it has been right for her. I've loved her for so long, it would be impossible for me to wish her any ill will."

They sat on the front steps and talked about the changes that had come to the small town. Bernie was the only soldier from Monson killed in the war, but several had been wounded. The influenza epidemic was a source of terror for every family in the close-knit community. Mrs. Johnson told Dale how sudden it had been for those who died from the dreaded disease. Monson had lost over thirty people within three months. His parents were buried on the hillside cemetery on the south side of town. She insisted on returning to her home a short distance down the road to get some lunch for him. Dale knew that to decline would be futile.

"You've got to eat, Dale," she announced, and left. A few minutes later, she returned proudly carrying a tray of food and placing it on the kitchen table. "If I remember correctly, you were always fond of baked beans. I just finished baking a pot of beans so you eat heartily. I also remember how you liked my Swedish boulla rolls. I brought along a supply of them, too."

"You're spoiling me already, Mrs. Johnson, but I love it," answered Dale good-naturedly. He was hungry and the smell of the sweet boulla breads whetted his appetite even more. "It's been a long time since I had a home-cooked meal. Thank you."

"Remember, there's more where that came from," she answered on her way out the door. She understood that Dale needed time to adjust to the idea of being home without his parents and without the companionship of Lenore. She knew in her heart that this would not be an easy period for him.

The small bungalow held so many warm memories. Dale could visualize his mother busy in the kitchen preparing meals for her two hungry men, and his hard-working father stomping mud from his shoes before entering the house. The distinctive aroma of his father's favorite pipe tobacco could still be detected in the parlor where his parents quietly spent the fading hours of each day before retiring to bed. That had been Dale's favorite time of day when he had the full attention of both parents without the distractions of household or outside chores. The glowing kerosene lamps had helped to create an intimate atmosphere where he felt secure and special.

Now, sitting at the large oak table in the center of the kitchen enjoying the warm food, Dale noticed that new electric lights had been installed while he was away. His mother had written to him about how great it was to have a room without flickering shadows from the dim oil lamps. The window beside the table looked out on the lakefront. He could see the dock his father had built out of cedar poles when Dale was a small boy. The sun was beginning to set in the west casting long shadows of towering spruce and pine trees that dotted the shore of the lake. The calm waters reflected the bright rays of the sun making the lake look as if it had just turned red.

Dale reminisced how often his parents had sat at the same table looking out the same window at the same view. It had not changed since he was a young child. It was a scene that held his attention like a campfire in the forest or a fireplace in the living room. Suddenly, Dale heard the front door open. At first, he didn't believe his eyes. Lenore was outlined in the doorway.

"I was at the house when Mom returned from bringing you the tray," Lenore explained breathlessly. "I just had to see you, Dale."

He was unprepared for her visit. He had often thought about what he would say to her when this moment arrived, but all he could do was invite her inside. "Come in, Lenore. I've just finished your mother's boulla rolls and they're still as delicious as I remembered." He felt weak and unsure of himself. She was as lovely as ever with her long blonde hair hanging free below her shoulders. If he wasn't careful he would make a fool of himself, for he had to fight an urge to take her into his arms. Her eyes had a sad beseeching look that touched him.

"You're looking well, Dale," she said self-consciously not quite realizing what she was saying. "You've lost a little weight, but you haven't changed at all. It's been a long time hasn't it?"

"It's been the longest two years of my life," stated Dale matter-of-factly, hoping that his voice didn't betray the nervousness he felt. "You're as pretty as I remembered you, Lenore. I hope you're happy with your new life."

Lenore, seeking the support of one of the chairs, watched him intensely, listening to every word. She held out a hand across the table to him and said, "I'd give anything to turn back the clock. I made a big mistake, Dale. I wasn't completely certain about it until I saw you here in the kitchen. Can you forgive me?"

"How am I supposed to interpret those words, Lenore? Our time has passed. It can never again be like it was."

"Yes, it's possible!" she sadly sobbed.

"No, we're no longer kids. Too much has happened. What we had was special, and I cannot deny that my love for you is as strong as ever, but…"

Lenore looked up at him, her brilliant blue eyes wet with tears. "Dale, I thought I'd never hear those words again."

"You must let me finish, Lenore," he cried, holding her hands in his. "There are others that must be considered. I've wanted to hate you for so long, but I can't. I've tried, believe me, I've tried!" Dale released her hands and stood up. He walked to the window looking out at the sunset but not seeing it.

"You haven't answered me, Dale. Can you forgive me?"

"Forgiveness comes easy for a person in love, Lenore. Sure, I can forgive you, but in that same breath I blame you for turning the dreams we shared into ugly nightmares. How could you so carelessly betray our commitment to each other for all those years? Our love should have been strong enough to transcend all temptations." Dale spoke with a trace of desperation in his voice.

"I've asked myself that same question more times than you can imagine," Lenore said softly. "I have no answer, Dale. If I had it to do over again, I'd handle it differently."

"That's not an answer, it's a product of hindsight. I'm not going to judge you, Lenore, I've loved you too long for that. I've been responsible for the loss of men's lives who were ordered to do things based on my individual and fragile judgment. No, Lenore, I'm not qualified to judge your actions. My responsibility to Bernie and his death still haunts me."

Lenore deliberately walked around the table, placed Dale's arms around her waist and passionately embraced him. "My gentle Dale. How you must have suffered in the war. Bernie wrote often about you. You made us all proud. I've walked in shame for a long time. Knowing that you can truly forgive me helps more than you know."

Dale could not help himself. He held her close to his heart and when her soft lips reached up to him he kissed her. It was an automatic response that he could not control. "I never stopped loving you, Dale," Lenore whispered in his ear and laid her head on his chest.

"I love you too, but love is not enough. There has to be trust and a willingness to sacrifice for each other, and strength of

37

commitment enough to overcome all temptations, Lenore. You've made a new life with another man and have a child to think of. It would be easy for me to step back in time and pick up where we left off, but it's too late now. Our time has passed. We're two different people. If we were to try again, we'd end up hurting other people and you can't find happiness at the expense of someone else. I'll always wish you much happiness."

"Wherever you go or whatever you do, gentle Dale, my love follows you," Lenore cried, breathing deeply. "I'm glad we had a chance to talk without being hysterical. There's wisdom in what you say. I'm sorry that my weakness destroyed something beautiful between us. I needed to hear you say those words, 'I forgive you'."

"Tell me honestly, Lenore. Is he good to you?" he asked.

"He tries too hard to be like you, but, yes, he's good to me. He's a good father to the baby."

"Then the three of you have a chance to work together for a common cause. There's hope for you."

"What are you going to do now, Dale?" asked Lenore, looking in awe at the battle ribbons on his chest.

"I'm not sure. I came home to build a new life for myself. I guess I had to have this conversation with you before I could decide anything else," admitted Dale.

"I've said a prayer every night for your safe return, and my prayers were answered. I must go now, I told Mom that I wouldn't take long. I'm sorry for my mistakes and hope that you can find happiness with a woman worthy of you. Good-bye, Dale. I failed us both and I'll carry that hurt to my grave. Take good care of yourself old friend." Lenore grasped him around the neck and kissed him warmly one last time before running out the door.

Dale stood motionless in the kitchen watching her disappear, feeling empty and terribly alone. A veil of darkness descended upon him.

Chapter Five

Dale had a torturous night's sleep in the same bed he had slept in as a child. He was pleased that Lenore had made the effort to speak to him, for he doubted he could have summoned the courage to approach her. For hours he tossed and turned trying to put his past with her into perspective, knowing that it was always there for him to revisit. Only the future held any possibility of fulfillment.

Dale spent the next day renewing old friendships in town and purchasing supplies for a trip to the family cabin on the Lake of Three Sorrows. He also visited Mr. and Mrs. Fred Olman and confided to them his desire to spend some time alone at the lake.

Fred Olman was a respected citizen in the small town. He was a short, dark-skinned man with balding hair and a small black mustache. His active energy and interest in town and school affairs was common knowledge. He was the most educated man in town, and people often sought him out for assistance with problems or questions in which he may be able to enlighten them. His patience and charity was sincere, and he enjoyed his role of being a patriarch and respected advisor to those who sought his advice. He was usually well-dressed.

Dale's father had been Fred Olman's closest friend, so it was only natural for Dale to turn to his former high school principal to discuss plans for the future. Mr. Olman was supportive and helpful, as Dale had always known him to be, and volunteered to return the rental Model T to Newport after he had driven Dale to Moosehead Lake. Dale also discussed the possibility that Colonel Nelson might be contacting him. Mr.

Olman promised to get word to Dale in such case. Dale spent the next day assembling and purchasing supplies for the trip. He had carefully packed his uniforms away in the dresser drawers of his bedroom, and retrieved good serviceable outdoor wear from the family storage trunks in the attic.

The next day, Mr. Olman rode to Greenville with Dale and helped carry his supplies to a canoe he had rented on Moosehead Lake. "Are you sure this is what you want, Dale?" asked Mr. Olman, concerned about his being alone in the wilderness.

"I've been looking forward to this for a long time," Dale replied enthusiastically. "Don't fret about me, I'll be fine. After all, I'm a forester and I'll be back in my preferred element, at last. I appreciate all the help you and Mrs. Olman have given me. Feel free to use the car for as long as you have a need for it. When I return to Monson, I'll make other travel arrangements."

"Good luck, son. I'll get word to you if it's necessary. Take care of yourself," Mr. Olman replied.

"I promise, Sir. Thanks again for everything," shouted Dale, shoving off from the Greenville dock.

Moosehead Lake was mirror smooth, perfect for canoeing. Sometimes the large lake could produce swells as high as four feet in stormy weather. The wary boater watched the western skies above the lake for any sudden changes in the weather pattern. If strong winds appeared evident, small craft were prudent to head toward shore. The lake was notorious for its ability to produce choppy wave conditions without warning, especially where the land masses constricted the water flow. Dale followed his father's routine and always stayed within a few minutes of the eastern shoreline. It might take a little longer to reach his destination that way, but being caught in a canoe in the middle of the lake in a sudden wind squall was unwise and risky.

Returning to the Lake of Three Sorrows invoked different emotions than those triggered by his return to Monson. Dale's memories of the lake were primarily associated with time spent alone with his parents. The Coopers had stayed there for weeks at a time without contact from any other person. Their family circle had grown stronger in the middle of this wilderness. Together, they had learned self-sufficiency, and developed a level of confidence that enriched all of their lives. The three of them had worked together as a team, yet each had maintained their individual responsibilities.

One chore that was inevitably assigned to Dale was the collection of small dead branches from the spruce, fir, and pine trees, into a large canvas bag. When the bag was full he carried it to the three-sided shed next to the cabin and piled the boughs against the inside wall to keep them dry. A small amount of the dry branches were also stored inside the cabin in a woodbox beside the small cook stove. The single outhouse was built against the back wall of the firewood shelter, and any person who used the facility customarily grabbed a couple of sticks of wood to bring back to the cabin. Consequently, a large supply of dry logs was always available in the kitchen.

The trip from Moosehead Lake traditionally took about three hours, with the final half of the journey being the more strenuous. The breeze across the lake was gentle and Dale was encouraged by his progress. A few slow-moving cumulus clouds floated in the sky, reflecting in the clear waters of the lake. The sun periodically hid behind the clouds then broke out unimpeded warming Dale's body. The sweet scent of balsam and spruce filled his senses. He headed due north toward Spencer Bay in the northeastern section of the lake; here he would make landfall at the prominent landmark known as Indian Point, which marked the end of travel on Moosehead Lake.

Dale was breathing harder than usual when he arrived at Stony River, a small stream which flowed into the lake at Indian Point. Traditionally, this was a good place for travelers to rest for awhile and eat something. A well-worn path ran along the first half-mile of river, to a portage of several hundred feet before the canoe could be placed back in the water again. After that, it was another mile to the Lake of Three Sorrows. Dale's family had tried dragging the fully loaded canoe along the trail, but experience quickly taught them that it was easier to make several light trips back and forth with a loaded backpack; the final trip could then be made with the empty and lighter canoe. The latter technique took longer, but it avoided the total exhaustion that usually resulted in trying to carry everything in one trip.

Dale made two trips back and forth with provisions. On the third trip he dragged the canoe over land to a place where it could be placed back in the water. The flow of the water down Stony River was drastically minimized for the next mile or so as it meandered along on an almost level riverbed. Halfway up the river a smaller stream branched off to the east from Stony River. This small stream was locally known as Savage Stream, after a trapper who had lived in the area over a century ago. Savage Stream flowed into the Lake of Three Sorrows from the north and eventually drained into Spencer Bay near the eastern shore.

Dale skillfully guided the fragile canoe into Savage Stream for about ten minutes, then he navigated it toward the western shore at a small cove nestled among large granite outcroppings and a few aspen trees struggling for life among the crevices of the rocks. The shore of the cove was sprinkled with small pebbles. Dale jumped out of the canoe and pulled its full length out of the water onto the shore. He had decided to come ashore at this point instead of following around the granite rock formation into the wider body of water that formed the Lake of Three Sorrows. A well-traveled overland trail from this location led directly to the Cooper cabin.

He loaded the sturdy open-topped pack basket, which had once been his grandfather's, onto his back and stepped off toward the cabin with a spring in his step. He stored the remaining supplies under the overturned canoe, planning to return later. The trail led through a dense stand of balsam fir and white spruce which formed an arched canopy of green overhead. Here and there a soft shaft of sunlight shone through small openings in the green forest canopy like a floodlight on a theater stage. Scattered along the path were sweetfern which filled the air with a heavy pungent aroma whenever Dale crushed the fragile leaves underfoot. The trail meandered around several large rocks as he neared the top of the small rise overlooking the cabin. The sun was still high in the western sky, and Dale rested against a rock to savor the view, humbled by the grandeur of the scene. He was home at last!

The small cedar log cabin below him was perched on a flat section of granite ledge at the water's edge. From there, a four-foot wide mooring dock jutted twenty feet over the lake. It was a great spot for fishing or swimming. Dale felt a sense of well-being wash over him the minute he started down the slope towards the cabin. The first thing he noticed about the cabin was that the supply of firewood under the shelter was a little lower than usual. Whenever he and his father visited the camp, their first order of business had been to start a firewood cutting and splitting project to replenish their supply of wood fuel. The process continued as long as weather permitted. A time-honored tradition in the north woods required that those who used the cabin, also added to the stockpile, an equivalent amount of wood used during their visit.

Dale stepped onto the porch and placed the box he was carrying on the swinging wooden settee that hung from the ceiling, then backed to the edge of the settee to remove his loaded backpack. Relieved of his load, Dale walked to the edge of the porch and absorbed the sights, sounds, and smells that assaulted his senses.

"Without a doubt the peace of mind that had so long alluded me, could be found in this beautiful place of refuge," he whispered to himself.

Gazing south across the Lake of Three Sorrows, Dale noticed that a large tract of forest land had been burned since he had left for duty in France. Gaunt black stubs of trees were the residual remnants of a fire that had burned itself out at the south shore of the lake.

His spine tingled with excitement. For the past four years he had dreamed of standing here on this very porch looking out across the lake. He had frequently doubted that he would survive the war. To be standing here alive and uninjured seemed a gift from the Heavens. The simple beauty of the lake and its surroundings, even the burned section, awakened his spirit.

All of a sudden, Dale smelled smoke in the air. Ever alert to the destructive force of forest fires, he leaped off the porch to the rock lookout behind the cabin so that he could observe the surrounding area. He didn't see any smoke in the distance, but noted a small plume of smoke rising from the cabin's chimney. Relieved that a forest fire was out of the picture, he ran to the cabin to see who was inside. Over the years, the cabin had been used by a number of forest travelers, so it was not unusual for it to be occupied now.

The front door of the cabin opened into the great room that served as kitchen, living room, and dining room. On the far wall was a massive stone fireplace with a few warm ashes still in the hearth. Dale's parents had slept in a bed to the right of the fireplace where his father had rigged a heavy curtain to enclose the area for privacy, it looked untouched. Dale glanced to the opposite side of the room where he had slept in a wooden loft built over the main room with an access ladder on the wall.

He scaled the ladder to the loft, uncertain what he would find. The loft was empty, but the bedding was lying on the mattress as if it had recently been used. Normally, bedding was stored in a chest suspended by wire from the middle of the ceiling to prevent rodents from making nests in it. Dale then noticed the bedding chest open on the floor. It was probably someone from the Great Northern Paper Company using the cabin. They traditionally signed the log book hanging on a rope beside the door. Dale checked the book and found no recent entry. The last entry was two months ago when a forester for the Great Northern had stopped by for a day to escape a rain storm. Dale stepped out on the porch and called, "Hello." No answer came.

Dale thought it odd that the stranger had not left a note. The cabin's door was never locked or barred, and there was always plenty of dry matches in a metal container and kindling wood for an instant fire. To someone lost in the wilderness, the cabin could be a welcome shelter, at times even a life-saving refuge. Food was stored in a small earth cellar entered by a trap door in the center of the floor. It was a place where canned goods, rice, flour, dried peas and dried beans were stored in metal containers, so that they would not freeze or be ravaged by wild animals. It was a place where excess foodstuffs were stockpiled whenever Dale's family left the cabin. He lifted the trap door to inspect the inventory. There was still a good supply remaining on the shelves along with extra containers of kerosene for the lanterns. Puzzled, Dale closed the trap door and scanned the room for clues.

It looked as if the table had been recently wiped clean, and the galvanized dishwasher tub on a bench near the door, held an unwashed coffee cup. The blue enamel coffee percolator was on the grate at the fireplace still warm and half full of coffee. Dale shrugged his shoulders. He was thirsty and hungry from his trip and decided to have a cup of warm coffee since it was already made.

He went out to the porch to get a small jar of peanut butter and a box of crackers from his pack. The dry crackers and peanut butter would go better with the coffee to wash it down. Finally, he sat at the familiar table and sipped the coffee. Even though it was not as hot as he preferred, he had to admit that it was a good cup of coffee! Dale was still a little perplexed about who the stranger could be.

While Dale was enjoying the coffee, a slim figure approached the cabin with an armful of firewood, climbed the steps on the porch, and walked through the door. Dale was startled by the footsteps, and rose to see who it was. The intruder screamed hysterically at the sight of Dale and froze, dropping the load of wood in the middle of the floor. The visitor was a young lady with long black hair done up in two braids that hung down the front of her shoulders!

45

Chapter Six

The young lady continued to scream, her eyes filled with fear. She started to run for the door. Dale blocked her path, attempting to calm her.

"My name is Dale Cooper. I'm the owner of this cabin. Don't be alarmed, I won't hurt you." The frightened girl stopped screaming as he spoke, but her eyes were like those of a trapped animal willing to risk everything, if need be, in a desperate dash for freedom. Dale had anticipated her instinctive reaction and placed himself in the doorway, intentionally cutting off her escape.

She fearlessly interpreted his motives and flung herself at him with such force that it almost knocked him over. Her cry of desperation alarmed Dale. With fists flailing like a windmill, she pounded at his chest and face in an attempt to force him out of the doorway. She managed to land several blows before he was able to grasp her arms and hold them pinned at her side, crazed with fear that her escape attempt had failed. Dale recognized that look all too well, he had seen it many times before when men came face to face with death. It frightened him, but he was at a loss as to how to calm the young woman.

"Please, lady," Dale pleaded. "I promise not to harm you. Do you understand what I'm saying?"

She continued to struggle, and started to scream again. Her high-pitched, piercing cries worried Dale that she would injure herself if her hysteria continued. So he slapped her across the face with his open palm and instantly regretted the decision.

"I'm sorry lady," he cried with self-reproach.

The blow resounded through the cabin rocking the woman's head sideways and throwing her so off balance that she started to fall.

"My God, what have I done?" he exclaimed, fearful that he had struck her too hard. He caught her limp body before she reached the floor and carried her to his parent's bed beside the fireplace and laid her on her back. Dale felt sick with concern that he had severely injured her. His first reaction after placing her on the bed was to check her wrist for a pulse. It was strong and regular and he sighed in relief. Next, he placed his ear over her mouth listening for the rhythm of her breathing. She was breathing freely. Dale anxiously watched her with questioning eyes.

The woman's copper complexion, prominent cheek bones and ink-black hair indicated that she was probably Indian, very likely from one of the native tribes in northern Maine. She appeared to be in her middle twenties and even in her present condition, extremely attractive. He now saw that her clothing was torn in several places and soiled with mud. Dale speculated that she had been lost in the forest. He wrapped her in a warm Hudson Bay blanket to prevent her from going into shock.

She still did not stir. Dale nervously picked up the wood she had dropped on the floor and neatly piled it in the woodbox. He searched in the box for some dried white cedar shavings to rekindle the fire, and within seconds cheerful flames were snapping in the fireplace. The longer the woman laid there, the more Dale was afraid he had seriously injured her. She was still unconscious when he left the room to get more firewood from the lean-to.

Outside, he noticed a fish line with two freshly-caught brook trout of good size sitting on top of a pile of wood. When he walked into the room with an armful of wood, the woman was sitting on the edge of the bed staring forlornly into the fire. She looked exhausted, but at least she was not screaming.

"Are you all right, Ma'am?" asked Dale, quickly dumping the wood into the box. "You had me scared for awhile. I didn't mean to hit you and I apologize for doing it harder than I intended. I just wanted to stop you from getting more hysterical than you already were."

"Yes, I'm all right," she told him, speaking in a soft melodious voice.

"I found your trout outside. If you don't mind, I'll clean and put them on the pan now that the fire is going. Are you hungry?"

The woman did not respond, but Dale was encouraged that she did nod her head to indicate that she was hungry. She continued to stare at the fire avoiding eye contact. Dale dressed the trout and placed them in a heavy cast-iron frying pan on a grate near the flaming logs. The woman turned her head away from him and quietly cried. Dale stood there feeling terribly ashamed of the way he had handled the situation. Awkwardly, he moved closer to her and placed a hand on her shoulder to console her. She jerked away from him.

"Please," Dale pleaded. "I'm sorry that I slapped you, be assured that I will not harm you. Is there anything I can do to help you?"

There were several seconds of agonizing silence. Finally, she replied. "No, you did not hurt me."

"You made coffee earlier and I finished off the last cup before you came in. Would you like me to make more coffee?" volunteered Dale, watching for a reaction.

She hesitantly shook her head and answered in a low voice; "I'd like that, thank you."

Dale grabbed the water pail and rushed to the lake, where he filled it with fresh water. The sun was beginning to set and the evening was growing cooler. The dark clouds gathering in the West were an indication that rain or cloudiness would be a part of the weather for the next twelve hours. Dale returned to the cabin and prepared the coffee, placing it on the grill to percolate while he put another log on the fire.

"This should hold us for the night," he announced doing his best to be cheerful. "I haven't had a taste of fresh trout for years. This will be a treat for me Ma'am. Thank you for catching them."

"It took me a long time," she answered, with a shy smile.

A smile! Dale's heart leaped, as he remained casual. "I've got some fresh boulla breads and some strong cheese I picked up in Monson. They'll go good with trout," Dale said, slicing the large loaf of bread and placing the cheese and bread on the table. Then, he searched his pack for a small jar of orange marmalade. The luscious aroma from the percolating coffee filled the room. Dale flipped the trout which were cooking nicely in the large cast-iron pan.

"It's been ages since I was this hungry. Come, supper is almost ready." Dale motioned for the woman to take a seat at the sturdy table. It was an awkward moment for both of them. She took a place and accepted the plate he set in front of her, eating ravenously for several minutes in silence. Evidently she had not eaten for a long time. There was an air of deliberate calmness and benign grace about her that was in sharp contrast to her first reaction to his presence.

"Please, help yourself to the bread and cheese," he urged. "You look starved. When was the last time you had something to eat?"

"Two days ago," she answered directly.

"The weather outside is not very promising for travel, so we're going to have to share the cabin for the night," Dale was unsure what her reaction would be. "I've got a lot of questions to ask you and I understand that you don't owe me any explanations, but please know that I apologize for striking you. I thought it was justified at the time, nevertheless, I still feel bad about it."

"I accept your apology," the woman answered, deliberately lifting her eyes to meet his.

Dale smiled in relief. "My name is Dale Cooper. My parents built this cabin years ago. I recently returned from Germany

49

and was looking forward to spending some quiet time here," he explained, realizing that his words might have given the wrong impression, he hastily added, "Don't think I resent your use of the cabin, because I don't. It has never had a lock on the door, and it never will as long as I own it. I would never deny its usage to someone in need of its shelter. I admit, I was surprised to find you here."

"My name is Iowaka. I found your cabin late last night and helped myself to your coffee," she said with serious eyes. "It was all I could find in the cupboard. This morning I searched for maps or anything else that might tell me where we are, then I spent the rest of the day trying to make up a fish line. When I returned to cook the trout, you were here," she declared simply.

Dale was still puzzled over the things she didn't tell him. "Iowaka, that's a pretty name. Are you from one of the Mic-Mac tribes in Maine?"

"No," Iowaka answered quickly. "My mother is a full-blooded Cree. My father is an Englishman who died years ago when I was small. I'm a half breed!" she stated defensively.

"To me," Dale replied casually. "That suggests that you have the best of both worlds in your veins. I had several Indians from Maine who served with me in France. One lost his life trying to defend his wounded friend when the Germans attacked our lines."

"Are you a soldier?" she asked curiously.

"I was a soldier for four years," Dale told her. "However, I'm changing my status to a part-time soldier this summer."

She seemed pleased with his answer, but did not volunteer any additional information about herself for the rest of the evening.

The rain began falling heavily before they had finished eating. The wind also picked up, driving the rain against the windows making small rills across the panes of glass. The howling wind gusts shook the windows with increasing fury. The stormy weather conditions seemed to make Iowaka nervous. She had that same withdrawn look of being trapped and at the mercy of a stranger. The fact that she was facing a night under the same roof with a total stranger was unsettling to her. The weather forbade any realistic thoughts of leaving the cabin. Besides, she didn't know where she was!

Dale pulled his chair nearer to the fireplace and lit up a pipe filled with his favorite smoking tobacco, Half and Half. He watched Iowaka sitting motionless at the table, her thoughts far-removed from the small cabin.

"I promise not to pry into your affairs," he assured Iowaka. "I also want you to understand that you're safe here. I pledge my word and my honor as an officer. You're a guest in this cabin, not a captive, and I will protect you from any possible harm. I noticed that you used the loft last night. Tonight, I'll give you a choice of the loft or the bed in the corner of the room. There are curtains that can be drawn for privacy."

Iowaka considered his offer. "If you don't mind, I'll take the loft. Thank you for trying to reassure me. I'm exhausted and would like to rest now."

"That will be fine. I'll keep the fire going for a while longer so that the cabin will be warm," said Dale.

"Goodnight, Mr. Cooper," she nodded and smiled.

"Goodnight, Iowaka. Rest well and please, call me Dale," he added.

"Goodnight, Dale," she said hesitantly, and turned in for the night.

During the course of the evening, the storm blew itself out. Dawn arrived with a beautiful sunrise which burned off the mist rising from the lake. It was a good omen.

Dale awoke and started the fire to prepare breakfast. He carefully checked the carton of eggs which he had carried from the canoe in his hands. Dale had a large appetite and a taste for a traditional breakfast of bacon and eggs, boulla bread and plenty of hot coffee. As soon as he put the coffee pot on the grate, he left the cabin to retrieve the second backpack he had left behind in the canoe. The pack contained some fresh clothing and his shaving supplies.

Dale had just finished shaving on the porch and started breakfast cooking when he heard footsteps. He turned to see Iowaka climbing down from the loft. He hardly recognized her this morning. She had undone her braids and let her hair fall around her shoulders. She was beautiful.

"Good morning," Dale acknowledged her. "Did you sleep well?"

"Yes, I was exhausted and fell asleep very quickly," she replied self-consciously eyeing the food he was preparing.

Dale did his best to be a gracious host. "I've taken the liberty of placing a pitcher of warm water and a wash basin with soap on the dresser beside the bed behind the curtains. It's the most private spot in the cabin. I found a comb and brush that my mother had used if you want them. Breakfast will be ready by the time you're finished, but, please, take as long as you need."

"Thank you for your thoughtfulness," she answered shyly, retiring behind the curtain.

A few minutes later, Iowaka rolled back the curtain from around the bed just as Dale was prepared to serve the food he was cooking. Her hair was tightly braided now like yesterday. The two ate heartily without much conversation. The Maine woods had a habit of creating healthy appetites in the forest people. When Dale had cleaned his plate, he sat back in his chair and leisurely sipped a third cup of coffee. He was pleased to see Iowaka enjoy the meal.

She glanced at him and smiled comfortably. "That was a very good breakfast. I can't believe that I'm eating this way."

"It's the fresh forest air that does it," he told her. "Tell me, Iowaka, may I ask a question or two?"

"If you wish."

"Two things have been on my mind all night. Where did you come from, and where are you going? You don't have to answer if you don't want to, for it really is none of my business.

It's just quite unusual for a young lady to be alone in the wilderness without any visible luggage."

"I understand your curiosity," she said, sipping her coffee. "I had just completed the nursing course at the Greenville Hospital, and there was a small graduation dance and celebration at the Town Hall which most of my classmates attended. There was a young man named Joe Landers at the dance who works at the hospital and whom I've known casually for several months. He asked me if I would like to come with him to another celebration in a small place called Kokadjo, north of Greenville."

"Yes, I know the place."

"Well," she continued, avoiding his eyes. "We left Greenville in his automobile. The celebration he had in mind was not what I had visualized. He became aggressive and tried to force me into the back seat of his automobile. I refused to go. He had been drinking and I was afraid of him. When I resisted his efforts he called me every vile name he could get his filthy tongue around. When I finally pulled myself free, I ran as fast as I could into the safety of the woods, where he soon gave up looking for me. During the struggle with him, I lost my purse, which had my return tickets to Canada and all of my money. That's why I'm in the middle of nowhere and afraid…" Iowaka finished relating her story and started to cry.

Dale was angered at what she had been forced to go through, and did his best to console her. "You were unfortunate in your selection of a friend, but take heart. You defended your honor with courage and conviction and you're to be congratulated for your effort. Your purse with tickets and money can be replaced. In the big scheme of things, money really has little value compared to our reputations, and our self-respect. So here," he offered pulling a clean handkerchief from his pocket. "Take this and dry your eyes. If you want to blow your nose, go ahead and blow."

His last remark brought a smile to Iowaka's lips. She turned her head and used the handkerchief to clear her stuffed-up nose.

"So you're a nurse, congratulations," said Dale once her tears had stopped.

"Yes, I'm lucky to have had the chance to go to school."

"Where do you live in Canada?"

"I live with my mother in a small Cree village on the north shore of Lac St. Jean, north of Quebec City. I want to return to the village and help my people with my new skills."

"Why did you come way down here to Greenville for a nursing course?" Dale asked.

Iowaka shrugged resignedly. "I'm not a white citizen. In many ways there is more prejudice against half-breeds than there is against purebloods. I tried several schools in Canada and was refused. Greenville was one of the few that accepted me, and it was the first to do so. It was a relatively simple thing to travel by Canadian Pacific Railways from Quebec to Greenville."

"I understand," replied Dale, growing increasingly impressed with this young lady sitting across the table from him. She held herself proud and erect and spoke with conviction. It was hard for him to imagine someone holding prejudicial views against her solely on the basis of the color of her skin. "Was it difficult in an all-white school?"

Iowaka hesitated before answering, surprised at how comfortable she felt talking with Dale, and was amazed at how personal their conversation had turned. "No, it was not difficult. Most of the students and staff were wonderful to me, and we had a lot of fun together. A few had trouble accepting me, and that hurt, but I learned to ignore them and continue with my studies. Most of the people in the village were very gracious and helpful. A couple of times in the past year, insensitive remarks were made about who and what I am. It made me uncomfortable, but that's the real world we live in. My encounter with Joe Landers is something I completely misread. He had one thing on his mind. I made a bad choice and should never have gone with him in the first place."

"That young man needs a lesson in manners. Maybe one that hurts a little," said Dale speculatively. "Listen, I have a plan in mind."

Iowaka's interest was piqued, but she told him, "I don't want to be a bother."

"Hear me out, Iowaka," Dale urged. "I'll take you back to Greenville by canoe today. You can pick up whatever you have left at the nurses' dormitory, and I can advance you the money you need for the trip back home."

Iowaka shook her head. "No, I couldn't accept that. You're very kind but we don't even know each other."

"Listen to me, please," Dale ordered with a stern note in his voice. "I just returned from the killing fields in Europe. During the war I got used to placing my life in the hands of young men I hardly knew any better than I know you. As a consequence, I've learned to respect my own judgment. If it makes you feel better, we can call it a loan. What do you say?"

She considered Dale's words and replied, "I'm flattered by your generosity. I'll accept on the condition that I will pay it back as soon as I arrive home."

"It's a deal then," Dale added, collecting the dirty dishes on the table. Together they cleaned the dishes and the cabin in short order and then left for the canoe. As they climbed the hill behind the cabin Dale turned suddenly to catch another glimpse of the view. Iowaka saw the look of pride and satisfaction in his eyes. She turned as well, admiring the same view, locking it into her consciousness. She would always remember this time and place where tragedy was averted by the kindness and generosity of a stranger.

Iowaka and Dale arrived at Greenville by noontime, and walked to the train station to check on the schedules. There was a train leaving for Montreal in a couple of hours. Dale paid for tickets to Lac St. John, and then, insisted on buying them lunch. Iowaka agreed provided she stop at the nurses' boarding house to clean up and change her clothes. She promised Dale that she would hurry so that they would have time for lunch together.

After she had freshened up, they selected a popular restaurant near the railroad crossing. Dale carried her two bags from the boarding house and placed them on a railroad cart at the station. As they approached the restaurant on the Moosehead Lake waterfront, Iowaka grasped Dale's arm and pulled him to one side. Her eyes were filled with fear.

"That man, Landers, just came out of the restaurant door! Try to ignore him," she whispered desperately in his ear.

Dale glanced in the direction of her gaze. Three young men were leaving the restaurant. Two of the men walked down the landing without giving Dale or Iowaka any notice. The third one, a short well-built man with black hair stared tauntingly at Iowaka. A surly laugh escaped his mouth. He turned to address them.

"Look at what we got here. Our little half-breed injun has made it back to civilization. What did you…"

He never finished the sentence. Dale wheeled on his left foot and landed a stinging blow at Landers' head with the back of his left hand. The slap sounded like a shot from a gun. The stunned Landers reached for his smarting cheek.

"The next time you open your mouth you low-life mongrel, it better be to apologize to this lady," Dale snarled, his voice barely above a whisper.

Landers checked Dale out. He was heavier and bigger than Dale so he predicted that he could take him. Landers attacked with all his strength, hoping to knock Dale to the ground and teach him a lesson. However, Dale anticipated the move and sidestepped from the path of his attacker, grabbing Lander's arm using the momentum of the blow to pull him off balance. As Landers was falling, Dale struck him a hard chop to the side of his neck just before he hit the dock with a solid thud. The savage blow stunned Landers.

Dale looked at the other two men with a menacing stare in his eyes. They saw the look and backed away, holding up their hands in front of themselves.

"This ain't our fight," said one of them to rationalize their backing down.

"Your friend needs a good lesson in manners," Dale told them, his eyes still flashing. "You warn him that I'll be glad to continue the instructions at anytime. Now get him out of here."

Joe Landers groaned as his associates rushed to help him off the dockside. Dale silently watched until they were out of sight.

Iowaka witnessed the incident in wide-eyed disbelief. Dale directed her towards the restaurant door with a gentle nudge.

"Don't think anything about it," he explained, still breathing heavily. "Sometimes you just have to act on instinct. I apologize for making a scene but he really asked for it."

A waitress who knew Iowaka from previous visits to the restaurant, showed Dale and Iowaka to a booth facing the water front. "Bravo, Sir!" the waitress exclaimed. "That jerk has had it coming for a long time. Are you okay, Iowaka?"

"Yes, I'm fine now," she answered, her face still flushed from all the excitement. "Betty, meet my newfound friend, Dale Cooper. Betty has always been here when we had time from our classes to stop in and have a cup of coffee and a sandwich."

Betty grinned in a friendly manner. "I'm glad to meet you, Dale. We're going to miss Iowaka's smiling face around here, now that she's graduated."

"It's my pleasure to meet you, Betty. I apologize for making such a ruckus, but…"

"You did what I've been wanting to do ever since the guy first came into this place. I'll get you a menu."

Dale and Iowaka spent the next hour enjoying a bowl of seafood gumbo and sandwiches topped off with a large piece of custard pie and several cups of coffee. They were still strangers, and yet each felt something comforting in the other's presence that neither would have been able to describe.

"Would you give me your address so that I can send you a check?" Iowaka finally asked.

"I'll give you mine if you'll give me yours," Dale grinned.

"Of course," she responded, writing it out on a pad of paper she pulled from her jacket pocket.

"Maybe we can write to each other," he suggested, watching closely for her reaction. He gave her his Monson address.

"That would be nice," said Iowaka politely, her face offering little indication as to how she felt about Dale's suggestion. "We should be heading over to the station now," she said, standing up, and waving to Betty who came around the counter to say good-bye.

"Good luck to you where ever you go, Iowaka," said the waitress giving her a warm hug.

"Good-bye, Betty. Thanks for everything."

"Get out of here, you're going to make me cry. I hate good-byes," Betty dismissed them, holding the door open for their passage.

They walked in silence to the nearly deserted boarding platform. There was something melancholic and sad about a train station. It reminded Dale of all the times he had said good-bye to loved ones, sometimes for the last time. The sentiment so overwhelmed him that Iowaka asked him if there was something wrong.

"No," he answered quickly. "I just have a hard time with farewells. I was thinking only of myself. I'm sorry."

"I hear the train in the distance," said Iowaka soberly. "There isn't much time to say it, and I'm not sure how to express my appreciation for your kindness. You've been a true gentleman, Dale, and I want you to know that the short time we've spent together has been special to me!"

"It's been great for me too," answered Dale.

The train chugged into the station spouting smoke from its stack and hissing steam from its brakes. Dale placed Iowaka's luggage on the transom of the train and turned to her. "Good luck, Iowaka. I hope your nursing career goes well for you."

"I'll send the money as soon as I can," promised Iowaka. "May God be with you, Dale."

"That'll be fine," Dale offered her his hand.

Iowaka grasped it quickly, drawing close to him and softly kissed him on the cheek. "I'm glad I met you, Dale."

"So am I," he replied. He watched her step onto the train and take a seat near a window where he could see her. She smiled and waved at him as the train moved slowly down the tracks. Dale saw her wave one last time before the train pulled around the bend and disappeared.

Dale surprisingly found himself consumed with an aching sense of emptiness at Iowaka's departure. He had felt the same way when he had said good-bye to Lenore, yet, he had known Iowaka for only a few hours. The mournful sound of the train whistle in the distance seemed to echo his loneliness.

Chapter Seven

Dale's recent chance encounter with Iowaka only added to the complexity of his emotional well-being and left him more uncertain than ever about the future. He was uncomfortable with the intensity of feelings he held for Iowaka, virtually a stranger. Now that Lenore was no longer a part of his life, Dale hoped that it was not a sign of fickleness on his part that whenever he met an attractive young lady he would immediately develop romantic feelings. It left him seriously questioning his judgment.

He walked down Greenville's main street in search of a store with a public telephone to call Mr. Olman before heading back to the cabin. He eventually located a telephone booth just outside the Indian House.

"Hello, Mr. Olman? This is Dale Cooper. I wanted to check and see if you had any messages for me."

"I'm glad to hear from you, Dale. I just received a call from a Colonel Nelson who was asking for you. I took the liberty of telling him that you wouldn't be available for a few days. He left a number for you to call. He wants you to call New York City 288J as soon as possible. He seemed anxious to settle something. I'll take the rental car back to Newport tomorrow, Dale."

"Thanks a lot, Mr. Olman. I'll call Nelson."

"Is there anything wrong, Dale?" Mr. Olman asked with concern. "It's a little unusual for you to leave the cabin the day after you arrive."

"The past twenty-four hours have been interesting," Dale smiled wryly. "I don't want to get into it right now, but I'll tell you about it the next time we're together. Thanks for everything."

"No trouble at all, Dale. By the way, this morning I ran into Lenore on the street. She asked me about you and where you were planning to work and stay. I know it's a touchy situation and I was noncommittal."

"I think that's the best approach. The past is history and we've got to move on," Dale replied firmly.

"I agree with you. Good-bye, Dale, take care of yourself."

"Good-bye, Mr. Olman."

Next, Dale called the number given to him by Mr. Olman for Gregg Nelson. An operator answered and transferred him to the colonel.

"Hello Dale, this is Gregg. Thanks for getting back to me."

"I'll soon be at an isolated location for a few days, so I wanted to call while I could," Dale explained. "What can I do for you, Sir?"

"Well, Dale," Gregg began. "I've been authorized to make a thorough study of a large tract of land in northern Quebec Province, which the bank is about to foreclose on. We're anxious to get started on the project."

"Winter comes early up there, Gregg," Dale cautioned. "You could see snow as early as September or October. Weather is a serious factor in dealing with the sub-arctic. It's now mid-June, so you really don't have much time to prepare an expedition for arctic conditions."

"I'm aware of the ramifications of weather, Dale," the Colonel replied knowingly. "Still, without going into minute detail, would you be interested in representing the bank and its shareholders by going to Canada to evaluate the property as time, weather, and logistics permit? I'm talking as soon as possible, Dale."

"Yes, I'd be willing to consider it," Dale thought about the proposition. It sounded like something he could do before he settled down to a full-time job. "If you want, I can come to New

York for briefings, but in the interest of time I would suggest you send me a detailed letter covering my duties, responsibilities and the absolute minimum amount of information that you need in order to make decisions on the property. If I remember correctly, you were always a stickler for brief and articulate field orders answering the questions of what, when, where and how; therefore, I'll get to see if you've still got the right touch." Dale smiled.

"Old habits die hard, young man. I'll try to be as specific as you require," Gregg answered with a chuckle.

Dale told Gregg, "I'll agree to be your representative provided that what's outlined in the material you send me is something I am capable of doing and which can be completed before winter. Once I receive your proposal, I promise to reply immediately. I'll remain flexible, but I must tell you that I intend to take a few days off for myself. How does that sound?"

"I couldn't be more pleased, Dale. I'll put an information packet out to you as quickly as I can work it up. And, by all means, take the time. God knows you earned the right to do so. If I could I'd be doing the same thing, but this situation has been demanding all my attention lately. Thanks Dale, enjoy your rest and relaxation."

After purchasing a pocket full of chocolate bars at a local general store, Dale returned to the cabin. He was physically weary and mentally exhausted. The proposed expedition would require a lot of planning on his part, but until the time came to execute the trip to Canada, he intended to fish, eat, and sleep, ignoring everything else.

The forest was where he belonged. Dale sat in the swing-couch on the porch sipping a cup of coffee, feeling at one with the wilderness world around him. It wasn't that he didn't like people, he did, but most of the time he just never felt a strong need for them. In his view, this was not anti-social behavior; rather, it indicated that his spiritual and physical worlds were operating in perfect harmony with each other. The solitude and serenity gave him the opportunity to connect with his inner soul, increasing his awareness and appreciation of the natural beauty that surrounded him. He had heard that the native peoples of the forest believed that all things, even trees, water, rocks, and the clouds in the sky, possessed a spirit and a soul, and Dale was not so sure they were wrong. When he was alone in the forest he could feel the presence of God.

For the first time since November, 1918, Dale took the opportunity to put his war-time experiences in perspective. He still had nightmares about the men he lost, especially those he knew on a first-name basis. While the nightmares were no longer as frequent as they had been, they were painfully vivid when they did occur. Sometimes, he awoke in a heavy sweat with the sound of guns still ringing in his ears, and the acrid smell of cordite filling his nose, just as if he had never left the battlefield. Dale feared these sounds and images would never leave him.

Combat can do strange things to man. A large percentage of combat veterans had been able to put the experience out of their minds allowing them to concentrate on their daily affairs. A small percentage had been unable to cope on their own, and needed rest and medical attention before they were capable of living a normal life. The remaining small percentage of veterans, including Dale, had chosen to study and analyze what they had gone through, with the intention of not making the same mistake twice. Dale's analytical curiosity helped to make him a fine leader of men, but it had also required a good deal more energy and effort for him to carry out those missions he had been ordered to implement. This trait partially contributed to the fact that Dale felt more responsible for the losses sustained by his unit than most other officers. That was his greatest burden to bear.

Dale accepted his need now for the sanctuary of the forest which, to him, was the embodiment of grace and form. He required its healing qualities as much as he did food to sustain his body. The four seasons framed the wilderness in unique harmony, enhancing its influence and lure as a temple to soothe the soul. He was grateful for this unhurried interlude, utilizing it as an opportunity for renewal and evaluation far from the distractions of civilization.

The fish in the lake were as plentiful as ever and Dale spent much of his time sitting on the dock with a fishing pole in his hands. All his actions were spontaneous and instinctive and he avoided making plans for the future. On one beautiful sunny day, he walked around the lake on an overgrown pathway he and his parents had often traveled. The birds singing in the nearby trees were accompanied by the gurgling of the river entering and leaving the lake, which was a large catchment basin. It was music to his ears. He never tired of hearing the birds; it was the one sound that had never penetrated the battlefield and for which he had often listened, but to no avail. What would birds have to sing about on a battlefield anyway, he reflected?

Several white birch trees next to the cabin were a favorite haunt for grosbeaks, warblers, and finches that played all summer long in the branches. They shared the stand of birch trees with a few flying squirrels, who raced through the canopy with ease as they climbed to the very top of one tree and then catapulted toward a neighboring tree, losing altitude in the jump. Yet they repeated the process over and over until they ran out of trees at the granite outcroppings, at which point they would simply reverse direction.

Every evening Dale would lie on the comfortable featherbed in the loft listening to the sounds of the night. The one he associated the most with the cabin was the hauntingly melancholic cries of the loons. Nocturnal creatures dominated the forest while man sought rest in his own instinctive cycle of behavior.

One night Dale had an unnerving dream that left him shaken and uncertain about its meaning. He had fallen asleep to the sound of loons calling from the lake. The first thing he remembered after waking was that he had felt as if he had been floating above the cabin, watching the mist rise from the lake, when a shrill cry had echoed across the water. It was the sound of a person experiencing extreme pain, and it sent chills through his body. His heart beat faster as he watched the lake from which the sound had originated. Then, he remembered, a bright light appeared as if the sun had been shining. Afraid of what was taking place, Dale remained motionless and continued to stare at the scene before him as if he had been hypnotized.

As he watched, the form of a young Indian mother who had drowned years ago, slowly rose from the water holding two small children in her arms. The mother lifted her head to the heavens and wailed in long, high-pitched tones as the children slowly slipped from her arms and sank beneath the surface of the lake. The mother's inhuman howl reached a crescendo and echoed again and again across the water. A few seconds later it was silent. A light mist then parted above the water, revealing the tormented face of the Indian Maiden as she slowly sank below the surface. It was the face of Iowaka!

The realism of the dream kept him awake most of the night trying to sort out what it could possibly mean. He thought of Iowaka at her village in Canada where she lived with her mother. He also thought about Gregg Nelson's proposition and the intriguing prospect of cruising some remote tract of forestland in that same region of Canada.

That next morning Dale awoke feeling unrested and confused. He cleaned the cabin and filled the wood box in preparation for a trip back to Greenville. The past few days had piqued his curiosity for the material that Gregg Nelson had promised to send him. Ever since he left France the same old question, "Where do I go from here?" had troubled him. He had a hard time staying idle for too long. He made the canoe trip without incident, leaving the canoe at Greenville, where Dale boarded the Hasey Maine Stage bus to Monson on its way to Bangor. By mid-afternoon Dale was checking his mailbox at the Monson Post Office. There was a letter from Canada, Dale noted with a smile, and a large manila envelope from Gregg's bank in New York. He tucked the mail into his backpack and rushed to his parent's home. He wanted to be alone and away from prying eyes when he read Iowaka's letter.

Dale sat at the large kitchen table devouring every word she wrote:

Mistassini, P.Q., Canada
June 30, 1920

Dear Dale,

Enclosed is the money that you let me borrow for my passage home. Thank you for your thoughtfulness and kindness. I'm sure that my experience in the Maine woods would have been most difficult if you had not arrived at the cabin when you did. I was lucky it was you instead of Joe Landers.

I have strange feelings about our short time together. I do not want to read anything into them that is not possible, and, at the same time, I don't want to deny something that may be real. A single day is not long enough to know someone, but in that short period of time I feel as if I've known you much longer, and this puzzles me.

Please excuse my ramblings. Sometimes I interpret feelings much differently from other people, and sometimes I forget that I'm a half-breed with the blood of two cultures in my veins and that civilized society frowns on tainted blood, be it Indian or Caucasian. It's probably better for me to understand my position and accept that which is expected of me. In many ways I'm still searching for where I belong. I can honestly tell you that, in the past, I never thought much about who or what I am, but on my train ride home I thought of nothing else.

If I've been bold and impetuous in this letter, I hope you are not offended. I have a habit of speaking my mind. I'd like to hear from you again, Dale. It was just one day, but I'll always remember it with fondness. I wish you well.

Thanks again for being so nice to me when I really needed it. Iowaka

PS: My Christian name is Ashley Huntington. I used my Cree name, Iowaka, when I went to nursing school, so that the people whom I studied and lived with would not misunderstand that I'm half Cree, of which I'm very proud. I'm also proud to be my father's daughter. Maybe using the name the way I did was defiant and confrontational, but I wanted my friends to learn who I really am. You may not be able to understand my desire to be true to my heritage. Some students at school resented me for it, while most were very kind and I treasure their friendship. Thanks for being so patient with me!

> Good-bye,
> Dale, Iowaka

The letter had a spontaneous tone to it that pulled a smile from Dale. The fact that Iowaka remembered with fondness the day they spent together was encouraging. Her honesty and directness warmed his heart. Her overtones of race irritated him because he had never given it a thought. He would like to see her again, but wondered if it was truly possible? After all, she was hundreds of miles away in a foreign country at an isolated location, and, realistically, their chances of becoming better acquainted seemed doubtful. Also, Dale's track record with Lenore had made him skeptical about long-range commitments. No matter how strong his feelings, he knew that he needed to proceed with caution.

Dale next opened the packet from Gregg Nelson and studied its contents. The tract of land in question had been well-defined by a detailed perimeter survey done ten years ago by a professional surveyor. The land was logically defined and described by the streams and ponds in the Mistassini area of northern Quebec Province and composed a total of twenty thousand acres. It had been purchased outright from a local Indian tribe. The original purpose of the purchase, and of the subsequent loan from Gregg Nelson's bank, had been to market some of the timber to a regional paper mill. Bodies of water and valid water rights existed for the transportation of logs and pulpwood to the paper mill, making it a potentially lucrative capital venture.

Gregg's letter failed to explain exactly what went wrong with the enterprise. Instead, he outlined what was expected from Dale:

(1) A complete inventory of standing timber and its growth potential, so that harvest projections could be estimated.

(2) Recommendation of an estimated annual cut applying the principle of "sustained yield" (average annual harvest never exceeds average annual growth), taking into consideration natural mortality and losses from fire insects and/or disease.

(3) A cursory examination of the tract for the possible extraction of asbestos and/or aluminum.

(4) An estimate of costs of conducting the appraisal.

Dale's immediate reaction to the project was amazement at the amount of information the investors required. Timber and mineral evaluations were not difficult for a professional such as Dale to document. The main challenge was getting to the remote tract in the first place. Then, if it took longer than expected it could mean trying to collect data under harsh winter conditions. That could be extremely hazardous unless they were well-prepared for the bitter cold and heavy snow falls normal in the area. It would be a major undertaking to establish a center of operations on the tract and to keep it supplied in the winter. There were no roads or railheads for over a hundred miles.

The more Dale examined Gregg's proposal, the more excited he became. The land was located below the permanent frost line in the boreal forest region of northern Quebec and over a hundred miles from Lac St. Jean, the nearest point of civilization. The presence of several bodies of water within the tract would make it feasible for float equipped aircraft to be used to transport the men and supplies required. When conditions turned cold and the area became snow covered, the planes could use snow skis for landing and takeoff. Dale grinned to himself. Completing the project would be a challenge and great experience. Besides, he could use the money.

It was near midnight before Dale, working on the kitchen table, completed a detailed response to Gregg's request for an estimate of costs. Work at such an inaccessible site would require a minimum of a two-man crew. Pilots would need to be located and hired for the shuttle runs necessary to supply the expedition. Dale thought it would be possible to complete the work before heavy winter conditions set in. Nevertheless, it would be prudent to prepare for winter, the dominant season of the north woods. As Dale well knew, forest dwellers are constantly preparing for winter, recovering from winter, or enduring winter, and to overlook its importance could be a deadly error in judgment. The native people of the forest claim their greatest achievement is survival, year after year, in such a harsh environment.

Dale put aside Gregg Nelson's proposal and read Iowaka's letter one more time. He knew it would be impossible to sleep until he composed a reply.

Monson, Maine
June 25, 1920

Dear Iowaka,

I left the cabin at the Lake of Three Sorrows earlier today and received your letter and money. I'm now at my family home in Monson. Thanks for repaying the money. You were very prompt as promised.

Today I received a job offer for the next few months that should prove interesting. I just completed my estimate of its cost and will mail the proposal tomorrow. I should have confirmation within a week or so.

It was great to be able to spend some time at the cabin. I relax easier there than I can anywhere else. It satisfies my need for solitude at this particular juncture of my life, but I don't like to sit and be idle for long. That's why I was glad to make a bid on a job I'm capable of doing. I'm excited about the possibilities.

I can truthfully tell you that when I returned to the cabin after you left Greenville, its usual charm was present as always, but you had given it a special "glow" that was missing. I don't know exactly how to interpret these feelings that I have and I thought it important you should know. I was pleased to read your thoughts about the day we spent together and I share your wonder and concern about what passed between us.

You are very harsh on yourself. You are a child of two people who loved each other. Isn't that the most important heritage any of us can have? Your English father and your Cree mother have given you a truly unique legacy that you should be proud to carry. Each of us is defined by the person we are, and the life we live. What matters is what's in our hearts, and that has nothing to do with race, culture, or skin color.

We're all unique human beings. We should get up each morning, look in the mirror, and rejoice at our own uniqueness - there's not another human being on the planet exactly like us! Isn't that enough reason to be proud of ourselves?

Now I'm the one who is rambling! I would like to continue writing to you. I wish you success in your nursing career, and across the miles I say goodnight, Iowaka. Until next time.

Thinking of you,
Dale Cooper

Chapter Eight

The next morning Dale called Gregg Nelson to let him know that the proposal was in the mail. Gregg gave him a conditional approval to do the job, suggesting that Dale prepare himself, so that when final approval was obtained from the board of directors of the bank, there would not be any delay in getting the expedition underway. Buoyed by the good news, Dale stopped at Monson's only restaurant for a cup of coffee and a piece of pie. He noticed Mr. Olman sitting in a booth reading the Bangor Daily newspaper.

"Good morning, Mr. Olman," Dale greeted him. "Mind if I sit down?"

"Please do," answered the bespectacled high school principal. "It's nice to see you, Dale. How was your stay at the lake?"

"More eventful than I expected," answered Dale, telling him about the encounter with Iowaka.

"Sounds as if it was a good thing you showed up when you did. You seem different today, Dale, evidently the visit did you some good. Have you given anymore thought to what you want to do?"

Dale mentioned the proposal he had been working on, and took the opportunity to quiz the knowledgeable educator about asbestos and aluminum mining practices. During their discussion, Lenore entered the restaurant. She didn't recognize Dale because his back was towards her, but she did notice Mr. Olman and approached the booth.

"Hello, Mr. Olman," she said. "Oh, hi, Dale. I didn't expect to see you."

"Dale and I were about ready to order a piece of pie," Mr. Olman told her. "Would you care to join us?"

Lenore hesitated. "Well, if Dale doesn't mind."

"No, of course not," stammered Dale. "Please sit down."

"It's a surprise to run into you like this, Dale." Lenore took a seat beside Mr. Olman. "You look much better than the last time I saw you."

Mr. Olman watched his two former students with interest. He knew what they had shared before the war. Now, Dale had matured beyond his years while Lenore was in many ways still a teenager in a woman's body. It seemed only yesterday that he had the two students in his classroom.

"Listen you two," commenced Mr. Olman in his lecturer's tone, which he had used in every class he had ever taught. "Why don't we just have a cup of coffee and try to enjoy each other as adults. I can remember in the not-too-distant past when you two were just adolescents thrilled at whatever the world had in store for you. Well, things didn't turn out the way you expected, and that's the way it is in the adult world. Nothing is gained by dwelling on the past or on a future that you can't control."

"I believe I've accepted it, Sir," said Dale soberly, taking care to direct his gaze at Mr. Olman instead of Lenore. "The hurt was hard to handle, especially since I was miles away from home. I believe I've risen above recriminations now. It's difficult to explain to someone who has never been there, but the pain was lessened by the simple fact that I was one of the lucky ones to survive the war. So many good men were lost, like Bernie. Really, my loss was not nearly as great as the one Lenore's family had to endure."

Moved by his statement, Lenore touched Dale's arm across the table. "I failed to appreciate what you went through over there. I never meant to hurt you, Dale. Really, I never…" Lenore abruptly stood up and darted out of the restaurant.

Dale and Mr. Olman finished their coffee in silence. Mr. Olman spoke first. "I apologize for that incident. I didn't understand how intense things still were between you two."

"How could things not be intense, Sir? This is only the second time I've seen her since I returned from Europe."

"I know, I know, son. I'm sorry. I thought the two of you were destined for each other. I guess we were all wrong."

"You could say that, Sir," Dale replied, anxious to leave the restaurant. He was not comfortable discussing his personal life with anyone, even a friend as dear as Mr. Olman. He finished his coffee, said good-bye, and returned home. He wanted to check the trunks of clothes stored in the attic for adequate field clothes for the expedition.

Dale was still the same size and weight as he was in high school and found several woolen outfits that would be appropriate for the harsh environment of the northern spruce-fir forest. Later, he was quietly working at the kitchen table on supply lists for the trip when the phone rang.

"Hello," he answered.

"Hello, is this Captain Cooper?" asked a sonorous feminine voice.

"Yes, but I'm no longer in the Army," he told the anonymous woman.

"I just wanted to confirm if you were the person being considered by the Acme Bank of New York to evaluate a property in Canada."

"Yes, I'm the person," he answered, surprised at the question. "What can I do for you?"

"I'm calling to ask if you would allow me to accompany you on the trip?" the woman inquired.

"This is very sudden Ma'am," Dale admitted, quite taken back by the request. "I don't know who you are and nothing was ever mentioned to me about having to accept another person."

"You mean a woman, Captain Cooper."

"Well, yes…," he responded truthfully.

"I'm willing to pay my share of expenses."

"Why do you want to go?" asked Dale, a little annoyed at her insistent tone.

"My father, Charles Kemp, purchased the piece of land in question, and I will inherit the property if finances can be agreed upon. My father initially purchased it to prospect for gold; he was told by parties unknown to me that the land was rich with the substance. However, he traveled up there three years ago and has never been heard from since. Our family has assumed that he had some kind of accident. So, when I learned from Mr. Nelson that you were being considered to appraise the property, I was hoping that I could come with you to determine, if possible, what happened to my father."

"I see," said Dale. "That sounds like a legitimate reason for wanting to go. I've prepared and submitted a proposal for myself and a guide. Besides, it's rugged country and I don't know how long the appraisal will take or what we'll find once we get there. The northern wilderness can be quite dangerous. We'll be a long way from doctors or a hospital in case of an accident or sickness. I'd really try to talk you out of it. I'll be glad to report to you after we've checked the area for any traces of your father."

"Gregg prepared me for the answer you just gave, Mr. Cooper," the woman said unhappily.

"Hasn't Gregg informed you of the dangers inherent in any undertaking to unknown territory?"

"Yes, but I want to go and find out for myself about my father," Rachel Kemp replied stubbornly.

"We can't settle anything right now, Miss Kemp. I haven't been authorized yet to carry out the project. Why don't you contact Gregg Nelson and let him know that I don't mind if you want to accompany us. I want you to understand that the primary purpose of the expedition is to evaluate the property. In doing that we'll end up reconnoitering most of it, which should provide some information about your father. How does that sound to you?" asked Dale, hoping he had not made a mistake accepting another member to the party.

"You sound as if you were still in uniform, Mr. Cooper," Miss Kemp sounded amused. "Gregg told me a great deal about you before I called. If he had not been as generous with his praise of you as he was, I would never have contacted you. In answer to your question, yes, I promise to not interfere with your work and to follow orders."

"Well," laughed Dale. "I didn't mean to sound so formal. For your information, I hope to have confirmation of my approval within a few days, and I'm prepared to head north the day after I receive it. Will that be a problem?"

"Not at all. I'll be in touch with Gregg and let you know if I learn anything new. I feel better about the trip already. Thank you, Mister Cooper, for understanding my situation."

"You're welcome, Miss Kemp." Dale hung up the phone and stared into space wondering about the odd request. Miss Kemp's presence in the party would make for complications that probably even she was unaware of. Being responsible for her safety would be a major consideration, and maintaining privacy in the forest could be difficult. At the same time, Dale understood and admired her determination to learn what happened to her father.

Gregg Nelson called Dale the next day with news that the board had approved his plan and provided a budget for the expedition. Contracts and legal papers would be awaiting him at the warehouse of the Northern Outfitters Company Mistassini, Province of Quebec, Canada, located at the northern end of Lac St. Jean. He was authorized to select anything he needed from their stockrooms. They were the largest fishing and hunting supply house in the area. Gregg had also authorized additional supplies for Rachel Kemp and for a local guide.

After Dale said good-bye to Gregg, his excitement began to grow. He contacted the Monson Post Office to forward his mail to the Northern Outfitters address, and called Mr. Olman to check on the house once in awhile. Mr. Olman gladly agreed. Dale also wrote and mailed a letter to Iowaka at her home in Mistassini informing her of his plans, hoping that he could arrange a visit with her before departing for the interior.

The next day, Dale rode the Hasey Coach to Greenville. From there he caught a Canadian Pacific train to Montreal where he stayed overnight. He was able to make a connection for a train to Quebec City the next day. The closer he drew to his jumping off point, the more excited he became. From Quebec to Lac St. Jean he had a choice of train or boat. He selected the train because it was faster even though he had to wait two additional days to start the trip.

When he finally arrived at Mistassini, Dale was impressed with the beauty of the forests and mountains. The town of Mistassini was located on the eastern side of the Mistassini River, a short distance from where it empties into Lac St. Jean. Mr. Callahan, a representative of Northern Outfitters, met his train and escorted him to a small inn strategically situated at a bend in the river near the railroad terminal. A box containing various papers was awaiting Dale at the inn where he would be staying until his departure north. Among other things, it contained an authorization to draw materials and supplies as needed, and a check book for expenses.

A large envelope with "Personal" written on the outside caught Dale's attention. As he expected, the information inside related to Rachel Kemp. Gregg vouched for her authenticity and approved the added expense of her accompanying Dale, at least until the end of summer. Gregg left it up to Dale's discretion when Rachel should return home.

Dale and Mr. Callahan spent some time going over plans. Dale's supplies were ready to be shipped as needed. The location of the tract was over one hundred miles due north with a small pond located near the center.

Dale was pleased to learn from Mr. Callahan that a small cabin was located near the pond. Working in such latitudes requires adequate shelter, for weather tends to be erratic and severe. The cabin meant that they would not have to transport tentage or build a shelter when they first arrived on site.

Later, Dale stretched out on his bed at the inn and reviewed his progress. He liked it when a well-formulated plan started to come together successfully. According to the Northern Outfitter representative, the only logical way into the tract with all the supplies for an extended stay was by aircraft. Dale objected at first, but was persuaded when the representative told him that planes equipped with floats on their struts, instead of wheels, could land on virtually any body of water. The use of aircraft had increased dramatically since the war. They were becoming more reliable and versatile as time went by.

The next morning, Dale was enjoying an early breakfast of steak and eggs in the inn's dining room, when he was approached by a Royal Canadian Mounted Policeman. "How do you do, Mr. Cooper, I presume. I'm Inspector Clough. I was hoping to talk to you about your expedition. May I join you for coffee?" the towering policeman asked in a friendly manner.

"Of course, Inspector, sit down," responded Dale, eyeing the man curiously. Inspector Clough was an aging man with gray streaks running through his reddish, curly hair. Tall and broad shouldered with prominent chiseled facial features, the Inspector presented a formidable presence.

"You may not remember me, but we met in France during the war, when I was Chief of Staff of a Canadian division on your left flank," the policeman said taking a seat at the table.

"Oh yes, I remember," Dale nodded. "Colonel Clough, of course. What a pleasant surprise, Sir. I recall our visit now and remember that you told us you were a policeman. What a small world. Please help yourself to the coffee." Dale was genuinely pleased at the chance meeting, motioning for the waiter to bring them more coffee.

"I confess we knew you were coming," admitted the Inspector. "The outfitters notify us whenever people are planning a trip to the interior beyond ten or twenty miles. Your credit voucher listed you as a former Army officer. When I first heard your name, I knew I'd met you but I had to refer to my war journals to be exact. Old age is beginning to work its magic, Laddie. Enjoy your youth as long as you can."

"What do you think of our preparations so far, Inspector?"

"They're sound and well thought out. You won't be able to carry all of your supplies on the first airplane trip though. I suggest that you have the pilot fly out to your site on a weekly basis. That will give you the necessary supplies and weekly mail service, and it's a good insurance policy in case you have to leave for sickness or an accident."

"The plan makes sense, Sir," Dale agreed.

"The flying service that the outfitters have contracted for you are an experienced outfit. They've purchased surplus Navy flying boats and they're meticulously maintained. I can vouch for the pilots, too, they frequently fly for the Force on special operations."

"I'm relieved to hear that," Dale confessed. "I've never flown and I'm a little hesitant about it. I agree that it will be much more convenient than trying to reach our destination by canoes or by foot."

"The police would also like more detailed knowledge of your itinerary. It helps make our job easier if we know beforehand exactly where forest travelers are going and when they expect to return. I'm getting too old to conduct these search and rescue missions that seem to be necessary on a regular basis," said Inspector Clough, helping himself to a piece of toast and marmalade.

Dale nodded. "What do you suggest I do for a guide?" he asked. "I'm aware of the advantages of working in remote areas with at least another person on the team. It helps insure success. We have another member of the party that will be joining us sometime soon."

"You mean the young lady, Rachel Kemp."

"Yes, I didn't realize you knew..." answered Dale with surprise. "I'm not exactly pleased with that development, it sort of came with the job."

"She won't make your job any easier, I grant you that. I don't like to see women come into the north when they have not been initiated to the rigors of life in the woods. There are some though, who get along better than most men. You'll just have to give Miss Kemp a chance, Mr. Cooper."

"Please, call me Dale," he requested, impressed with the Inspector's experience. There was an air of congeniality and confidence about him that made him feel comfortable.

"Dale it is, then. Just so you know, we have a Mounted Police station at Lac St. Jean and we monitor who comes and goes. We're not a police state, of course, but it helps the small number of men we have to cover such a large area, and it simplifies our ability to enforce Canadian laws. In regards to a guide for you, there are a number of competent men available for a fair price. One of the members of the local Cree tribe would be a good selection. I understand you've had the good fortune of becoming acquainted with one of my favorite persons, Miss Ashley Huntington, or Iowaka as she sometimes calls herself."

"Yes, I've met her, Inspector," cried Dale, dumfounded by what he was hearing. "In fact, I had hoped that I'd be able to meet with her again before we jumped off for the 'bush' as you say. Is her tribal reservation very far from here?"

"Only a few miles from here, Dale. I spoke to her this morning on my way from the station, and she asked me to give you this note." The Inspector searched his brown tunic pocket, and extracted a letter which he handed to Dale. "You'll be able to hire one of her tribal members for a guide. They're the best there is. Take it from an old hand."

"I will Inspector, and thanks for all your help. It was good to see you again."

"I've got a busy day ahead of me, Laddie, so good luck on your great adventure. If you want to go out to the reservation, the Inn has an automobile that you can hire." Inspector Clough reached across the table with his large bony hand and grasped Dale's firmly. The grip was like a vice. "Oh, one more thing, Laddie. You may be interested to know that Miss Huntington has been instrumental in establishing a regional infirmary on the tribal grounds. It's not just for tribal members, anyone who needs help is welcome. She's one of our angels of the north and we intend to make sure no harm comes to her. I'm not threatening Laddie, I'm just letting you know that she's one of our shining stars and we're privileged that she's returned to this unsettled region to share her newly acquired nursing skills. For special people like her, we take extra care to see that she's protected and assisted in every way possible."

Dale smiled at the Inspector's remark. "I would expect nothing less for her, and it's exactly what I would do if I was one of your policemen, Inspector."

"I think we're going to get along, Yank," he said, slapping Dale congenially on the shoulder as he left the dining room.

Alone at last, Dale picked up the letter and read:

Dear Dale,

I just received your letter and spoke to Inspector Clough at the police station. It's hard to believe that you're here in the north woods.

I'll be happy to see you at the infirmary if you can find time to visit.

Iowaka

Dale carefully folded the note and tucked it in his pocket, determined to see Iowaka as soon as possible. Upon leaving the dining room, he stopped at the lobby and asked the innkeeper to arrange for a taxi to the infirmary. It was available for immediate use, and Dale raced to his room to get a jacket.

The short ride to the Cree tribal lands gave Dale an opportunity to view the area. The hunting and trapping lands were owned by the native peoples of Canada. The position of the Indian in Canadian society was not as well assimilated as

Dale had imagined it to be. They managed their own lands with the assistance of Provincial and Federal Departments of Indian Affairs.

The small village where the infirmary was located was neat and orderly with log cabins all the same size. The two-story infirmary was a recently constructed building of processed lumber instead of logs. Dale asked the driver to wait for him. He was nervous and approached the front door with an uneasy feeling. Iowaka appeared at the entrance and greeted him warmly.

"Welcome to Canada, Dale!" she said excitedly. The Iowaka before him had the same confident air that Dale remembered, her radiant attitude rivaled by the brightness of her brown eyes. Her white nurses' uniform made a lovely contrast with her dark complexion.

"It's nice to see you again, Iowaka," responded Dale. "What a coincidence that this project brings me here so close to where you live. Another marvelous coincidence is Inspector Clough. I met him in France during the war."

"Really, that's wonderful. Inspector Clough is our guardian angel and we love him. He may look strong and tough to you, but inside, he's all heart," Iowaka smiled. Noticing that the driver was waiting, she suggested, "If you want, you can send the driver back to the Inn and come inside awhile."

Dale discharged the car and returned to the infirmary. Iowaka led him down a hallway, smelling of disinfectant, to a utility room furnished with several arm chairs and a coffee pot percolating on a small gas range.

"This is where the staff likes to relax. Can I get you a cup of coffee?"

"Sure," answered Dale, taking a seat at a small table. "I never refuse coffee."

Iowaka grinned. "I remember that first cup of coffee you fixed for me in Greenville. I was scared, cold, and exhausted. The warm aroma of that cup helped dispel some of my misgivings. I'll always remember your kindness to me."

Dale watched her pour the coffee and take a seat beside him, her relaxed easygoing manner making him feel at home. "You seem content with your work here. The Inspector told me how busy the infirmary has been. He's very proud of you and the staff."

"Of course it's been difficult at times, and we're still learning as we go. There's a desperate need for a facility like this. Since I returned from Greenville, I've assisted at ten births and patched up a lot of injuries. I'm glad to be able to help those who need us."

They talked freely about Dale's expedition and his need for a guide. Iowaka didn't hesitate to recommend her cousin, Edward Blake, with whom she had gone to school. Ed had served in the Canadian Army during the war and fought in France for two years. She promised to have Ed Blake call Dale.

A short time later another Cree nurse interrupted them in the utility room and offered to take over Iowaka's duties for a while if she wanted some time off with her friend. Iowaka thanked her and turned to Dale.

"Would you like to meet my mother? I've told her all about you and she'll be pleased to meet you."

"Sure, I'd like that," Dale answered. The invitation seemed natural.

They left the infirmary and walked along the Mistassini River towards her mother's cabin. Iowaka filled him in on some of the history of the region.

"Some of the men in the village work at the waterfront businesses. The paper mill hires most of them and some women also. That's where my father worked; he was an engineer for the paper company. He came from England as a young man and helped build the plant on the lake. He was not much of a businessman, but he was a brilliant engineer," she explained with pride. "My mother is the leader of the local tribal council. She fell in love with my father the first time they met. They had a wonderful life together, even though the marriage was not accepted by everyone. I think you'll like her."

"If she's like you, I'm sure I will," Dale answered honestly. Iowaka looked at him and smiled.

"We live in the next cabin. When my father was alive, we lived in a house closer to the town of Peribonka. After his death, my mother moved here where she was more comfortable." Iowaka opened the cabin door and announced their presence. "Mother, I've come with a visitor."

The cabin reminded Dale of the one on the Lake of Three Sorrows. The kitchen and dining room were combined in one great room with a large stone fireplace built into the back wall. Bookshelves standing at least eight feet tall were built on both sides of the stone chimney and filled with books of every description. A small ladder leaned against the wall to reach books on the top shelves.

A soft voice wafted from the room on the right. "I'll be right out."

When Iowaka's mother did appear Dale was stunned by her beauty. Other than white streaks in Mrs. Huntington's hair, Iowaka and her mother could nearly pass for sisters. Mrs. Huntington wore a light blue dress with a high lace collar that accented her smooth bronze skin. Her hair hung loose down her back. She had a regal air about her that was complemented by her naturalness and warmth.

"Mother, would you believe it?" said Iowaka. "This is Dale Cooper, the man I told you about in Greenville. He's come to survey some forest land in the north country. Dale, this is my mother Miriam Huntington."

"Welcome to our cabin, Mr. Cooper," greeted Mrs. Hutchington. "My daughter has talked a good bit about you, and I'm glad to have the chance to thank you for being the gentleman you were when she needed help."

"It's wonderful meeting you, Mrs. Huntington. Anyone else would have done the same thing. This is my first trip to northern Canada, and I must say that its beauty exceeds my expectations."

"Beauty is in the eye of the beholder, Mr. Cooper, but I'm glad that you find our portion of the country beautiful," she smiled, grasping Dale's right hand with both of hers. "It's been a long time since we've had a visitor from the United States. Please sit down and make yourself comfortable."

"Thank you," said Dale, taking a seat on the large couch in front of the fireplace. "Your library is impressive. I read a lot when I was a young man. I haven't had much of a chance lately."

"You were in the war," said Mrs. Huntington, taking a seat beside him. Iowaka settled into a chair facing them.

"That's right, I was an infantry captain in the American Army," Dale replied.

"He's also a forester, Mother. That's why he's been commissioned to carry out an evaluation of the land."

Dale settled back in the comfortable couch to absorb the cordiality of the cabin. The steady glow of embers in the fireplace was not the only source of warmth. There was an air of naturalness and informality that made Dale feel at ease. The three of them talked freely for an hour or so about their lives. Mrs. Huntington reminisced about her deceased husband and the problems they had in a society semi-hostile to mixed marriages.

"How did you handle it?" asked Dale.

"My husband was a very gentle man with strong convictions," stated Mrs. Huntington proudly. "He answered the snide, obnoxious remarks with silence, and always said: 'When those critics have a marriage as good as ours, then I'll pay attention to what they have to say.' I loved him for that. I love him just as much today." Her voice was sad.

"What a wonderful legacy for Iowaka. I wish I had known her father."

Iowaka was growing a little uneasy about the direction of the conversation and suggested that they call it a night. She had duty early in the morning. Dale rose from his seat thanking Mrs.

Huntington for her hospitality. She made him promise to come and see her again.

Dale escorted Iowaka back to the infirmary and called for the taxi from there.

"They said it would be right over," he told Iowaka.

"I'm glad you stopped by. It's been nice. I'll send Ed to talk with you tomorrow. If I don't see you again before you leave, I wish you good luck on your project."

"Thank you. I liked your mother. It's really been nice," Dale told her, filled with feelings he could not completely describe. "I won't write for a while, but I'll keep my promise to your mother. Also, Iowaka, I have a question that's been on my mind since we first met. Are you engaged or committed to someone?"

"No," she answered quickly, smiling at the inquiry. She laid her head against his arm. "There have always been opportunities for me to meet young men and I occasionally go out with friends, but I do not have anyone I would call 'special'. The girl who gave you up must have been a fool. Tell me Dale, are these feelings I'm having real or are they just a ridiculous infatuation? Is there something between us that we both share?" She lifted her head and stared, aghast at her spontaneous declaration of feelings.

Dale responded with a simple "Yes," taking her into his arms and kissing her. She returned his caress.

"Be careful on your trip," she whispered. "There are a lot of things that can go wrong in the wilderness. I'm so happy you came. Good-bye, Dale. Until next time."

Dale looked down at her. "I promise to be careful. Don't worry about me. Until next time."

He started to say something else, when she touched her finger to his lips and said softly; "Not now. Don't spoil this moment. I want to remember it until you return."

Chapter Nine

Dale awoke the next morning to the sound of rain driving hard against the window in his room. It was dark and dreary outside. He was amazed at the size of the white-capped waves churning on the lake. They were as large as he had seen on the ocean. The desk clerk intercepted Dale on his way to the dining room for breakfast, announcing that a Miss Rachel Kemp had checked in last night and wished to see him as soon as possible.

"Miss Kemp is in room 202 at the head of the stairs." The round-faced young clerk had a smirk that bothered him, arousing Dale's natural curiosity.

"Is she accompanied by anyone?" Dale asked.

"She was with an older woman who seemed to be out of place this far from civilization," replied the clerk.

"Please let her know that I'll be happy to meet at her convenience. Right now, I'm interested in having some breakfast."

"I'll tell her, Mr. Cooper."

Dale selected a table by a window with a view of the lake and ordered breakfast. Shortly after, a taller-than-average young woman with short blonde hair dressed in a dark maroon dress, entered the dining room anxiously observing each person. When she spied Dale, she confidently walked toward his table and asked; "Excuse me. Are you Mr. Dale Cooper?"

"Yes, I am," he answered, rising to greet her. "You must be Rachel Kemp. You certainly made good time getting here. I didn't expect you for another day. Please, sit down."

"Thank you. I've never been so far from civilization in my life," she admitted with a nervous smile. She shook Dale's hand and took a seat opposite him. Her flushed cheeks and hazel-green eyes mirrored her nervousness, but that did not prevent her from inspecting Dale carefully and perceptively. So far, she was not disappointed.

"This is mild compared to what's ahead of us," Dale stated truthfully. "You know, Miss Kemp, the trip will be difficult at best." She was a very pretty lady he thought, doubting if she could handle the rigors of the planned expedition into the wilderness.

"I've given this a lot of thought," she declared with certainty, meeting Dale's penetrating look. "I understand that it's unorthodox, and I'm sure you're correct about the conditions. Nevertheless, I'm determined to carry out my plan. The fact that you're a perfect stranger to me doesn't make it any easier, but Gregg Nelson has assured us that you can be trusted as an officer and a gentleman."

"What do you mean by 'us'?"

"My mother, Andrea Kemp, has accompanied me to this jumping off point to assure herself that I'll be in good hands."

"Fair enough," responded Dale, enjoying Rachel's pleasant smile and unpretentious manner. The apprehension she exhibited at first soon dissipated. She did not appear to be a vain or self-centered person as some attractive people tend to be; instead, he found her to be direct and spontaneous. Dale inquired seriously, "Miss Kemp, once we get to the forest tract, exactly what do you intend to do about your father? It's most likely that someone has been to the cabin on the property since you first realized that something was wrong. If he had been injured or took sick, surely the Mounted Police would have been notified."

"Mr. Cooper," Rachel responded firmly. "If you were in my shoes, wouldn't you want to find out, first hand, if possible, what happened to your father? Even if we fail to find him, I'll be able to rest easier knowing what his world in the north woods was like. Every friend and acquaintance I've talked to has taken the same position that you have. No one seems to take me seriously when I say that I'm committed to do this."

"I certainly don't mean to question your resolve, Miss Kemp, or to go back on my promise to you. If I were you, I'm certain I'd do the same thing."

"Thank you for saying that," said Rachel, relieved.

"I do have a question that's been bothering me. Please don't think I'm trying to pry or take offense, but have you faced the possibility that your father never intended to return?"

"If you knew my father, you'd never suggest such an outrageous possibility," Rachel cried indignantly. "To answer your question, yes, I have considered it, and dismissed it as totally unlike him. Now, I understand that my decision to make the trip imposes an obligation and responsibility on your part and I'm sorry for the inconvenience. However, I promise to not be a burden for you. I expect and intend to do my share of work. I simply wish to impress upon you how much I need to make this journey."

Dale nodded, recognizing serious determination when he saw it. He would not question her motives again.

Later that day, Dale contacted a flying service capable of transporting the expedition members and their supplies into the interior. The pilot explained that it would be impossible to lift all of their supplies and passengers in one trip, so a follow-up trip could be made within three days, weather permitting. He also suggested that Dale should consider a weekly supply run. Dale agreed.

Edward Blake stopped by the inn late in the afternoon looking for Dale. Dale met him at the hotel bar and took a seat beside him. The bar was practically empty at the time.

"Hello, I'm Dale Cooper. Are you Ed Blake?" Dale asked.

"Yes, Sir. Iowaka asked me to speak with you about the possibility of acting as your expedition guide." Blake had a deliberate, self-confident quality about him that Dale instantly liked. He was shorter by three or four inches and probably outweighed Dale by ten to fifteen pounds. His face was clean shaven with closely cropped black hair. Dale noticed a scar running beneath his left ear down into his neck.

Ed Blake saw Dale look at it. "In case you're wondering about the scar," he said, trailing his fingers along the edge of it.

"None of my business," said Dale. "I didn't mean to stare."

"I was lucky," Ed Blake shrugged his broad shoulders. "It happened in France when the Germans surprised us one night. I can tell you this, the German soldier that did it to me never returned to his lines." It was easy for Dale to imagine this sturdy Canadian Cree as a soldier.

"Thanks for stopping by, Ed. Please, call me Dale. You come highly recommended."

"Well, Iowaka exaggerates sometimes," answered Ed. "I've spent a lot of time in the interior north of Lac St. Jean, and I've been to the area you're interested in cruising. As a matter of fact, I stopped by the cabin back in 1919 right after I got out of the Army. I visited with a gentleman there who told me that he was prospecting for gold. I may be mistaken, but I believe he owned the land."

"You mean you actually met Charles Kemp?" Dale asked.

"Yes, Sir," Ed continued. "We talked for a few hours. I'd been out exploring for a new trap line after my medical discharge, he offered to put me up for the night. I was anxious to return to my own base camp so I refused the offer. Why does that sound so unusual?"

"We're going to be accompanied by a woman, Rachel Kemp, who claims to be Charles's daughter. Her family hasn't heard from him for three years, and they've been assuming he's dead. Whatever information you have about Kemp, will be of interest to Rachel," Dale paused, collecting his thoughts. "Did you say that you were medically discharged?"

"Yes," Ed replied. "I received some nasty gas burns under my arms and chest, and of course the cut on my neck when our Canadian battalion held a portion of the line at Vimy Ridge.

89

Then, just months before the Armistice I was wounded in the leg by German machine gun fire. I was determined to not let it limit my life so I exercised vigorously after it healed. I'm as good as I ever was on my feet, Sir."

"I don't doubt that, Ed," Dale replied, encouraged by Ed's quiet self-confidence. "What rank did you hold?"

"I was a sergeant in my rifle company."

"I had a feeling you were a sergeant. You talk like one," Dale smiled. "Right now we've both left the Army behind, so no more 'Sir' stuff. It's just Ed and Dale."

"Does that mean you want to hire me, Dale?"

"You bet," Dale responded emphatically. "I'm fortunate to have you. If weather is favorable for flying tomorrow, we can leave as soon as the pilot gives the word. Can you be ready by then?"

"That's fine with me. I've flown with the pilot that will take us into the bush. He shot down two German planes when he was in the Royal Air Force."

"That makes me feel better. I've never flown before. By the way," Dale shook his head. "We did not talk about your salary. How about two dollars a day?"

"That's very generous and I accept. I think tomorrow will be suitable for flying. If there's nothing else to discuss I've got lots to do before I leave," said Ed, rising from his seat. "Incidentally, does Miss Kemp know about her father's activities after he left for the north woods?"

"I can't speak for her, but as far as I know, she and her mother have not heard a word from him in years. Like I said, they assume that he's dead," said Dale, wondering about Ed's measured question. "Do you have anything to add?"

"I have no knowledge of what happened to him," Ed replied.

"I'll see you in the morning, Ed. Thanks for taking the job." Dale watched the stocky figure leave the room.

It had been a productive afternoon. Dale sat at the table in his room and drafted a letter to Gregg Nelson informing him of the progress of the operation, and that it might be possible to submit weekly reports depending upon the weather. Dale also wrote a letter to Mr. and Mrs. Olman, bringing them up to date on his movements and intentions. He was interrupted by a knock at the door.

"The door's open", Dale called out.

The desk clerk opened the door. "Excuse me Mr. Cooper, Mrs. Charles Kemp and her daughter wanted to know if you could meet them in the dining room for the evening meal."

"Tell them I'd be glad to," said Dale. "What time would be best?"

"We serve dinner between six and eight o'clock. I suggest seven o'clock."

"That'll be fine," answered Dale, checking his gold pocket watch. It had been a present from his family when he was commissioned a second lieutenant in the Army. He was hoping to see Iowaka before his departure the next morning and was disappointed to have committed himself for a portion of his last evening.

The Inn was a busy place for such a small community. Mistassini was a popular jumping off point for people entering the remote regions of the northern forests. Vacationers and sportsmen were the most prevalent. Occasionally a gold prospector gambled that he could find the mother-lode if he just tried one last time. Some of the forest travelers went into the bush by foot, but the improved reliability of the airplane had made it the increasingly preferred mode of transportation, and sparked a whole new industry of adventuresome entrepreneurs whose knowledge of the northern wilderness and love of flying was their stock and trade.

The dining room was filling up rapidly when Dale made his way through the lobby to a vacant table. Minutes later, Rachel Kemp entered the room with an elderly lady in tow. The head waiter directed them to his table.

Rachel made the necessary introductions. "It's my pleasure to meet you, Mrs. Kemp. Please sit down," invited Dale warmly.

"Rachel insisted that I meet you before leaving for the north," said Mrs. Kemp. She was a tall, thin woman whose prominent nose and forehead gave her a hawkish appearance. Her once proud blond hair was now streaked with gray and white. There was an elitist air of formality and self-sufficiency about her that irritated Dale. Her daughter, by contrast, exhibited a refreshing excitement about the great adventure that was unfolding for her. The waiter accepted their dinner orders and left.

"Are we going to leave early in the morning?" Rachel asked eagerly.

"Yes. Everything is all set for our departure. The weather looks promising and I've made arrangements with a guide familiar with the area, a young Cree by the name of Ed Blake."

"Do you mean an Indian is going to be a permanent part of your expedition?" exclaimed Mrs. Kemp.

"Yes, Mrs. Kemp."

"Well, I hope you'll be able to protect Rachel. After all one never knows what people like that are capable of."

"Mother," gasped Rachel. "I can't believe you said that."

"Your daughter will be safe on this trip, Mrs. Kemp. You can be assured that I'll live up to the promise. I don't share the same sentiment that you entertain for the native peoples. I trust Ed Blake, a veteran of the war, by the way."

Mrs. Kemp was about to comment further, but Rachel interjected, "Mother, let's drop the subject, please." Dale liked the firm resolute look Rachel gave her mother. She was more her own person than he had imagined.

"If you say so, dear," said Mrs. Kemp, turning to Dale. "I came this far to try and talk Rachel out of the fantasy she holds about her father being alive. Now, I see that she is more determined than ever to follow through regardless of my protests. Mr. Nelson assured us that she would be in good hands. Now that I've met you, I can only pray that he's right."

"I'm flattered by your endorsement, Mrs. Kemp," replied Dale with a touch of irony. At that point the waiter served their dinners.

As the evening continued, Dale began to see Mrs. Kemp in a more favorable light. Whenever she spoke of her concern for her husband, her eyes glistened with suppressed tears that lingered for a long time. Dale sympathized with her and hoped that the expedition would dispel some of the uncertainty regarding Charles Kemp's disappearance. It was also evident that Mrs. Kemp loved Rachel very much and was probably guilty of sheltering her more than necessary. While Rachel returned her mother's affection, she also let it be known that she was in control of her own destiny.

The dining room customers were slowly thinning out. Dale and the Kemps were casually enjoying a final cup of coffee when Dale caught a glimpse of Iowaka, still wearing her uniform, standing at the entrance foyer of the dining room. He motioned for her to join them. She approached the table cautiously.

"I'm glad you came, Iowaka." Dale stood up to greet her.

"I hope I'm not intruding," she said.

"Not at all," Dale replied, pulling out a chair for her. "Please have a seat. I'd like you to meet Mrs. Charles Kemp and her daughter Rachel Kemp. This is Iowaka, she works at the infirmary here in town."

"I'm glad to meet you, Iowaka," responded Rachel sincerely. "What a lovely name."

"Hello, young lady," said Mrs. Kemp. "Are you a nurse?"

"Yes, I'm a graduate nurse practitioner," answered Iowaka. She had detected an undertone in Mrs. Kemp's remarks that made her a bit defensive.

"You must be very proud," said Rachel, anxious to deflect any potential conflict. "You caught us just as we were about to leave, Iowaka. If you'll excuse my mother and me the two of you can talk in private. It was nice meeting you. I'll be ready first thing in the morning, Mr. Cooper."

"That will be fine," answered Dale, standing as they left the table. "Goodnight."

"Good night, Mr. Cooper," said Mrs. Kemp ignoring Iowaka.

"Well!" Iowaka said after the Kemps left the room. "I gather she doesn't approve of me. There are a lot of ways to register unacceptability. The most hurtful is silence."

"I apologize for her rude behavior. At least her daughter has some common decency."

"I didn't mean to break up your evening. I just finished my shift and took a chance that you would be here. I wanted to wish you good luck and 'bon voyage'. What did you think of Ed Blake?"

"He'll work out great. Thanks for sending him to me. Rachel will be coming along on the expedition, too. She wants to find out firsthand what happened to her father."

Iowaka hesitated a moment and said, "I spoke to Ed before I came here and he asked me to tell you privately that when he saw Charles Kemp at the cabin, there was a Cree woman with him. It was obvious that they had been living there together for some time. The woman was pregnant!"

Chapter Ten

"What?" Dale demanded. "Is he sure of this?"

"I don't see why Ed would make up such a story. At first, he considered it would be better not to tell you, but the more he thought about it the more he felt that you had a right to know. Does this complicate the trip for you?"

"I hope not. Anyway, we'll deal with it when it becomes a problem. Have you eaten?" Iowaka was uneasy.

"I ate at the infirmary," she answered. "I hope that I didn't interrupt your evening, Dale. I really must go." She rose from the table quickly, an unsettled look on her face.

Dale grabbed her by the arm and said, "What's wrong, Iowaka? You're not yourself tonight."

"Nothing really…"

"If you insist on leaving may I please take you home?" Dale felt frustrated.

"If you don't mind, Dale. I only wanted to wish you well and ask when you expected to return."

Dale called for the Inn's taxi to take them to her home. They rode in silence for awhile until Dale asked the driver to let them off so that they could walk along the river. The wind was brisk but refreshing, and the evening stars were aglow in the blue-black sky. It was a beautiful night.

"You know, Iowaka," said Dale reaching for her hand. "Not everyone is like Mrs. Kemp. I'm sorry you were the object of her rudeness."

"I've had to deal with her type all of my life. You'd think I'd be used to it by now," she exclaimed, breathing hard. "It makes me feel dirty and cheap and I resent it. I can forgive her for thinking the way she does, but I'll never understand it. I accept the fact that I'm a half-breed, and am proud of who I am. What I object to the most is that attitude of inconsiderate people often makes me feel ashamed of what I am."

Dale stopped walking as a shooting star arched across the sky, leaving a plume of fiery light that shone from horizon to horizon. He confronted Iowaka holding her at arms length so that he could see her face in the limited light available. "Stop that kind of talk. Do you remember what I told you back in Maine?"

"Yes, and I believe you were sincere when you said it. That doesn't change the facts. Even my mother has cautioned me not to reach too far unless I was prepared for the consequences. To be honest, Dale, lately I've thought more about it than ever before."

"Because of me?" Dale asked.

"Yes, because of you. When my imagination starts to work overtime, I visualize ugly situations like tonight happening all the time." Iowaka leaned her head disconsolately against his chest. Dale had never seen her like this. The feelings they had for each other were so strong and so new that neither of them quite knew how to handle the phenomenon.

"The first time I met you, Iowaka," Dale struggled to find the right words. "I knew that something special and wonderful had come into my life. I can't pretend to know what it's like to experience prejudice, but I do know that nothing is impossible if two people want something badly enough to make it work."

Iowaka sighed. "When I'm with you, everything seems to be right with the world. Yet, if it's right, then why does it hurt so much?"

"You ask too many questions," Dale told her, tilting her chin upward and kissing her lightly. "I'm a believer in fate. I've seen men die in combat while others two feet away remained untouched. There has to be some reason why things happen the way they do, even if it's beyond our comprehension. If we share the same feelings for each other, then we shouldn't question it."

"It's just so hard to trust, Dale," she whispered. "Still, love can't be wrong, can it?"

Dale felt a warm glow within. "No, love is never wrong."

Hand in hand they walked the rest of the way to her mother's cabin in silence. Words were no longer necessary to speak what was in their hearts. The soft glow of candles in the windows of cabins along the route guided them to Iowaka's mother's home.

"Would you like to come in for a while?" asked Iowaka.

"It's getting late and your mother may be resting. I don't want to disturb her. I'm not sure how long this trip will take, but I'll contact you as soon as we return. The plane will be making weekly supply runs, so maybe we can send messages through them."

She squeezed his hand. "I'll keep in touch, and pray for your safe return. I'll miss you, Dale."

"I'm so glad it was my cabin you ran to in Greenville," he told her. "Otherwise I would never have met you." They held each other for a long time before saying good-bye. Dale watched her disappear behind the cabin door.

Early the next morning Dale, Ed Blake, and Rachel were racing north through the clouds. The two-engine float plane soared easily above the limitless green forest with nothing below but a carpet of green canopies interspersed with ponds, lakes, and streams of various sizes. Intermingled with the spruce-fir forest type, Dale noticed numerous golden brown bogs filled with meadow grass and stunted spruce trees a few feet tall.

The noise in the cabin of the plane was deafening. Each of the three passengers were a bit apprehensive about flying. Ed Blake's attempt at nonchalance was unconvincing. He held his head tight against the seat he was strapped to and his knuckles were white from gripping the arm rests. Rachel, on the other hand, tried little to hide her fears. She looked faint as she stared out the window astonished at how high she was above the ground. Dale was nervous but he had developed a "what-the-hell" attitude during the war that allowed him to overcome his fear. The continuous forest below was fascinating; the longer he looked, the more detail he observed. The streams and rivers were lined with a thin strip of deciduous trees producing a lighter hue of green than the coniferous spruce-fir forest type.

Sections of forest that had been clear-cut were evident in those areas closest to streams where the logs could be floated to market. From the air it was possible to appreciate the checkerboard-like squares of land, several acres in size that had been cleared of all trees for pulp and lumber. Provisions for regeneration of the harvested areas was insured by the residual blocks of forest left uncut surrounding them. Prevailing winds swept the bare openings with seeds from nearby trees. The system had been in operation for generations, and those areas harvested several years previously were now covered with a lush green stand of young saplings, primarily spruce, which develops faster from seed in mineral soil and full sunlight than its companion, balsam fir, which develops easier in partial shade. The young forests are more productive than the mature forests, sustaining a more diverse wildlife population and improving water quality by allowing snow to accumulate on the ground instead of in the canopy, where it melts quicker.

One hour from the time the plane had left Lac St. Jean, they were approaching their destination. The pilot banked the plane to position it for a landing on the small body of water below them. The plane slowed and began its descent miles from the pond, the tree tops below them drawing nearer and nearer. The pilot shut down the engines as soon as the floats touched the water, sending up plumes of spray on both sides of the plane. Finally, the aircraft gently slowed to a stop at the far end of the pond.

They had arrived! Dale scanned the shore to locate the cabin. The simple log structure was a welcome sight, even if it did look a bit small for three people. Ed Blake jumped into the water to secure the plane to a nearby tree. The pilot told them that he wanted to unload their supplies as quickly as possible. Weather conditions shifted rapidly in the northern latitudes. Dale helped Rachel from the plane into the shallow water. She jumped in without hesitation, thanking God to be back on solid ground. They all helped to unload their small amount of luggage and supplies. The pilot told them that he would return in two or three days with a full load of supplies. Ed released the tethering line and helped Dale push the float plane into deeper water.

The three adults stood on the shore watching their only link to the civilized world fade from view. Dale was elated that his great adventure was about to begin, yet a feeling of abandonment momentarily rushed over him as the drone of the plane's engines grew fainter and disappeared altogether, leaving them in the silence of the immense sub-boreal forest, closer to the arctic circle than to the equator. Ed picked up his ax and walked toward the cabin. Rachel was on the verge of tears when the reality of her situation finally hit her. "I'm not sure I realized what I was in for," she said.

"Take heart, Rachel," Dale smiled. "So far so good. We've arrived in good shape with provisions intact and good weather to organize our camp before nightfall. Come, let's check out the cabin."

"I never thought it would be quite so desolate and harsh," she admitted, following Dale toward the cabin. "But you're right, so far, so good."

The cabin was less than half the size of Dale's cabin. It would be tight for three people. The northern wall of the cabin was covered with a stone fireplace. The floor was smoothly packed earth, scattered with bits of leaves and spruce cones. The only piece of furniture was a small table made from two split pieces of straight grained white ash fastened together, attached to the eastern wall. Two split logs served as seats. Facilities were rough but serviceable. There were no utensils or evidence of recent occupancy.

"Well, we've got one piece of furniture to start with," said Dale cheerfully lighting a candle he had taken from one of the packs Ed had placed near the door.

Dale and Ed checked the condition of the field stone chimney chinked with clay, determining that it was perfectly safe to use. It was colder on the ground than expected, and it looked as if a fire was going to be a daily necessity. Therefore, Dale established the production of a supply of firewood as their first priority. He had anticipated the need for axes and saws and had included them in the supplies that accompanied them.

Dale was resolute that they work as a team to make the expedition a success. Rachel immediately began to collect fir branches for use as a broom to sweep the cabin clean. Such initiative would help her adjust to wilderness routines much faster, thought Dale.

"What do you think about using the west wall, opposite the table, as your sleeping area, Rachel?" Dale asked her. "We can rig some curtains for your privacy and build a platform of soft branches for a mattress."

"That will be all right. I don't want to be a bother."

"Listen, young lady," he told her. "We might as well have an understanding here and now. There are certain things that you have a right to as a woman. A place to sleep and dress in privacy is a minimum of what should be made available to you. When I said that you could come along on this trip, I anticipated making provisions for your personal needs. So, it's not in any way a bother to Ed or myself. We'll work together and look out for each other. That way, everything will go much easier. So, no more about being a bother, okay?"

"Okay," answered Rachel grinning uneasily.

Ed was in his element. He had already begun collecting dry firewood and dragging it to the cabin site. Dale volunteered to saw the wood scraps into usable lengths and stack it in a pile against the cabin wall. Once they had accumulated enough wood to last a couple of days, they could concentrate on the reason they had made this journey in the first place.

Rachel cleaned the walls and floor of the cabin while Dale and Ed worked on firewood. She also organized their supplies and piled a large stack of firewood beside the fireplace. Then, using some dry cedar shavings that Dale had whittled for her, she started their first fire in the fireplace.

Their spirits rose immediately as they watched the flames grow. The sparse cabin was instantly cozier and more cheerful. As soon as the sun disappeared behind the trees on the horizon, the air turned cooler. By the time they sat down to a supper of baked beans and biscuits, they were exhausted. Ed had baked the biscuits on a small reflector oven he had packed, and it was to become one of their most prized items.

After eating and scrubbing their plates in the lake with sand, Dale and Ed rushed into the dense stands of timber to gather princess pine and caribou moss for Rachel's bed, before it became too dark. Princess pine is a small bush, six to ten inches tall, that grows as a ground cover beneath spruce and fir stands. Caribou moss is a white colored lichen that grows in similar locations. They have provided comfortable and fragrant cushioning material for forest travelers for generations.

As Dale and Ed dumped several armloads of the material on the floor of the cabin, Rachel fashioned a thick mattress by tightly wrapping them with two blankets, and fastening them together with safety pins. When she was finished, she had a mattress almost ten inches thick of the soft vegetation.

"Thank you, Dale and Ed," said Rachel pleased with the success of her new bed. "I'm so tired, I could sleep anywhere, but this will feel good tonight."

"We've got just one more thing to put together tonight," said Dale. "I included two large tarps in our supplies that we could have used as tents in case the cabin wasn't usable. Since we don't need both of them, we can use one to partition off a part of the west wall for your privacy. For tonight, Ed and I will use the other tarp as a lean-to outside."

He and Ed fashioned a curtain out of one of the tarps for Rachel's sleeping area. She retired shortly after they completed the installation. That evening, Dale made his first entry in a daily log book, in which he included everything worthy of mention.

Then, Dale and Ed stepped outside to erect their lean-to. Dale had purchased three sleeping bags heavy enough for the chilly climate and especially suited for the outdoors. A thin sheet of rubber on the bottom of each bag protected the user from wet ground.

The night was dark and cool. A soft breeze swept across the vast forests from the northwest saturated with the sweet bouquet from spruce, fir, and cedar trees. The scent at times was so strong that they could almost taste it. Dale breathed deeply pulling the clean air deep into his lungs. Laying snug and comfortable in his sleeping bag, Dale watched the stars in the dark sky feeling as if he was alone in the universe at the top of the world. The plaintive howl of wolves across the lake were answered by other members of the pack north of the cabin, only intensifying his feeling of utter loneliness. Their piercing cries filled the midnight hour as the illusive spirits of their ancestors caressed the landscape. The nocturnal creatures took control of the night.

Inside the cabin, Rachel lay on her makeshift bed and watched the dying embers in the fireplace slowly fade from red to gray. She was exhausted, yet, found herself unable to sleep. She was proud to have come this far to solve the mystery of her father's disappearance, and was willing, even eager, to do her share in this harsh environment. It was both intimidating and inspiring. Rachel could not help thinking about her father. Her life in the city had not prepared her for this primal wilderness, but she was determined to do all she could to solve the mystery of his disappearance. At last, her eyes closed and she drifted off to sleep.

While they slept, the heavens put on a show that would have dazzled any audience in the world. The famous northern lights, the aurora borealis, erupted in glorious color, filling the skies with brilliant red, green, and yellow designs always in motion, rolling and curling across the cobalt-blue sky in erratic designs. At one time it looked like a river of diffused light tumbling down a pathway like a waterfall. Snapping and hissing sounds accompanied the symphony of color, resembling a dreamy illusion like waves of misty light churning across the sky.

The next day, Dale and Ed set out to explore the tract. Rachel decided to remain at the cabin to try her luck fishing in the pond to supplement their rations. Dale oriented the cabin and lake, and the position of the sun with his compass. The parcel of land was rectangular in shape, with the borders tied into streams or other water bodies. Rarely did the map make any reference to unique land formations in the area. When Dale and Ed checked the western north-south line, they found blaze marks on trees which coincided with their determination of the boundary line. Someone had clearly marked the boundary two or three years ago!

The discovery of the marks kindled a spark of enthusiasm in them, offering hope that they might be able to learn something about Rachel's father. They followed the western line to the juncture of the northern boundary, which ran east-west, and found a pile of rocks with a spruce branch inserted in the center. The branch had been cut from a live tree about three years ago. They found similar evidence of human activity all along the northern border to the juncture of the eastern boundary which ran north to south.

Dale and Ed spent several days marking and documenting the boundary lines, concluding that there were no complications with abutting properties. They found an unusual situation near the southern boundary not far from the cabin. Large rock out-crops filled an area, fifteen to twenty acres, with very little soil. The glaciers had scrapped this section of northern Canada down to bedrock, which became known as the Canadian Shield. Crops were next to impossible to grow on the shallow soil. When tree growth eventually developed, it was frequently affected by windthrow because the roots were unable to penetrate deep enough in the barren soil to hold the large trees upright. They scanned the uprooted areas for evidence of mineral deposits, noting that one location had mottled, dark green rock formations which they believed to be asbestos.

They also found evidence of aluminum within the blowdown area. Clay, slate, shales, schists, and granite all contained large amounts of aluminum oxide. The deposit Dale was most impressed with was creamy white in color, with streaks of yellow, brown and red. He made a note of its location in his journal with a thought that it might, some day, be of commercial importance. Minerals without access to transportation systems were worthless. Still, the future potential was noteworthy. They retrieved several samples of bauxite and asbestos for evaluation in a laboratory.

Rachel's fishing attempt had been successful that first day. She had caught three good-sized trout which they all enjoyed for dinner. She was always alert for something that would clarify the disappearance of her father. She had discovered a set of initials that might have been his carved on a log near the cabin. Several feet behind the cabin she also discovered an old refuse dump partially covered with caribou moss which, from a distance, resembled a blanket of snow on the ground. The dump failed to yield any substantive clues except that the last person to occupy the cabin had consumed a lot of canned baked beans and tea. She had hoped to find some sort of link to her father, but she found nothing. There was no evidence of clothing or personal items, like a watch or a comb or a hat, that might have been left behind. She was discouraged. It was as if he had never existed!

On the morning of the third day, all three of them were heartened to hear the drone of engines in the distance. An airplane was approaching. They ran to the pond to watch it land. It was a smaller aircraft than the one that had brought them north, but it was the same pilot. He threw Ed and Dale a line to pull the aircraft closer to the shore.

"I would have come yesterday, but we had engine trouble on one of the planes," said the pilot they knew as Pete, opening an access door on the plane's fuselage. "I've got all the supplies

I could carry on this trip. Not as much as you hoped for, but it's the best we could do. I'll be back within a week's time to make sure you're not short."

"It's reassuring to have you return on schedule," replied Dale, helping Pete and Ed unload the supplies.

As soon as the plane was unloaded, Pete thoroughly checked the undercarriage of the empty aircraft. "I'm always concerned about floating debris and logs. It doesn't take a hell of a lot to collapse the pontoons. By the way, do you have anything for me to take out for you?"

"We've got some ore samples for you to deliver to the outfitters," replied Dale, passing them to Pete. "They're expecting them. I've included some observations and notes with the samples. I was hoping I'd have a letter or two to post, but there wasn't time. I'm sure I will on your next trip." Rachel ran into the cabin to get a letter she had written to her mother, and gave it to Pete.

"I almost forgot. Inspector Clough gave me an envelope and asked that I deliver it to you," said Pete, reaching into the cockpit of the plane, and handing it to Dale. "I'm not going to stick around long. We're expecting some unsettled weather tonight. I'll see you in a week."

They watched the plane circle the small pond and disappear with some misgivings. Rachel had a sad gleam in her eye as if she had given up hope of finding some evidence about her father's disappearance. The agonizing uncertainty of never knowing what happened to him was discouraging. Ed shrugged his shoulders as they headed back to the cabin. He had taken the job as much for his cousin, Iowaka, as he had for the money. Therefore, the quicker they completed their task, the sooner he would be able to return to his family.

Dale was anxious to see what was in the large envelope from Inspector Clough. He sat on the ground in front of the cabin with the sun facing him and read the note inside:

Dear Mr. Cooper,

I am sending you this packet of messages, one for each member of your party, in the hope that word from the outside world will make your stay in the bush more tolerable.

Also, I wanted to remind you to be on the alert for whiskey peddlers. They appear to be bolder than ever this summer and will get worse before the heavy snows come.

Best wishes on your project.

Insp. Gerard Clough,
RCMP

Dale smiled. It was as if the Inspector had read their minds. "Ed and Rachel," he shouted. "I have mail for you."

"Mail for me?" asked Rachel, running from the cabin.

"Yes, this was in the packet," Dale explained, handing the letter to her. "You have one also, Ed."

"I bet it's from my wife," he said, accepting the letter with a smile.

"I didn't know you were married, Ed," said Dale, surprised.

"You never asked, so I never told you."

"Do you have any children?" asked Rachel with interest.

"My daughter, Linda, is one year old," Ed announced proudly. "She and my wife, Tasha, live at the same village as Iowaka. I'm not worried about their safety, but I miss them."

Ed and Rachel stepped back inside the cabin. Dale tore open the envelope marked for him from Iowaka. He devoured the words.

Dear Dale,

Inspector Clough guaranteed me a place for this letter on the first supply flight to your base of operations. I miss you already and you've only been gone for two days! When you're not with me I have difficulty believing what has happened between us. It's been so quick and I worry about that fact as much as I do the different cultures we come from.

I will not dwell on the negatives. You are always in my thoughts, and I relive the events in Greenville over and over, trying to understand what we've been experiencing. I look forward to your return and wish you success in your project.

Take care of yourself and say 'hi' to Ed and Rachel. Until next time, Dale. I love you.

Iowaka

The weather changed rapidly soon after the plane had left. The skies turned black and winds increased in velocity enough so that Dale and Ed moved their sleeping bags inside. By the time they got the fire in the fireplace going, the heavens were emptying themselves. It poured with a vengeance. The rain was whipped into a greater fury by winds which now approached hurricane proportions.

"On a night like this a man can be thankful for basic comforts such as a roof over his head and a warm fire," declared Ed, his strong profile silhouetted against the glow from the fireplace.

"A woman, too," admitted Rachel. She turned to Ed. "My admiration and respect for your people has grown these past few days. Just surviving up here is an accomplishment. My life back in New York was so different, we take so much for granted. I've experienced more feelings since I came north than I ever thought I had in me. You know, even while I was scared to death in the airplane, there was something satisfying about going forward in spite of the fears."

Dale watched her with an amused smile. The lovely lady with the short blond hair looked like a stereotype of her social birth; however, there was a strength and grace within her that she was just beginning to discover. Dale admired how she never complained about anything and eagerly approached the discoveries that each day introduced. He watched her grow in confidence and self-reliance, learning to trust her own ability to adapt to her surroundings. Many of her peers would have been rendered completely helpless in the same situation.

"How is your mother?" Dale inquired.

"She wrote to tell me that she's returning home," Rachel answered. "It's just as well. She would be miserable staying in Canada, and probably she'd make everyone around her feel the same way if she had stayed."

The shrieking wind and driving rain continued until dawn. Then, the storm stopped as quickly as it had started. The early morning sun warmed the wet earth, causing dense sheets of mist to rise and dissipate into the air.

Shortly after he awoke, Dale stepped outside to check on weather conditions, hoping that they would be able to continue their forest inventory of the property. Heavy clouds in the west dictated they should stick close to the cabin in case of sudden shifts in weather. As Dale and Ed prepared to set out, Rachel asked if she could be a third member of the inventory team. Dale was gratified at the proposal. He would never have imposed upon her to participate, but he was pleased that she wanted to contribute. She promptly took on the task of recording the diameter and height measurements of the different tree species as Dale and Ed measured them within the selected plot samples.

By midday, Dale realized, they had progressed half again further than they would have without her. It was time for a break, and they stopped for lunch near an open ledge. Rachel had insisted on carrying the small pack containing their sandwiches so that the men could move more freely around the sample plots.

"Do we have to continue our line into the blowdown area?" asked Rachel, passing out the sandwiches.

"We should do a few plots," answered Dale, sitting down on a rock. He took a bite from his sandwich. "I'm starved. This bannock bread you make is pretty good, Ed. I've heard about it, but this is the first time I've ever tasted it."

"It's a staple food for trappers and hunters in the forest," Ed acknowledged the compliment with a smile and continued in his relaxed, deliberate manner. "It isn't bad, but I prefer the yeast bread my wife bakes in a regular oven. In the bush you're usually so hungry anything tastes good."

"I think you're right Ed, out here anything would taste good," teased Rachel. "I better watch what I say or you'll be asking me to do the cooking, and that would be a disaster for all of us." Playful banter passed easily between them.

After lunch Dale followed a compass line into the blowdown area. The bearing took him through a recent landslide that had toppled several large trees from the crest of a prominent knoll. The momentum of the slide scoured the soil and vegetation from the side of the hill making it impossible for Dale to continue in a straight line, so he offset a few feet to the east in a line that took him over a portion of the denuded hilltop.

Rechecking his compass bearing, Dale had the feeling that something was not right. He carefully scanned the side of the hill that had been denuded by the slide and discovered a black opening in the rocks to his right. He was curious, and went to investigate. To Dale's surprise, the mud slide had uncovered an opening to a cave.

A broken tree trunk blocked a portion of the cave opening. Dale pulled himself over the trunk and dropped on the other side near the cave's entrance. He struck a match to light the black interior and knelt to see what was on the cave floor when the flame went out. He lit a second match which illuminated the floor at his feet and let out a startled cry. On the floor of the cave lay the skeletal remains of a human being!

Chapter Eleven

The small match did not give off enough light for Dale to see beyond where he stood. The skeleton at his feet appeared to be a male. The clothing that remained looked like remnants of a plaid Hudson Bay mackinaw. His first thoughts were that the body might be Rachel's father.

"Dale, Dale," hollered Ed. "Where are you? Are you all right?"

"I'm fine, Ed," Dale answered, climbing back over the fallen tree in front of the cave entrance. "Stay where you are, I'll be out in a second."

"What happened? We heard you cry out?"

"I'll tell you in a minute," Dale said, wondering whether to tell Rachel what he had found.

"Did you hurt yourself?" asked Ed, waiting on the other side of the fallen tree.

"No, I got a little tangled up in a recent mud slide," Dale replied, trying to hide his excitement.

Rachel studied the look on his face and knew that something unusual had taken place. "You've found something haven't you, Dale?" she questioned. He realized that any attempt to keep information away from her would be futile.

"You're looking a little pale," admitted Ed.

"I was going to keep it from you, Rachel, until we could be certain. Yes, I found a cave on the other side of the fallen tree with human remains inside."

"My Father," screamed Rachel, her composure gone. "Lead us to it."

"Not now, Rachel," Dale answered firmly, holding her by the arm. "First of all, it's completely dark, we can't see anything inside the cave. We should return to the cabin for a lantern and candles so that we can explore the interior, and bring notebooks to record what we find and where it's located. I think we should treat the discovery as if it was a crime scene, since it may very well be, don't you agree?"

"Yes, that's for the best," answered Ed quickly. "We can send for the police when the next plane arrives."

Rachel sat down on the rock where she had eaten her lunch to collect her thoughts. There was no doubt in her mind that the skeleton was her father. At first, she was eager to rush to the scene to make a positive identification, but the more she thought about it, the more reluctant she was to view the remains.

"Perhaps I shouldn't go," she cried in a shaky voice.

Dale knelt beside her. She was like a child in many ways. He didn't think it would be healthy for her to see the skeleton. It would leave an unsightly memory of the last view she had of her father.

"I think that's a good idea," he replied. "Why don't we go back to the cabin? Ed and I will pick up a lantern and return. We'll let you know what we find. What do you say to that?"

She nodded meekly. "Okay. I can't look at his body just now. I want to remember him as he was, tall and strong and full of life. I don't want to be a burden to you but I'd appreciate it if you and Ed would find out what happened."

"We'll do our best," Ed replied, understanding her position.

Dale checked his watch and concluded that they had enough time to return to the cabin and check the cave before darkness limited them. Meanwhile, Rachel promised to start a fire and prepare supper.

Dale and Ed quickly grabbed candles and lanterns and headed back to the cave. It turned out to be as large as the cabin with a ceiling high enough for the men to stand upright. They carefully explored every inch of the interior with the lanterns. There was a single corpse on the earth floor with a revolver in its right hand. It looked as if he had shot himself in the temple. Dale and Ed exchanged glances. This was not what they expected to find.

They went through the man's pants and shirt pockets being careful not to disturb the body, which had not been completely stripped of flesh by rodents, but the remainder had started to mummify. All they found in the tattered clothing were a few .32 caliber cartridges for the pistol in the man's hand.

"It looks as if he had been living in here for a while," Ed called from the back wall of the cave. "There's a small wooden box of personal items next to what must have been a bed at one time."

Dried balsam fir boughs had been stacked several inches deep in a corner of the cave. Closer examination of the area also turned up a rusty hunting rifle propped against the wall beside the bed and a tin cup on the floor.

"Let's bring that box out closer to the entrance where the light is better. Wow, this thing is heavy," Dale remarked. A candle had melted down over the cover of the box, leaving a stub affixed. They removed the cover revealing three moose hide bags filled with gold dust.

"My God, there's a fortune here," Dale cried, carefully lifting the bags out of the container and checking to make sure there were no holes. In the bottom of the box was a leatherbound ledger wrapped in an old shirt imprinted with the initials of Charles Kemp. The ledger was filled with writing. Dale did not take the time to read it thoroughly, but saw enough to determine that Charles Kemp had been locked inside the cave by a landslide. The journal indicated that he had survived for several days until thirst became so unbearable that he chose to take his life. He had left notes describing what had happened to him after he had come to northern Canada. Dale closed his eyes for a moment. What a horrible way to die. His heart ached for Rachel.

"What is it?" asked Ed eagerly scanning the contents of the ledger.

"There's a note in here to Rachel and her mother." Dale added. "I have a feeling we should contact Inspector Clough as soon as possible. It'll be a week before the supply plane returns. Is there any way we might get a message out sooner?"

Ed considered the question. "As far as I know, the closest village is at Fort Lewis, probably sixty miles northwest of here. There's a Mounted Police detachment there."

"That's too far for us to travel," Dale shook his head. "I guess we'll just have to continue with our work and wait for the plane. What do you think, Ed?"

"We could build a large brush fire with green wood that would send up lots of smoke," suggested Ed shrugging his shoulders. "If anyone was in the area they might check out the source of the smoke. Of course you never know who you're going to attract. My gut feeling is that we should keep this to ourselves and wait for the plane."

"I think you're right, Ed," said Dale. "We should leave the body and the contents of the cave as we found them, and move the wooden box to the cabin for safe keeping."

"Rachel is going to feel awful when she finds out how her father died. Should we tell her?" Ed posed the question that had been on both of their minds.

"We owe her the truth," replied Dale, testing the weight of the gold bags. "I think she'll be able to handle it if we explain the ordeal of a prolonged death from lack of water, but it's not for us to tell or not tell her. She'll find out when she reads the ledgers. After all, this belongs to her. If I carry two of the bags can you carry the box and the third bag? That way we can make it to the cabin in one trip."

"Sure," Ed replied.

They helped each other climb out of the cave and set out for the cabin with mixed emotions. They were in high spirits over the discovery of Charles Kemp's whereabouts, yet, it did not dispel the sadness and sorrow which Rachel would have to bear. Ed was in the lead when they broke through some dense brush into a clearing near the cabin. Suddenly, without warning, he dropped to his knees and motioned Dale to do the same. "There's someone besides Rachel in the cabin," he whispered in Dale's ear. "We had better hide the gold and box here under some brush and check out what's happening. If it's the hooch peddlers that have paid us a visit, then Rachel could be in danger."

"How many did you see Ed?"

"I saw one outside the door and another one passing through the door out of sight. There may be more. I'm glad we brought our sidearms. Come, we'll hide this stuff and hit the cabin from the rear."

They located a slight depression in the ground where a clump of small fir trees had been toppled over, and placed the box and gold bags in the hole, covering it with several layers of branches. They both checked their handguns. Dale carried his service Colt automatic pistol with him at all times in a shoulder holster, while Ed wore a Webley service revolver in a holster on his belt. Dale had been concerned about Rachel's safety those times she was left alone at the cabin, and decided he would teach her to use the only rifle in the party - a Remington 0.35 autoloader carbine. It was light and easy to carry.

"Let's go Ed. It may simply be some trappers or hunters passing by."

"It's possible, but I have a hunch they're not paying us a friendly visit. However you want to handle it, I'll back you up."

They approached the cabin from the rear and split up so as to flank the cabin door from both sides. It was agreed that Dale would call for Rachel from the western side of the cabin until the strangers came out to investigate who it was. Ed was to remain out of sight until the men came out to confront Dale. Dale slapped Ed on the shoulder and took off at a run toward the door.

"Ahoy there, Rachel are you ready for supper," Dale shouted as loud as he could to announce himself. A moment later, a head popped out the door checking both sides. Ed was nowhere to be seen so the stranger stepped through the door in front of Dale.

"Hello," Dale greeted him as casually as if he were out on a stroll. The man was wearing a pair of coveralls and a wide-brimmed hat. A heavy beard covered his face making it impossible for Dale to determine if he was a white man or an Indian. Either way he presented a scruffy appearance. He wore a pistol belt and was holding the revolver in his hand pointing it menacingly at Dale.

Dale was hoping to draw all the men out of the cabin knowing that he had to remain alert and cautious. He continued walking toward the door. "Rachel, are you all right?" he shouted. "It's me, Dale."

Her muffled cry indicated that something was wrong. Dale threw caution to the wind and faced the intruder. "I don't know who you are stranger, but I'm warning you to put that gun back in your holster or use it, because either way I'm walking through that door. Even if you shoot me, I promise to take you with me." His boldness left the man uncertain as to what to do except to fall in behind Dale, which was exactly what Dale was hoping he would do. A few feet short of the door, Dale pivoted on his right heel and caught the man behind him square in the face with his elbow, knocking a tooth loose, and splattering his face with blood. He followed up with precisely-aimed blows to the man's midsection, and, finally, a knee jerk using every ounce of strength Dale could muster to the man's groin. The intruder doubled over in pain.

Then, Dale signaled Ed to come forward. So far there was no sound from the cabin. The door was closed but not latched, so Dale propelled himself against it, forcing it open with a crash and immediately rolled to the floor with his .45 automatic cocked and ready. The light from the fireplace was enough for him to see what was taking place. Rachel was wrestling on the floor near her bed with one of the intruders and a third man was standing menacingly over him with a knife, poised to

115

attack. Instinctively Dale fired twice at the threat and was on his feet before the man fell to the floor.

Dale leaped for the man struggling with Rachel, wrenching him to his feet and savagely pistol-whipped him in the face and neck. The assailant cried out covering his face with his hands. Ed plunged through the door and grabbed him by the arm and threw him outside, where he tripped over his companion Dale had disabled.

Dale's fury was still high, but his main concern was for Rachel. She was sitting on the floor with her knees drawn to her chest crying hysterically. He sat down beside her and placed an arm around her. "I'm so sorry this happened to you, Rachel," he tried to assure her over and over. "Are you hurt, are you all right?"

After a few minutes her sobs began to diminish. "Thank God you came when you did. That pig attacked me as soon as he came through the door," she said still trying to catch her breath. "I thought I was going to die."

"You did great, Rachel," Dale said, trying to comfort her. "You held them off long enough for us to make it inside. They'll never do this to anyone again. I'm proud of you."

Ed had finished tying up the assailants and stepped into the cabin. "We've got them now," he said. "They won't bother you again, Rachel. Did they hurt you?"

Rachel continued to cry accepting Ed's comforting hand. "You two are wonderful. The last thing I expected while you were out was for three men to barge in and start making lurid remarks to me!"

Ed checked the man on the floor. "He's dead," he said quietly. Dale helped him drag the man outside near his colleagues, who were still dazed about what had taken place.

"All three of them are white trash whisky runners. You were fabulous, Dale. I heard the crack of the blow when you hit him with your elbow. He's still groggy, and he'll probably be hurting for a while."

"The one who grabbed at me… I want to see him," requested Rachel in a clear rational voice. Dale looked at Ed nodding his head in approval.

"He's right outside, Rachel. He doesn't look as formidable as he did," Ed triumphantly told her.

Rachel and Dale followed Ed to where the two live attackers were tightly bound. The one Dale had hit outside the cabin was not very alert, but Rachel's attacker still had a sneering smirk on his face even though his nose was bleeding profusely. He spit at her when she came close. She looked him straight in the eye and said, "If I were a man I'd kill you with pleasure, but since I'm not, you'll have to settle for this."

Balancing herself on one foot Rachel kicked as hard as she could at the man's unprotected groin, dropping him to the ground pulling his tethered companion on top of him. He laid on the ground moaning. She turned to Dale and Ed smiling, "Maybe that was not the right thing to do, but it sure has made me feel better."

Dale escorted Rachel back inside where he helped her straighten out the cabin. Ed ordered the prisoners to remove their shoes and belts, and to empty everything in their pockets on the ground. This was not the time to question them, but Ed informed them that they would remain tied together until the police came along. In the morning they might have some questions for them. Ed had only one question for now, "Where was their supply of hooch?"

The men made no reply. Ed tightened the ropes fastening their hands behind their backs, and routed the rope around their necks binding their bodies so that when they made the slightest movement it choked the other person. At last, the one Dale had hit with his elbow pointed to a stand of small balsam fir at the edge of the cabin clearing. Ed trotted out to take a closer look and dragged back two packs filled with bottled whiskey. "This will make good evidence for Inspector Clough," he said, casually placing the packs against the cabin and stepping back inside.

Dale and Rachel were sitting quietly at the table. Dale took Rachel's hands. "Now we've got a number of days to contend with the prisoners outside. Tell me honestly, are you going to be able to handle their presence until the plane comes? If their proximity to the cabin offends you or makes you afraid, Ed and I'll move them to a location farther away and take turns standing guard over them."

"I can't ask you two to do that," Rachel protested, shaking her head. "I'll be fine. I'm fortunate to have friends like you two. You warned me about making this trip. I never dreamed that I would be threatened like I was."

"Rachel, you're probably safer within the confines of this vast northern wilderness than you are on the streets of New York," Ed told her seriously. "You had the misfortune of falling prey to a few scavengers that roam the forest in search of victims. They are not native people but intruders upon our sacred land. If either of your abusers had been natives I would probably have killed them and turned myself in to the Inspector."

The three of them agreed that the prisoners would sleep beneath the tarp Dale and Ed had used the night before and remain tethered until the next plane arrived. No attempt was made to make them comfortable. Ed and Dale took turns checking their ropes hourly throughout the night.

The next morning, Rachel awoke rested and refreshed. Ed and Dale observed her improved spirits and told her what they had found at the cave. Dale whispered in her ear that they had cached the three bags of gold and a box with some messages from her father. They all agreed that it would be prudent not to let the prisoners outside hear them talking about what they had found. Rachel was less concerned about the gold than she was with the possibility of locating some last word from her father. Dale and Ed went to the hiding place behind the cabin and returned with the box of gold and the ledger. The prisoners had no knowledge of anything out of the ordinary.

Dale and Ed stayed close to the cabin that first day adding to their supply of firewood, and constantly checking the predators, while Rachel sat on her bunk and read every word her father wrote. Several times she was reduced to tears, but she continued to the end. She stared at the red coals in the fireplace and looked up at Dale when he opened the door to check on her. Her face was white with shock. He quickly went to her side and knelt down. She turned to Dale and said, with quivering lips, "My father has a son by a Cree woman."

Chapter Twelve

Dale was not surprised. Later that morning, a soft rain started to fall. The prisoners positioned themselves under the tarp so that they would not get wet, but the dampness soon penetrated their clothing and they were shivering. Ed gave them the bedding they carried in their packs to keep warm.

At daybreak, Ed untied the two men, one at a time, so that they could move about to restore circulation and satisfy their bodily functions. He stood close by with his revolver drawn, confident that they would not try anything. When their exercise period was over, Ed had them stand back-to-back so that he could tie them together. Then he ordered them inside the cabin with the stern warning that he would shoot at the slightest hint of trouble.

Rachel was sitting on her bunk with her back against the log wall as Ed marched the prisoners through the door. Hatred filled her eyes. She still hurt from the struggle with them, and shuddered at what might have happened if Ed and Dale had not returned when they did.

"Ask them if they knew my father," Rachel asked Ed.

"I'll untie one hand on each and bind them together, so that their other hands are fastened behind their backs. That way they can eat something and still be secured." Ed turned to the prisoners and asked in French, "You heard the lady, speak up." The order was greeted with silence as if they did not understand. "If we're going to share our food with you," Ed explained standing over them with a bowl of whitefish and rice. "We demand some information from you. It'll be several days

120

before the police arrive so you're going to be mighty hungry unless you cooperate with us."

This time the two men responded in French which no one but Ed understood. He conversed with them for several minutes and nodded for Dale to let them have a bowl of food. They ate ravenously.

Ed turned to Rachel, "I'm not certain if they can speak or understand English. They claim that your father did have a Cree woman that lived with him for a while. She returned home to her village and gave birth to a baby boy. As far as they know, the woman died giving birth. They knew Charles Kemp and they also claim that he disappeared shortly after the birth of his son."

Rachel listened quietly without a trace of emotion and asked, "Do they know where the child is now and who is caring for him?"

"They did not say, but I can tell you that it would be the duty of the mother's family to see that the child is raised properly. If the woman gave birth among her family members and friends, the baby has been well cared for," Ed assured Rachel. He questioned the prisoners further and after a few exchanges he once again turned to Rachel. "They say that the tribe caring for the child is east of here towards Fort Lewis. I've been to the camp they described. We can check it out if you want."

Dale had been listening closely and offered a suggestion. "Do you think it would be possible to walk to the village and back by the time the plane returns on its regular run?"

"I think so," answered Ed, watching the prisoners' faces for any sign of comprehension. He was not yet convinced that they did not speak any English. "Why don't we take these two back outside and tie them up for the day?"

"Good idea," agreed Dale, motioning for them to stand and walk out of the cabin. Ed secured them to a nearby spruce tree. Then he and Dale returned to the cabin to discuss their plans.

"Could you take Rachel to the village with you, Ed?" Dale suggested. "I'll stay here to watch the prisoners. That way, if you're not back when the plane arrives, I'll send them out. Are you up to the trip, Rachel?"

"Yes," Rachel replied eagerly. "I've been thinking about it since Ed first mentioned the village. I'm anxious to see the baby," she said, her cheeks flushed with anticipation.

Dale smiled at Rachel's enthusiasm. "The sooner you get started, the sooner you'll get back. You haven't said much, Ed. What are you thinking?"

"I've been wondering about the village elders and what they might think about us laying claim to the child. Or, is it your intention to ask for the child, Rachel? You should be prepared for the possibility that the child's mother may have had other children and that the elders will want the boy to be left with his brothers or sisters if there are any."

"I hadn't thought of that," answered Rachel with a frown. "What is the right thing to do for the child? If it's truly my father's son, then I have a responsibility to him."

"Is that the same thing as wanting him?" asked Dale, pointedly.

"I'm not sure, Dale, I think so," Rachel considered the question.

"Let us try to find the child first," Ed recommended. "We don't have to settle this now. This is a matter that the police will have to arbitrate anyway. If we gather our supplies we can leave within an hour. Are you comfortable with the prisoners for several nights, Dale?"

"They won't be a problem," Dale replied confidently. "I'll stick close by them fishing and gathering firewood. It'll be just for a few nights."

Rachel nodded in relief that a workable plan had been developed and helped Dale and Ed gather supplies for the trip. Ed insisted that everything be placed in his pack so that Rachel would not be burdened with a heavy load after her ordeal yesterday. He double checked his revolver and ammunition supply and said good-bye to Dale. "We'll be back as soon as we can. Don't worry, I'll watch over her, Dale."

"I know that, Ed. I don't speak any French but our visitors won't have any trouble understanding my instructions. We'll get along fine." Dale embraced Rachel. "Be brave on this trip, Rachel. You don't know what you're going to find. I wish you luck and will see you in a few days."

"Thanks, Dale," she answered, quietly following Ed's footsteps around the opposite side of the cabin out of sight of the prisoners.

The prisoners remained quiet all day. However, as they began to realize that Rachel and Ed were not around, they jabbered loudly, in French, well into the night trying to unnerve Dale and deprive him of sleep. When they were not talking loud, they were kicking the cabin wall continuously, failing to respond to Dale's protest. Since Dale had never required much sleep, the commotion did not bother him as much as the men had hoped.

The next morning the two prisoners were smug and belligerent. Dale was determined to teach them a lesson. He placed a large packing box on the ground in full view of the men and poured a cup of coffee from the big black percolator. Then he carried a heaping bowl of baked beans and a tray of warm biscuits and placed them on the box. The gentle breeze carried the aroma of the food to the prisoners. Dale returned to the cabin once again for a small jar of strawberry jam before he sat down on the ground to eat his breakfast. The men watched every mouthful that he ate. When he was finished, Dale left the jam and biscuits on the box in plain sight but did not offer the men any of the food. He knew that they could survive for a day without food, and it would help make them more manageable.

On the second day the two men were compliant with Dale's orders if they could have something to eat. He gave each of them a cup of water twice during the day, and spent much of the day fishing in the pond where he could easily watch the prisoners.

On the third day after Ed and Rachel had left for the native encampment, a float plane circled the cabin and landed on the pond. Dale was sawing wood when he heard the drone of the plane's engine and anxiously walked to the edge of the water. This was not the same plane that had previously brought their supplies. As soon as the pilot shut down the engine, Dale waded out into the water to help pull the plane closer to the shore. The pilot and two passengers were Mounted Policemen.

"Welcome to our camp," Dale greeted warmly. "I'm relieved that you're here. There's no way to get ashore without getting your feet wet. I apologize for not having better accommodations."

"We meet again, Mr. Cooper," exclaimed Inspector Clough, jumping from one of the plane's floats. "We received a message that you've run into some trouble. We came as soon as the plane was available."

"Hello, Inspector Clough," Dale was sincerely glad to see the policeman. "You might say we had some trouble!"

"The pilot is Constable Jenkins," the Inspector introduced his two companions. "The other young man is Corporal Haynes."

"Welcome," Dale said, shaking hands with the two young policemen.

"A runner came into our Fort Lewis Barracks from a nearby encampment with a message that you'd had a shoot-out with some rum runners. Is that correct?" Inspector Clough asked looking around the cabin.

Dale told the policemen what happened when he and Ed returned to the cabin from the cave. He also told them about the body they had discovered and the rest of their findings at the site.

"We've kept knowledge of the gold from the prisoners. What they don't know can't hurt them," Dale pointed to the secured prisoners beside the cabin. They approached the cabin at a quick pace.

"A wise precaution, Yank," said the Inspector, making some notes in a notebook. "Haynes, why don't you and Jenkins check out the two men. Place them under arrest and prepare them for the flight to Lac St. Jean."

The two sturdy policemen walked authoritatively towards the prisoners and ordered them to stand. They did so reluctantly. Corporal Haynes took a good look at the men and hollered: "I recognize both of them, Inspector. You've been suspicious of these two for some time. The partner that Mr. Cooper shot was part of the same ring of distributors."

"I shot their companion when he lunged at me with a knife," Dale confessed. "Rachel and Ed will verify that it was self-defense. The taller of the two prisoners had attacked Rachel and was in the process of having his way with her when we broke in on them."

"You've done the right thing, Yank," Inspector Clough responded. "We'll see to it that these thugs are kept out of circulation for as long as the law allows. Was Rachel injured?"

"A few bruises from the physical battering she took. He attacked her as soon as he saw that she was a woman. I couldn't get off a shot at him without endangering Rachel."

"I understand. It would have served him right, but I'm glad you restrained the impulse," said the Inspector.

The policemen had untied the prisoners' hands and secured them behind their backs with handcuffs by the time Dale and Inspector Clough approached them. The taller prisoner looked at Dale with unfettered hatred, and spit in his face when he got close enough to make contact. Dale calmly wiped the spittle off his face.

"Rachel was so angered by his bestiality that she involuntarily lashed out at him with her foot like this," Dale added, promptly delivering a swift kick to the man's groin, dropping him to his knees.

"Yank, you've got to control yourself better than that," demanded Inspector Clough, restraining him with a vise-like grip. "They're our prisoners now and we're obligated to protect them." The man Dale had kicked moaned heavily.

"This attacker," announced the Inspector turning to the policemen. "Is a bad apple, with a long history of brutality and battery against men and women. Secure them in the plane. Jenkins can take them to Lac St. Jean and return for us the next day."

While the pilot and Corporal Haynes were busy loading the prisoners, Dale took the Inspector into the cabin and showed him the box containing the gold and messages left by Charles Kemp.

"As you already know, Rachel and Ed have gone to the native encampment to check on the child," stated Dale matter-of-factly. "Are there any legal complications about the child, Inspector?"

"That's not easy to answer, Yank." The Inspector continued. "If the child has an aunt or uncle, then they have as much claim on the infant as Rachel and her mother. We'll just have to see what they find when the child is located. The child is the rightful owner of the gold if Charles Kemp proves to be his father."

"Could there be any doubt that the body in the cave is Rachel's father?"

"Only if there is tangible evidence to refute what he wrote in the ledger," cautioned Inspector Clough. "Knowledge of the gold could bring the rats out of the woods. I hope that Ed and Rachel are shrewd enough not to mention the gold to anyone."

"I doubt they would do that." Dale told him. "There's a fortune in the gold, and you're right, it does have a way of bringing out the worst in men."

Constable Jenkins unloaded a tent, two sleeping bags and a backpack from the aircraft before starting the engine. The prisoners were secured to their seats, and ready to take off. The remaining three men waded into the pond to push the airplane into deeper water. Dale was relieved to be free of responsibility for the prisoners.

Dale led the two policemen to the cave, carrying a large lantern to illuminate the cave's interior when the plane took off. He pointed to the exact location of the wooden box and stressed that nothing else was disturbed except their search of the deceased man's jacket and pants pockets. The Inspector noted everything he saw in his journal.

"The real question unanswered by the existing evidence is why was he in the cave instead of the cabin?" asked the Inspector.

"Do you suppose that he found the cave an easier place to defend himself and the gold?" suggested Corporal Haynes.

The Inspector considered the possibility. "Perhaps, Corporal. We'll never know for sure unless the tribal elders can add anything more to the mystery."

"Should we bury the body?" Dale consulted the Inspector, wondering what Rachel might want.

"We could bring it close by the cabin where you partially buried the intruder," Inspector Clough offered. "That way, Miss Kemp can do whatever she wishes at a later time."

"You know," observed Dale. "We would never have found this cave if it hadn't rained hard enough to undermine the soil holding the big trees that blocked Charles Kemp in the cave in the first place. The shallow unstable soils in the region are responsible for extensive areas of forest blowdown. I've never seen anything like it."

"I guess you could say that it was Divine Intervention that brought you here, Yank," remarked Inspector Clough. "Many things happen in this world that we can't explain. I have a feeling that the presence of Miss Kemp might have something to do with your discovery of the body."

"Maybe you're right, Inspector," said Dale.

The three men returned to the cabin for the evening. Darkness came rapidly after sundown. Corporal Haynes erected the silk service tent for him and the Inspector to sleep in for the night, and dug a small trench around the tent's perimeter so that water could be collected and diverted from the tent floor in case of rain.

They prepared a meal from the fish Dale had caught the day before and included some canned beans and bannock bread. Afterwards, they sat around the campfire smoking their pipes and discussing their impressions of the discovery of Charles Kemp's body and his gold. Inspector Clough was not aware of any gold prospecting within his patrol area and the gold in the cave baffled him. If a major find had been discovered, it would have triggered a stampede of gold-lusting adventurers to the area.

"I hope I never see such a thing. The lure of the yellow dust has been the undoing of many a good man," contemplated the Inspector. "We should bury Kemp's body tomorrow before his daughter returns from the village. Now that the barrier has been removed from the cave, it's vulnerable to any of the forest creatures. Do you have a shovel, Dale?"

"Yes, it's out back where we used it to dig the latrine ditch," Dale replied, listening to the increasing howl of the wind outside. "Are you sure you two don't want to sleep inside tonight?"

"We'll be all right. The tents are sturdy and waterproof," answered the Inspector. Corporal Haynes was engrossed in the journal. "Have you found anything that gives us a clue as to what happened, Corporal?"

"Nothing that I can determine," said Haynes, lifting his eyes to look into the fire. "The man certainly had grit. He writes very eloquently about the child and about his love for Rachel. She must have found his last words comforting but excruciatingly sad. I'd give anything to know what he intended to do about his son and wife."

"Rachel accepted the presence of the child with a lot of grace. She didn't elaborate on how he would be perceived by her mother," reflected Dale pensively staring into the fire. "I only hope for the sake of the boy that something can be worked out that doesn't place a stigma on him."

The Inspector scoffed. "You know as well as I do, Yank, the fact that his mother is Cree is stigma enough for some people, let alone that he was born out of wedlock."

"You're probably correct, Inspector. I'm not sure if I was a prejudiced person before I met Iowaka. I'd never been around many people of different ethnic backgrounds. Iowaka has had some bad experiences with bigoted people, in fact, that's how I met her in the first place. I just can't imagine anyone having unkind thoughts or feelings towards her simply because she's half white and half Cree."

The Inspector shrugged his shoulders in resignation. "Ah, Yank, the world's filled with all kinds of people who use race to define others so that they can feel superior to them. Arrogance and pomposity gone amuck - what a waste of talent and energy. Iowaka is an angel of mercy at her village, and is blessed with a physical loveliness our Lord usually reserves for his angels."

"I can vouch for that," added Haynes.

Dale was not sure if the wily Inspector was testing him or lecturing him, but when Dale caught the twinkle in Inspector Clough's eyes, he smiled and looked away. Dale gazed into the crackling fire. Suddenly he saw the face of Iowaka looking sadly back at him. An uneasiness immediately settled over Dale. He continued to stare at her face until it slowly disappeared deep into the burning embers.

That night the wind wailed around the cabin. The sky was again filled with an electrical performance of the northern lights, which illuminated the earth and created shadowy vistas across the landscape. Dale lay awake thinking of Iowaka and trying to deduce the significance, if any, to the sudden appearance of her face which had reflected great sorrow. It disturbed him for the rest of the evening. In the distance the howl of a wolf was answered from the opposite side of the pond against a steady yipping of foxes and noises of other nocturnal creatures. The night's cacophony contributed to his restlessness. He blocked the sounds by pulling the blanket over his head. Shortly thereafter, he fell asleep.

That morning, the three men checked the shallow grave of the third intruder that Dale had shot. The body was still partially uncovered when Corporal Haynes checked his identity. Inspector Clough insisted on uncovering the body so that they could search his pockets. They decided that another temporary grave could be dug nearby for the remains of Charles Kemp. It would be a grisly task but they had an obligation to give Rachel's father a decent burial before wild animals disturbed the cave.

Dale suggested that they take a blanket to wrap around Kemp's body, to facilitate carrying the remains from the cave. Inspector Clough and Dale went to retrieve the corpse while Corporal Haynes volunteered to start digging the grave.

It took the three men most of the morning to complete the grave and erect a cross. The Inspector read a committal prayer from his Mounted Police manual and then joined Dale and Corporal Haynes in a moment of respectful silence for the mysterious man they had just buried. Just as they were walking back to the cabin from the gravesite, Dale noticed a movement at the clearing in the East. Ed came in to view followed by Rachel holding the hand of a young boy walking beside her.

"We're back with my father's son," she shouted triumphantly.

Chapter Thirteen

Dale had never seen Rachel look as happy as she was leading the small child across the clearing. Surely, their journey was successful. It showed on their faces even though Rachel was tired from making the long trek. They were glad to join Dale and the policemen.

Ed had done most of the talking with the tribe. After a few inquiries, they found Charles Kemp's son living with one of the elder council members. No one objected to Rachel's claim on the boy once she and Ed described Charles Kemp and displayed a picture of Rachel and her father standing together in their driveway in New York. The council members recognized the man and released the boy to her care without objection. As Ed told Dale and the others, he had a feeling that the child had been a burden to the older couple and they were relieved to be freed of the responsibility. Rachel had promised to help the tribe with medicine and food supplies as soon as she returned to Lac St. Jean.

The small boy was two and a half years old and was of lighter complexion than most of the other native children at the camp. He seemed healthy and alert and had already attached himself to Rachel and Ed. At first he was apprehensive at the sight of all the strangers, but he grew noticeably more at ease when he saw that Dale and the two policemen were friends of Ed's and Rachel's.

"What did the villagers call the boy, Rachel?" Dale asked.

She smiled. "Everyone at the village called him Nakota. The elders nicknamed him White Owl because he was so quiet and lighter-skinned than the other children, and because he was intelligent and quick to learn new things." The boy stared wide-eyed at Rachel when he heard his name.

"What are the legal procedures for me to take him out of Canada to the United States, Inspector?" asked Rachel.

"Legally, he's a citizen of Canada and the United States," Inspector Clough stated hoping to allay her fears. "With his father's citizenship in the States and his birth on Canadian soil, I don't see any problem with him being awarded citizenship in either country. As soon as you arrive in Lac St. Jean I'll see to it that the customs and immigration departments grant you clearance to the United States. Are you certain that no other member of the tribe has any claim on the boy?"

"None, Inspector," Ed replied firmly. "We inquired throughout the village and got the same answer. The woman that gave birth to the boy had no other children or family as far as we could determine. For some reason, it seemed as though the mother was not particularly well thought of. Perhaps it was the fact that the child is a half-breed. That might help explain why they relinquished him so easily, too. The boy seemed to care for the couple he lived with and he was well provided for. The tribal council decided unanimously that Rachel should immediately assume responsibility for the child."

"In that case, preparing papers declaring him a United States citizen should be a routine matter," promised the Inspector.

"I appreciate any help you can offer me with this, Inspector Clough. So much has happened in such a short time, I feel overwhelmed. The boy does understand some English. The couple he lived with spoke it quite fluently and they passed it along to him."

Dale knelt down in front of little Nakota, offering him a chocolate bar. "You may have this if you want it."

With some hesitation, Nakota accepted the chocolate square and took a tiny bite.

"How do you like it?" inquired Dale in a calm voice.

"Mmmm…," answered the boy with a shy smile.

The smile warmed Dale's heart. "I'm glad things have worked out so well for you, Rachel."

"I'd like to think that I'm a better person now than I was before we started this journey to the wilderness," she remarked. "I've found a part of me that I didn't know existed."

"The wilderness can be a rigorous test of people's inner strength," added the Inspector. "It destroys some men and strengthens others. Those who grow from a forest experience are those who honestly examine themselves and have the discipline to take control of their lives. Finding that strength we all possess is a wonderful encounter, and you my dear Lady have blossomed with the discovery."

Rachel blushed at the compliment.

"I hear a plane in the distance," Ed pointed to the East.

They watched the plane come into view over the tops of the trees and circle the pond. It was the Royal Canadian Mounted Police plane returning to pick up the Inspector and Corporal Haynes. Constable Jenkins was at the controls. He guided the plane towards the cabin before shutting down the engine. Then, he stepped out of the cockpit onto one of the pontoons and opened a compartment in the fuselage, removing a large box of foodstuff.

"We'll leave you with some extra food in case your supply plane doesn't return on schedule," explained the Inspector, preparing to leave. He shook hands with Dale and Ed, and turned to face Rachel. "I'll start your paperwork as soon as I arrive at Fort Lewis where we have a radio link to the outside world. I'll alert the detachment at Lac St. Jean to your situation. Good luck, Miss Kemp. I admire what you're doing. Incidentally, I don't intend to mention anything to the authorities about the gold, as far as I'm concerned it belongs to you and the child. The less said about it the better. If you could see your way to help the tribe that raised the boy, I'm sure they'll appreciate anything you may offer."

"I plan to do that on a regular basis, Inspector. Thanks so much."

The two policemen climbed aboard the plane while Ed and Dale turned it around and shoved it away from the shore. The pilot increased the speed of the engines, breaking the floats free of the water, and lifted the craft into the air. The plane made a circle around the cabin then turned east towards Fort Lewis. Nakota watched in awe as the plane rose high into the air. It was the first time he had ever seen an airplane up close. He continued to cling tightly to Rachel's leg until the plane was out of sight.

Ed was the first to speak. "I don't know about the rest of you, but I'm starved," announced Ed, heading back to the cabin to start a fire.

"How are you going to handle Nakota with your mother?" Dale asked, watching Rachel's protective instincts toward the child. He was immediately embarrassed. "No, forget that I said such a thing. It's none of my business and I didn't mean to pry. I'm sorry."

"Dear, Dale," Rachel smiled and linked her arm around his. "When Gregg told me that he had every confidence in you, I was skeptical that any person could really be so trustworthy. You have proven me wrong. You've been my defender and you've become my dear friend, and you have every right to be concerned about my mother and Nakota. You saw her reaction to Iowaka and Ed. I'm afraid that if she knew the truth of what had happened here, it would hurt her terribly. I was going to discuss this with you before we left Canada, but since you brought it up, I'll ask your opinion now."

"I promise to be candid," Dale told her.

"Before I ask you the question I have in mind, I should tell you that Gregg and I are engaged to marry."

"Well I'll be," Dale's face lit up. "You and Gregg... I'm happy for the two of you. Gregg was a great commander. I respect him a lot. He's lucky to have a girl like you."

"Thank you," responded Rachel. "Now, for my question. What do you think of the idea that Gregg and I adopt Nakota, and say nothing to my mother? Is that being deceptive? Is it wrong to begin his new life under a cloud of lies? Or is it simply being realistic about my Mother's prejudices? I'm sure that Gregg will support the idea. I know that I can love him as if he was my own. In fact," she confided breathlessly. "I think I already do."

Dale took both of her hands in his and looked deep into her beautiful blue-green eyes. He saw his own reflection. "I'm not qualified to answer all of those questions, Rachel. The fact that you've already given this much thought to the subject indicates that silence might be a wise course. The worst that could happen is that your mother would somehow learn the truth, and you'd have to defend your actions. Whatever you decide, you have my pledge never to breathe a word of this conversation to anyone except Iowaka, and I know she will support you too. I believe I speak for Ed, also."

"I have the most wonderful men sharing my life. Thank you, Dale," cried Rachel, kissing him on the cheek. "I have so much to be thankful for. I've lost a dear father in this world of endless forests, but I've gained two dear friends and a son, who promises to grow into a fine young man. I'm grateful for that."

The next two days were warm and sunny. Dale and Ed took advantage of the good weather to continue their forest inventory work while Rachel cared for Nakota at the cabin. Whenever the men were away, she took the precaution of carrying a small .32 caliber revolver on her person. It was an extra weapon that Dale usually carried in his backpack. The revolver gave her a greater sense of security, and she became quite proficient in its use.

After discussing various options, the three of them decided that Rachel and Nakota should return to the Inn on the Mistassini River at Lac St. Jean on the next supply plane, which was due any day now. Dale and Ed insisted that she take the three gold bags with her and deposit them at the closest bank she could find, so that she would not have to worry about them being stolen or discovered by curious strangers. Rachel wanted to give Dale and Ed one bag apiece, but they refused her generous offer.

The plane arrived the following day. It brought mail for Ed and Dale and more food supplies. Rachel's belongings were already packed. She promised Dale that she would call Gregg Nelson and make a progress report. Dale also asked her to look up Iowaka and bring her up-to-date on events of the past two weeks.

"All set," said the pilot, packing Rachel's luggage in the fuselage of the plane.

An awkward silence gripped each of them when it became time for Rachel and Nakota to board the plane. The three of them had been a close-knit team, and each one felt disappointed that it was coming to an end. Rachel had proved to be an able partner and her upbeat attitude would be missed by the two men. The bond they all felt would last a long, long time. With some misgivings, Rachel hugged and kissed her two friends and protectors and climbed aboard the plane. Dale passed Nakota to her and helped to fasten him in the seat, waving to them as the pilot started the engine.

Dale and Ed stood on the shore and watched until the plane disappeared behind the tall spruce trees on the south side of the pond. They remained motionless until the sound of the engine was replaced by the soft breeze flowing out of the west, combed and sifted with the aromatic scent of cedar and balsam.

"I have a confession to make," said Ed, staring aimlessly across the pond. "When you told me that a woman was coming on the trip, I was skeptical. When I met her, she looked like your typical spoiled socialite and I was even more concerned. Yet, every day she was with us she proved me wrong. I have to tell you, she was a real trooper on our trip to the village. She never once complained and she insisted on doing her share of the work. She's a lovely lady all the way around, and I was glad to have her with us. I'll miss her."

"I feel the same way," Dale smiled. "She certainly rose to the challenge of roughing it in the bush. The man she's engaged to was my regimental commander in France. He's a good man. He's in for a surprise when she informs him of what has taken place way up here in the wilderness! Well, what do you say, Ed? Shall we hit the woods and wind up this project as soon as possible?"

"Sounds good to me. I'm anxious to return to my family and I know who you're anxious to see again," replied Ed with a grin.

Within two weeks after Rachel's departure, Dale and Ed had completed the field inventory work, and collected additional bauxite ore samples from several different locations. All that remained to be done was to compute the inventory figures and compile the information in a typewritten report to Gregg Nelson. They spent a day digging a cellar hole inside the cabin to store excess food supplies and fabricating a cover for the cellar out of small trees tied together. They rolled all of the bedding material into one tight roll and suspended it from the ceiling in the center of the cabin to discourage rodents from building nests in it.

When the last plane arrived. Dale and Ed were ready to go. They lifted their packs into the fuselage and strapped themselves in the seats. Dale asked the pilot to make a pass over the tract so that they could see what the property they had become so familiar with on the ground, looked like from the air. Then, they headed south toward the mid-day sun. The wilderness tract they were leaving behind would remain highly significant to four people, Dale, Ed, Rachel, and little Nakota. An enduring friendship had grown out of their wilderness experience.

Chapter Fourteen

Dale opened his most recent letter from Iowaka on the plane. She described how an outbreak of smallpox had hit the infirmary and parts of the village. The French referred to it as "le mort rouge" (the red death). He knew that the disease was contagious and worried about her for the duration of the flight.

The dark blue waters of Lac St. Jean were a welcome sight to Dale and Ed. The plane stopped at the Royal Canadian Mounted Police dock where Dale and Ed parted company.

"I hope your family is well," said Dale, shaking Ed's hand. "I'm glad you were with us on this trip, Ed, and I hope that this isn't the end for us. Let's keep in touch."

"That would mean a lot to me," Ed replied. "I'm glad you feel that way. After you've had a chance to get settled in and checked on Iowaka, my wife and I would be honored to have you meet the rest of the family."

"I'd like that."

"Give Iowaka my best," said Ed, briskly walking the plank ashore.

A policeman took Dale to the Inn where he had previously stayed. His first order of business was to take a long, warm bath to remove weeks of sweat and grime from his body. He called the infirmary immediately after he stepped out of the tub. When he asked for Iowaka, the person who answered the phone asked him to hold a moment. A few seconds later, he heard her voice.

"Hello, Dale?"

"Yes it's me," he said. "I just got in and finished scrubbing off layers of dirt. How are you Iowaka, I've been worried sick about you since I read your letter."

"I'm all right," she assured him. "This has been a very busy place lately. We've lost several patients to the pox and the high fevers."

"That's why I worry about you. Is it necessary for you to risk getting the disease?" asked Dale.

"Yes. I'm a nurse, Dale, and it's the sick people that need me the most right now. That's why I became a nurse in the first place. I can't walk away from this, Dale," she responded firmly.

"I was only thinking of you," Dale replied.

"I know, and I appreciate your thoughts. The rest of the staff and I are scrupulously careful how we care for the patients. We sterilize everything that comes in contact with the sick."

"Will I be able to see you today or this evening?"

"No," Iowaka replied, with a trace of regret in her voice. "The staff has voluntarily agreed to remain at the infirmary until this epidemic runs out. That way we won't contribute to its dissemination. I'm sorry, Dale, I want to be with you too. Be patient. Our self-imposed quarantine may save a lot of misery and some lives."

"I understand," Dale sighed. "Of course, you're correct. I'm just being selfish."

"Listen, Dale, why don't you visit my mother?" suggested Iowaka. "She would love to see you, and I'll bet a good home-cooked meal would taste good to you right now."

"You better believe it," Dale answered. "I waited to eat, hoping that you might be able to join me."

"Do you want me to call Mother for you?"

"Thanks, that would be great. Tell her I'll be over as soon as the Inn's taxi is available."

"Okay. It's nice to hear your voice again, Dale. Are you having any change of heart?" she asked boldly.

"Well, to be honest, I have, Iowaka."

"You're teasing me…."

"No, I'm dead serious," Dale told her. "Being away from you has made my feelings stronger than ever. I'm afraid you're stuck with me."

Iowaka laughed gleefully. "Me too! Isn't it wonderful?" Dale loved to hear her laugh. There was a little-girl quality about her that was endearing. Her voice was soft and melodious. "I have to get back to my patients, Dale. I'll call Mother now and tell her that you're coming over. Feel free to call me here as often as you want. I love you, Dale."

Dale's heart beat faster when he heard those words. "I love you too, Iowaka."

An hour later, the hotel taxi dropped Dale off at the cabin Iowaka shared with her mother. Prior to his arrival at Mrs. Huntington's cabin Dale had the driver stop at the Northern Outfitter's warehouse, where he picked up a small package they were holding for him. He carried it to the cabin and knocked on the door. Mrs. Huntington opened the door with a welcoming smile.

"Ashley called to let me know you were coming. Please come in."

"Hello, Mrs. Huntington. It's nice to see you. I was hoping to meet with Iowaka earlier, but she told me about the quarantine. She suggested that I come here instead."

Mrs. Huntington led him into the great room of the cabin. The faint scent of heliotrope filled the air. Dale noted the fragrant plant with the delicate bloodstone-colored flowers on a small table near the fireplace. The room had a warm comfortable feel to it. The kitchen table was set for two, and a coffee pot was slowly percolating on the wood-burning cook stove.

"Please make yourself comfortable," said Mrs. Huntington, motioning for him to take a seat at the table. She sat down across from him. "I started to get ready for you after Ashley called. I haven't made a meal for a hungry man in a long time."

"Well, I've been eating my own cooking in the bush, Mrs. Huntington, and I can assure you that I'm hungry," grinned Dale.

"Then you came to the right place," she replied. There was a natural graciousness about her that made being with her enjoyable.

"I noticed you called your daughter Ashley," he remarked. "What do you think she wants me to call her, Ashley or Iowaka?"

"I think she's comfortable with either one. I'll leave that for the two of you to talk about. I use Ashley most of the time for the precise reason she uses Iowaka. I want her to remember that her father was English, and she needs to be reminded of that on occasion. She uses Iowaka with every stranger she meets to make the statement that she is a Cree. She likes to see how people react to the fact. It might be difficult for a white man to understand, but people's reaction to her racial status helps her to evaluate their character."

"That doesn't surprise me. She made her race an issue when we first met."

"That sounds like Ashley. Well, coffee is ready and I have some fresh bread and a casserole in the oven. Do you like macaroni and cheese?"

"It's one of my favorite meals, Mrs. Huntington. I haven't had it in a long time."

She seemed pleased. "It was my husband's favorite too. Good cheese used to be difficult to find, but here in Mistassini it's plentiful," said Mrs. Huntington, removing the casserole dish from the oven and placing it on the table beside Dale. "Please, help yourself."

And he did. Dale thoroughly enjoyed the meal she had prepared. Eating at the kitchen table reminded him of being home with his mother and father. Mrs. Huntington ate sparingly obviously enjoying seeing him eat so heartily. He went back to the casserole three times. The macaroni and cheese was delicious. He hadn't eaten since early morning when he finished off the bannock bread Ed had baked the night before.

"If I eat one more mouthful I'll burst," Dale smiled, taking a drink of coffee.

"You did very well, Mr. Cooper," said Ashley's mother. "A cook is always pleased to watch a guest enjoy his meal. I'm glad you liked it."

"I have a gift for Iowaka." Dale removed a small package from his coat pocket. He took a small figurine out of the box and placed it on the table. "I'd like to know what you think."

The figure was that of a young woman sitting on a stool gazing longingly at the portrait of a soldier. When Dale turned a small key on the bottom of the figurine, the plaintive melody of Lili Marlene filled the air while the mourning woman slowly turned with the music. He had often heard it sung at the front lines and other gathering places during the war. When he saw it in a catalogue he ordered it for Iowaka.

"It's a beautiful melody isn't it?" asked Mrs. Huntington. "I'm sure Ashley will be pleased."

"I've heard that song many times under unusual circumstances, and it never fails to touch me," he confessed.

"The war was a terrible thing. My sister's son Ed returned from the war a changed man. He's more like a son to me than a nephew. He and Ashley are very close."

"I was fortunate to have Ed with me. I could not have completed the job without him. I'm proud to call him a friend," said Dale, remembering the calm and confident way Ed went about doing whatever had to be done.

"Did you know that he's the recipient of the Victoria Cross?" asked Mrs. Huntington.

Dale looked surprised. "No, he never mentioned it. As a matter of fact, he never talked about his war experiences except to say that he was a sergeant in the Canadian Army."

"That's his way. He's reticent about things closest to his heart. Now that your project is completed, I believe he plans to start working at the paper mill."

"I hope my project didn't keep him from a permanent job elsewhere."

"I doubt it. Ashley asked him and he was more than willing to postpone the job at the mill. He would do anything for her."

"She mentioned that to me," Dale smiled. "Ed invited us to his place, but, unfortunately, I won't be able to see Iowaka for a while until the threat of the disease is over."

"That's a shame. I worry about her," Mrs. Huntington shook her head at the mention of the smallpox outbreak. "However, she's absolutely devoted to caring for the sick. I pray for her safety. This outbreak is bad enough, but the winter of 1911 was the most heartbreaking one I've ever experienced. Thousands of my native people died from starvation and exposure to the severe weather. More than fifteen feet of snow fell on the north country that year, making it impossible to hunt for food or gather firewood. In fact, it was during that winter that Ed lost his mother and father from a disease that's unique to the north country - frosted lungs. It was horrible to watch my sister slowly deteriorate, gasping for breath while their lungs decomposed piece by piece. In the later stages of the disease she coughed constantly and often bled at the mouth as her lungs fell apart. I hope I never have to watch such a death again. I don't know how my lovely Ashley does it every day. I love her for the dedication she displays."

"It takes a special person to fill such a crucial role. I share your pride and love for your daughter, Mrs. Huntington," admitted Dale without thinking what he had said.

Mrs. Huntington was smiling. "I've known it ever since you and Ashley came for a visit. It showed in your eyes."

"Do you approve, Mrs. Huntington?"

She considered the question. "I'm not sure an approval is that important, young man. I fell in love with an English engineer and defied everything my family held dear. Yet, we probably had one of the most beautiful love affairs and marriages that two people could possibly have."

"Should I interpret that as an approval?" Dale nervously questioned.

"Yes," Mrs. Huntington conceded. "If you think it's necessary. My Ashley is a very special woman. As long as I see you making her happy I'll be your friend and your biggest supporter. If you fail her, I promise to be a most formidable foe." Mrs. Huntington looked straight into his eyes as she spoke.

"I couldn't ask for more," he replied. Dale told her about his experience with Lenore and his childhood in the small town of Monson. For the rest of the evening they sipped coffee, talked and became better acquainted with each other. By the time he was ready to leave, he felt as comfortable with Iowaka's mother as he would have been with his own.

"I want to thank you for a very pleasant evening, Mrs. Huntington," Dale told her truthfully. "I can see why your husband loved you the way he did."

"Why, thank you, Dale Cooper," Mrs. Huntington replied, embracing him and kissing him lightly on the cheek. "I do believe my Ashley has chosen wisely."

When Dale returned to the Inn, he found a letter waiting for him at the desk. He recognized the handwriting immediately - it was Rachel's.

August 4, 1920

Dear Dale,

    Just a line to let you know that the paper work has been completed for Nakota's adoption. I'm leaving for New York tomorrow. I'm most anxious to see Gregg.

I've already discussed the situation with him and he is in favor of it. You should be aware that he is in on our secret...

Now that I'm out of the forest and back to civilization, it's almost as if I never left in the first place. However, my heart is filled with memories and visions of how it was. I know now that it was a trip I had to make. Thank you again for making it so worthwhile for me. Please give my regards to Ed, another dear friend I'll never forget.

I've told Gregg about everything that happened on our expedition and he's awaiting your report with interest. I talked a few times with Ashley and her mother when I came back to the Inn at Mistassini. They are wonderful people! Don't lose her, Dale, she's a rare individual and worthy of any sacrifice.

Wish us well dear friend,
Rachel and Nakota

The next day, Dale made up his mind to return to Monson. Since he could not see Iowaka or spend any time with her, it made sense to write the report at his home. It would be more comfortable and would save the expense of staying at the Inn. He wrote a letter to Iowaka to explain his decision:

August 18, 1920

My Dearest Iowaka,

A note to say "au revoir". I'd stay here if I could see you once in a while, but since I can't, I've decided to return to Monson to complete my report to Gregg Nelson. I appreciate your need to honor the quarantine and I'm very proud of your dedication.

I spent a wonderful evening with your mother. I think we are going to be good friends. You are a lot like her in many ways. I hope you never change.

I want to check on the house in Monson and the cabin where we first met. I also want to check on the chances of getting a full time job as a forester somewhere. I'm most anxious to report for duty at the Maine National Guard on a part-time basis. By doing so, I can maintain my captain commission.

I'll be back to see you as soon as the quarantine has been lifted. I miss you more than I can say. I felt close to you when I was with your mother. She's a lovely lady just like her daughter.

We'll see each other soon. I pray for your safety, Iowaka. I love you.

Dale

PS: There is a little surprise for you at your mother's cabin. I hope you like it.

He arrived in Greenville at noon the next day. The summer season was nearing its end. The waterfront shops and businesses were still busy with tourists. The Hasey Maine Stage line still made daily trips between Bangor and Greenville, running through Monson. He waited an hour for the next bus.

Moosehead Lake was calm and glistening like a sheet of glass. There was a hint of autumn in the air, and it made him think how lucky he was to have completed the project in Quebec before severe winter weather descended. He felt oddly detached, a typical feeling following an extended absence from familiar surroundings. The farther away from home one traveled, he reflected, the longer the absence seemed to be. He missed Iowaka, but at the same time, he was glad to be on his way home.

When Dale arrived in Monson, he left his bags at the general store and walked across the street to Dutra's Garage. Dale noticed an automobile in front of his barn with a "for sale" sign on the windshield. Mr. Dutra had a good reputation in town for honest dealings and competent repairs. An automobile, Dale thought to himself, would make his life a little easier and would give him added mobility. Dale had not spent much money on himself since coming home from the war, and decided to check it out. The one year old Studebaker light six coupe had very low mileage. After a test drive down main street, Dale decided to buy it. The price was four hundred dollars. He paid Mr. Dutra in cash, and picked up his bags at the general store, and proudly drove his new car home.

The house was just as he had left it. The small stack of firewood piled against the old barn reminded him that he should be making arrangements for additional firewood for the coming heating season before it was too late. His father had used about ten cords of firewood a year. There were only three or four cords piled outside and in the shed next to the kitchen.

The first thing he did was to call Gregory Nelson. Dale wanted to inform Gregg that he could be reached at his family home in Maine. He also briefly outlined what had happened in Canada, and promised to have the written report completed within a week.

Next, Dale contacted the Headquarters of the Maine National Guard to inquire about available positions. He was pleasantly surprised to learn that a company commander's billet for a captain was open. He promptly informed them that he was interested in the position. The company headquarters were located at the armory in Dover-Foxcroft. Dale promised the enlistment officer that he would be down to sign the papers later that week.

Pleased with what he had accomplished in such a short period of time, Dale organized the kitchen table as a desk, so that he could compute the field notes and prepare the final report. First things first, however! He built a small fire in the kitchen cook stove and placed a pot of coffee on the front lid, then made himself a peanut butter and jelly sandwich. He was preparing for a long productive evening of intense calculations when a knock sounded at the front door. He walked to the front entrance wondering who it could be? He opened the door, it was Lenore.

"Hi, Dale, I hope I'm not disturbing you. I saw you drive through town earlier," Lenore explained hesitantly. Her cheeks were flushed and she looked uneasy.

"Come in, Lenore," Dale said automatically. It would have been so easy for him to reach out for her and make believe it was yesterday. She was extremely vibrant and attractive, and there was still a small spark within him that she could ignite if he was not careful. "You're looking well. How are your mother and father?"

"The family is fine," she said stepping inside. "I'm staying at home for now. Stanley and I are going through a rough period." Suddenly she was overcome with tears.

"Have a seat at the table if you can find room," said Dale, clearing papers from one side of the table. "I have a fresh pot of coffee on the stove. Would you like some?"

"Thank you," she said, staring at the work notes scattered about the table. "You're always busy working at something. Stanley has trouble keeping a job. I know now that our marriage was a big mistake."

"I'm sorry to hear that," Dale told her. "Regardless of what has happened between the two of us, I would never wish you any misfortune."

"I know that. The past few days have been a nightmare for all of us, including my parents. When I saw you come out from Dutra's I knew that I had to talk to you. Remember how we used to be able to read each other's minds and share our feelings about different things? I haven't been able to do that since Stanley and I got married." She seemed a little more composed now, sitting in the warm familiar kitchen talking with Dale.

Getting involved in the personal affairs of Stanley and Lenore was something Dale definitely did not wish to do. He was not an impartial observer despite all the time that had elapsed, and it was painful to attempt to arbitrate their problems rationally. He poured each of them a cup of coffee and sat down at the table across from her. She looked exhausted.

"I'm not an unbiased onlooker, Lenore. So maybe you're talking to the wrong person. If I were in Stanley's shoes, I'd probably be pretty upset about your discussing personal affairs with a former fiancée."

"Oh, you can't imagine how bad he gets when he thinks of you. Everything I do or say he throws back in my face, accusing me of still being in love with you."

"We can't turn back the clock, Lenore," Dale warned, concerned about the direction of the conversation. "Perhaps I should tell you that I've found someone that means a lot to me. You don't know her, but I believe it's real and I know that I miss her when I'm away from her."

Lenore looked stricken. "Do you love her as much as you did me?" she asked, pleading for an answer.

"Come on, Lenore. That's not a fair question to you or Ashley." Dale realized that he had used Iowaka's English name for the first time. Was it a subconscious effort to hide her Cree heritage? "I met her at the cabin on the Lake of Three Sorrows. She's a graduate of the Greenville Nursing School and she's half Cree Indian."

Lenore listened closely, every nerve in her body attuned to Dale's words. "She's a Cree Indian?" she cried in disbelief.

"Yes," answered Dale defensively. "I thought you should know about Ashley and me before you assumed too much or started taking this unsettled period between you and Stanley as an opportunity for some kind of reconciliation between us. I loved you once, Lenore. We can never recapture what we had, it's over. You're an adult with a child to think of now. There's no point looking backwards. If we look ahead we can shape our futures. So try to make it what you want it to be."

Lenore continued to sip her coffee closely watching Dale from the other side of the table. "Have I really lost you then, Dale?" she asked. "Is it really true?"

Dale's eyes were sad as well. "Lenore, you lost me the day you married Stanley. The memories we've shared will always be important to me, but you alone shaped your future to exclude me and you did it on your terms, that's the reality. It's a different world out there now. We can be friends and I'll always wish you well, but we each have a life to live and it's destined to not be together." His words sounded harsh. Only he knew the knot of pain in his heart.

"Old dreams die hard. I know you're right," Lenore blinked back tears. "I have to be responsible for my own choices, but I had hoped that somehow I could fix past mistakes and that there could still be a place for you and me."

"Listen to me, Lenore," said Dale, reaching across the table to squeeze her hands. "I understand, I really do. Things have changed. Now you should embrace the future with a happy heart for yourself, Stanley, and the baby."

"I'm sure that if Bernie were alive today he'd tell me the same thing," mused Lenore staring into her coffee cup.

"Of course he would. He loved you very much, and only wanted you to be happy."

Lenore pushed her chair from the cluttered table. "Thank you, Dale. I needed to have this talk with you. I wish you and Ashley well. I hope she's worthy of you. Who knows, we might end up being good friends in the future."

"I hope so," smiled Dale.

Lenore embraced him before she disappeared into the darkness.

Later that evening, Dale was finishing some of the calculations for the report when the telephone rang. It was almost midnight, and his experience was that calls at such odd hours of the night generally meant bad news.

"Hello," he answered apprehensively.

"Hi, Dale, this is Iowaka."

"Are you all right?" he asked quickly.

"I'm fine," she replied. "I apologize for the late hour. I just got off my shift and felt like talking to you."

"It's nice to hear your voice again. It's only been a day and I miss you already," he confessed truthfully.

"I'm so sorry about the quarantine, Dale. I'm also calling to thank you for the beautiful music box. My Mother brought it to me in a box of clothes she left at the door of the infirmary. Thanks for your thoughtfulness."

"I'm glad you like it. I wish I could have given it to you personally. How are things at the infirmary?"

"About the same." Iowaka's voice became serious. "We lost one patient last night, an elderly lady. We're taking every precaution possible to isolate the outbreak. I know our methods will be effective in the long run regardless of how disruptive they are at the present time."

"By the end of the week I should have the report completed and off to Gregg Nelson," he told her enthusiastically. "Then, I'm going to report to a National Guard Armory and sign up. I'll be able to maintain my captain commission by participating a couple of weeks in the summer and once or twice a month the rest of the year."

"Is that what you really want?" Iowaka asked guardedly. "I thought you were out of the Army."

"I am, but the reality is that all officers are subject to recall in case of national emergency. I want to use the Reserves to help me maintain a reasonable degree of readiness skills in case I'm ever called up again. Do you understand?"

"Yes, I suppose so. I don't like the thought of you leaving for another war, but I do support whatever you feel is the right thing to do," she exclaimed in a low voice.

"I appreciate that. Someone has to defend our country. I've been trained as a soldier and I consider it my duty to uphold the American ideals. Ed understands what I mean."

"I understand what you mean, too, Dale. If I were a man, I'm sure I'd feel the same way. I only pray that peace prevails in our lifetime."

"So do I," Dale stated earnestly. "I'm also going to check into the availability of permanent forestry jobs. When your quarantine is lifted, let me know and I'll be up to see you for a few days. I spent a wonderful evening with your mother."

"She enjoyed your visit too. I think you've made another conquest, Dale," she laughed. "I've got to get off this line. I'll let you know when the quarantine is released. I love you."

"I love you too, Iowaka, thanks for calling. My day is complete now that I've spent some time with you. Oh, by the way, I bought an automobile today."

"That's wonderful. I'm glad you're enjoying it. Until next time, Dale."

"Until next time, Iowaka. I love you."

Chapter Fifteen

Four days after Dale arrived in Monson, he mailed the completed report to Gregg Nelson and drove his new Studebaker on its first road trip to the National Guard headquarters at Dover-Foxcroft. There he was informed that the company commander billet was still available, so he applied for the opening. The adjutant there told him that the job was his as soon as his active duty files were retrieved from the Regular Army.

Dale had forgotten how much he missed being with troops. He met several other veterans at the headquarters who had been a part of the Guard when Dale's unit was activated in 1917. The men had recently returned from their annual summer training schedule. Generally they went to Camp Drum, New York, but this summer they were sent to New Brunswick to train with the Canadian Army. Later, Dale ate lunch at the officer's mess, talking over old times with officers he knew personally.

After lunch, he drove back to Monson. The report was on its way to Gregg and he had committed himself for duty with the National Guard. It seemed to him that a trip to the cabin at the Lake of Three Sorrows would be a perfect way to end the day. He pulled into Champion's Mobil gasoline station in the middle of Monson to refuel. A former high school classmate, Henry Brown, was working as an attendant. Dale told him that he was going to the cabin that afternoon.

"I heard that Great Northern Paper Company is constructing a new roadway around the northern rim of Moosehead Lake," said Henry, topping off the fuel tank.

"They're probably pretty close to your folks' cabin. Have you heard anything about it?"

"No, Henry, I've been out of town for several weeks. Where did you get that information?" Dale asked.

"I heard it from a truck driver who stopped for fuel on his way to Kokadjo a month ago. He was transporting one of the biggest steam shovels I've ever seen."

"That's interesting, Henry, thanks a lot."

"Sure, glad to help. Nice to see you again, Dale."

Henry had roused his curiosity, and he headed north toward Greenville. Indian Hill, located on the main road south of the village proper, offered one of the most spectacular views in the country. The vantage point looks northwesterly down at the dark blue waters of Moosehead Lake and the small islands scattered throughout. With the silver-white clouds hanging overhead reflecting the dying rays of the setting sun behind Kineo Mountain, Dale thought it was the most beautiful spot in the world.

It was too late in the day for Dale to rent a canoe for the trip to the cabin, so he drove towards Kokadjo on the east side of the lake to check on the status of any construction that might be underway. The cabin was six miles northeast of Kokadjo. When he arrived there, he noticed a concentration of construction equipment and supplies in a large holding area and stopped to inquire about the roadway at a trailer with an "office" sign above the door.

"Hello," Dale called as he knocked. He could see a man sitting at a large table covered with maps.

"Come in. What can we do for you?" asked a young blond man about Dale's age.

"I heard you were building a road up here. I'm the owner of the cabin on the Lake of Three Sorrows, and was wondering how close the roadway will be to it," said Dale, adjusting his eyes to the dim light of the kerosene lantern hanging above the table.

"Well, you can see what's happening here on the map," explained the young man, pointing to one on the table. "If you can read blueprints, this map should answer any questions you have."

"Thanks. My name is Dale Cooper. I'm a forester and quite familiar with maps. I appreciate the chance to examine it," he said extending his hand.

"I'm John Weeks, the project engineer," replied Weeks shaking Dale's hand. "Glad to meet you, Dale. This is our latest print of the project. You can see that we're starting at Kokadjo running northwest barely missing Spencer Bay. Your cabin is here," he said pointing to a black square dot on the map. Dale leaned over to study the map. The new road bordered the northern tip of the Lake of Three Sorrows. Access to the cabin would be convenient from the new road.

"You can drive out to the lake and park your car off the roadway," Weeks suggested. "We haven't finished yet, but it's suitable for a passenger car now. I checked on your cabin, what a great spot."

Dale smiled. "We've enjoyed it over the years. This road brings mixed blessings. It'll make the cabin more accessible. I only hope it doesn't detract from the privacy I have there now."

"You mentioned that you're a forester, are you looking for work?"

"You must have read my mind, John Weeks. You bet I am." answered Dale.

"The regional manager of Great Northern Paper Company mentioned the possibility of putting a forester on the payroll for long term planning or maybe using him as a consultant on a contract basis. You can check it out if you want, he'll be around tomorrow. I can send him over to your cabin if you're interested."

"I certainly would like to talk to him," Dale replied eagerly. "I appreciate your help, John. I'll be at the cabin all day tomorrow. Much obliged for everything."

"You're welcome," answered John grinning slyly. "I'm going to guess that you were a captain during the war, maybe a company commander. Am I right?"

Dale was floored. "Is it that obvious?" he responded with a grin.

"I was a lieutenant platoon leader," Weeks told him. "It's a game I play with veterans I meet. What division were you with?"

"The Second Division. I stayed on in Germany for occupational duty after the Armistice. I'm sure glad to be back home though, and I'm more than ready to start on a regular job."

"I hear you, Dale," Weeks replied. "I'll see to it that the big boss pays you a visit. Good luck to you."

The newly constructed road leading toward Spencer Bay was in better condition than Dale had expected. With the darkness coming on, he was uncertain if he would recognize the terrain north of the cabin, even though he had hiked and walked the area many times in his youth. When he recognized a small knoll covered with a stand of pole-sized white birch, he instantly knew where he was. He drove another quarter mile and carefully pulled the Studebaker off the right-of-way. If his instincts were correct, the trail leading from the Savage stream to the cabin was just a few hundred feet south of where the car was parked.

Taking a flashlight from one of the pockets on the driver's side door, Dale walked confidently into the woods picking up the familiar trail that led to the rock formation behind the cabin. The cabin door was unlocked as usual. He lit a lamp on the table and checked out the cabin interior. Everything was as he had left it, except for the fireplace. Someone had laid dry cedar shavings mixed with white birch bark and kindling, perfect for starting a quick fire. He touched a match to the shavings and shortly the room was filled with flickering light.

He placed a pot of coffee on the grate beside the firebox and checked to see what was available for foodstuff in the root cellar. Canned baked beans, corned beef and a variety of peaches and pears had been added to the cache since he left the cabin for Canada. The people who had used the cabin vindicated his principle of welcoming strangers with an open door. The unwritten golden rule of the Maine woods was alive and functioning well!

Familiar sounds filtered through the cool air. The lonely call of the loons pierced the silence of the night. He was struck with a sudden longing for Iowaka. He would never forget the terror in her eyes when he had first confronted her in the cabin. He didn't think it was possible, but he fell in love with her that very first night, and it had seemed the most natural thing in the world.

Dale awoke at dawn the next day and headed to the lake with his fish pole, spending several hours catching fish for breakfast and dinner. He had just landed a large trout when he heard a voice calling him. Looking up he saw a middle-aged man coming down the rocky ledge behind the cabin.

"I'll be right with you," hollered Dale, reeling in his line.

"Are you, Dale Cooper?" asked the stranger.

"Yes, Sir," replied Dale, shaking his hand.

"The project manager, John Weeks, told me that you were looking for a job. I'm Les Billings, Regional Forester for Great Northern Paper Company."

"Good to meet you, Mr. Billings. I'm a forestry graduate of the University of Maine. I recently got out of the Army and I'm looking for a job."

"I'm a Maine graduate too," claimed Billings in a calm clear voice. He was medium height with an athletic build and walked with a smooth fluid motion. There was a tendency for him to squint his eyes when he looked at Dale as if he was appraising him. It made Dale uncomfortable and gave him the impression that Billings had found something about him that was unsatisfactory. It didn't take long for Dale to discover that his habit of squinting was simply a part of the way Billings viewed the world around him. He was all business and not inclined to encourage familiarity.

"Would you be interested in a job collecting and recording basic data for a comprehensive forest management plan of lands owned by Great Northern Paper?"

"I would if the terms were right," Dale answered.

Billings nodded. "I had mentioned to Weeks that the company would be willing to hire a man and place him on the payroll as a permanent employee. If, however, you preferred to be hired as a consultant, we could work that out too. The job is basically independent of harvesting operations. What we're ultimately looking for is the establishment of a new set of data for the various compartments so that we can develop a more meaningful and accurate cutting budget, based on a sustained yield principal for all the land holdings."

"That's a tall order, considering the thousands of acres you own," remarked Dale, impressed with the magnitude of the undertaking.

"That's one of the reasons we're flexible on how the work is to be done. You could start out on a per diem basis and as you develop a better feel for what's involved, you could sign on permanently or even bid the cost of inventorying the compartments. If I was going to take on the job, I'd prefer an arrangement like that."

"That sounds good to me," answered Dale. "It would also give me more flexibility to work on other projects if the opportunity arose."

"I have a more detailed job description and employment requirements here," said Billings taking a large envelope from his jacket pocket. "Why don't you study it and let me know. The salaries offered are reasonably firm but the methodology is optional. Come up with any proposal that's workable and you'll find me flexible. My phone number and address are on the papers. I hope things work out Mr. Cooper, and look forward to your reply."

"Thanks for looking me up," said Dale. "Does a formal application have to be made or do you have the authority to approve the position? Also, do you object if I take a few days to discuss this with someone else?"

"That authority rests with me," Billings nodded briskly. "I'll hold the position open for the next ten days. I hope we can get together," Billings added, smiling as he shook Dale's hand.

"I'm sure we can work something out," added Dale.

Dale felt like yelling for joy, watching Billings retrace his steps up over the ledge. A chance for a job at a good rate right at his back door. He was anxious to share the good news with Iowaka. The fresh trout he had just caught would be a suitable meal to celebrate his good fortune.

After eating lunch, Dale rushed to Monson and called Iowaka as soon as he arrived at the house. She was not available but the person that answered the phone told him the quarantine was going to be released in two days. Upon hearing the good news, Dale made plans to travel to Quebec City with his Studebaker, where he could stay over-night and park the automobile while he took a train to Mistassini. It was too far to drive all the way, and the roads were nothing more than wagon tracks from Quebec City.

Mid afternoon of the next day he was in Quebec, where he went shopping for an engagement ring. In the very first store he found the ring that he thought was right. He stayed overnight at the Hotel Frotenac. The next day, Dale boarded a train to the interior. He hardly noticed the beautiful scenery outside the window of the speeding train as it cut through the dark green forests. His thoughts were dominated by Iowaka and the surprise he had for her. She was just beginning her long-awaited opportunity to serve her native community as a nurse. Now a stranger from a foreign land was coming to ask her to be his bride. Was that asking too much? Was he being selfish asking her to give up everything for him?

The familiar Inn at Mistassini welcomed him like an old friend. The desk clerk even offered him the use of the Inn's automobile for the evening. The quarantine's release was big news in the community and Dale called the Huntington home on the chance that Iowaka might be home. Mrs. Huntington answered the phone.

"Mrs. Huntington, this is Dale Cooper. I just arrived at the Inn. Is Iowaka at home or still at the infirmary?"

"Your timing is perfect, Mister Cooper. She just got out of the bath. I can call her if you like, or may I suggest that you come over and join us for supper? Ashley's so weary from the past few weeks and your visit will do her good."

"I'd like nothing more, Mrs. Huntington," Dale responded at once. "Thanks for asking. I'll be there within the hour."

"We'll be expecting you, Mr. Cooper."

Dale freshened up and changed into clean clothes as fast as he could.

"Give our regards to Miss Ashley," said the desk clerk. "She and the others at the infirmary have been wonderful to us. My mother was terribly sick from the disease, and they nursed her back to health. They don't come any better than that young lady," the clerk attested passionately.

"I agree with you, Sir! Thanks for the use of the car."

Dale parked beside the Huntington's cabin and knocked on the door. A familiar face opened the door - it was Iowaka. "My mother couldn't keep it from me. It's nice to see you again," she cried, slipping into his arms.

Dale was overcome. "I couldn't stay away once I learned you could leave the infirmary," he whispered in her ear. "You've been on my mind since I left." Dale held her at arm's length, there was something different about her. She seemed preoccupied and distant. He was about to ask her if something was wrong when Mrs. Huntington called from the kitchen.

"Welcome back, Mr. Cooper. Please, make yourself at home, supper will be ready shortly. We're having salmon tonight. Ed dropped off two big ones for us."

"That sounds great, Mrs. Huntington," he replied. "Coming here for your home cooking is beginning to be a habit."

The fireplace was alive with red coals. Iowaka selected another log from the wood pile and placed it on the glowing embers and took a seat on the couch. "Come sit down until Mother is ready. She can be a tyrant if anyone gets in her way in the kitchen," commented Iowaka in a serious mood.

Dale couldn't keep his eyes from her. She looked drained and tired, and yet, incredibly lovely. "You've been through quite an ordeal, Iowaka. I've been worried about you. I hope you have a chance to rest for a while now that the emergency is over." He took her hands in his and kissed them gently. His world was complete now, she was with him.

"How did you find the cabin on the Lake of Three Sorrows?" Iowaka asked in a hushed tone.

"I was there two days ago. It was the same as when you and I left it. I felt your presence and saw your face everywhere I looked."

"You're teasing me," she accused.

"No, I'm not teasing. You came to me out of the forest one day and I have never been the same since."

Iowaka smiled, clearly touched. "You always say such nice things to me. I think often of our encounter in the cabin. In fact, I want to talk to you about something."

Dale was prevented from asking what was on her mind when Mrs. Huntington again called them. "All right you two, dinner is on the table!" Dale followed her into the kitchen portion of the great room with grave concern.

The meal was delicious and Dale ate more than he had expected. Something was wrong! There was tension in the air that affected everyone. Dinner, though delicious, was awkward. When they were finished eating, Iowaka and her mother cleared the table, and then Mrs. Huntington announced that she was going next door to visit the neighbors. Dale appreciated the chance to be alone with Iowaka. Her mother graciously smiled at him as she was leaving.

Dale stood in front of the fireplace staring at the flickering flames waiting to hear what Iowaka had to say. She came to him and took his hand and began to trace the lines in his palm with her forefinger.

Finally she spoke. "I'm glad you came to see me, Dale. I had bad thoughts again when you left. I imagined that once you returned to familiar surroundings you would soon forget about me."

"If you only knew what is in my heart and how often I think of you," he replied, watching the reflection of the flames on her face. Listening to his words, Iowaka hesitantly lifted her dark eyes to his. He thought she was the most beautiful woman in the world and held her close. "I have something for you," he said releasing her to reach into his pocket withdrawing a small box. "This is for you."

She accepted the gift, her trembling fingers lingered on his. "You always bring me gifts," she said surprised.

Dale collected the outer wrappings as she peeled them off. When she opened the box and saw the engagement ring inside, Iowaka stared at him and began to cry.

"I had a long speech all memorized for this moment, but all I can say is, will you marry me, Iowaka?"

He could feel the emotion and tension running through her body. She continued to cry with her head buried against his chest. It sounded more like a cry of desperation than of happiness.

Dale clutched her tight to comfort her. "What is it, Iowaka? What's wrong?" He was terrified at what her answer might be. She clung to him for a moment, withdrawing from their embrace, and gently took him by the hand to sit down on the couch. "My God. What's happened to you? What have I done?"

She sat beside him and stared aimlessly at the burning embers. "I'm flattered by your proposal, Dale. Any woman would be honored to be your wife. However, I must tell you that I can never accept your offer of marriage. It's not because I don't have feelings for you. To the contrary, it's because I do love you that I must refuse your proposal."

Dale couldn't believe her words. "You're talking nonsense, Iowaka. We're at the threshold of a whole new life, it doesn't make sense for us not to be together."

Iowaka buried her tear-streaked face in her hands. Dale touched her shoulder and she recoiled. "Please, don't ask me to explain, Dale," she said firmly. "I'm not worthy of your request and don't ask me why. I can't tell you."

Dale was at a loss, overwhelmed with frustration. "Are you saying that what we thought we had is over?" he asked incredulously. "Do you want me to go?"

"Yes," Iowaka replied. "It would be best if you forget me and leave."

Dale shook his head in disbelief. "I believe I'm entitled to more of an explanation than that. How can I just go away and forget you? How?"

"My shame is mine alone. It has nothing to do with you and me. I must bear it and I must bear it alone."

"It still doesn't make any sense to me. How come things have changed so quickly? I love you."

"I can't answer your question," screamed Iowaka on the verge of emotional collapse. "I just can't. Please leave, Dale. I want to be alone."

Dale had often made split-second decisions on the battlefield in moments of grave danger, now he was at a complete loss as to what to do. He stood silently in front of the fireplace for what seemed an eternity trying to fathom what was going on in Iowaka's mind. The hysterical woman before him was no longer the woman he had fallen in love with. He had no intention of remaining where his presence was not welcome. Dale knew defeat when he saw it. Without another word he opened the cabin door and walked aimlessly into the cool evening air, crushed by the stinging denial.

Chapter Sixteen

Thirteen Years Later (June, 1933)

Dale sat on the porch of his cabin reading the newspaper enjoying the morning breeze. A notice for Monson Academy graduates in the *Piscataquis Observer* caught his eye: "A homecoming celebration for the graduates of Monson Academy will be held on Saturday at Tarr Hall, Tenney Hill Road, Monson at 8:00PM. All graduates are encouraged to attend, especially the Class of 1913 who is celebrating their twentieth reunion." It was an affair that should do him good, and he decided to attend.

Lifting his eyes from the newspaper, Dale looked across the Lake of Three Sorrows in a pensive pose. The tract of forest land that had burned while he was in France during the war was recovering rapidly. Beneath the scattered, rotting tree trunks was a lush green carpet of spruce and fir saplings so thick it was difficult to walk through. The forest had changed, thought Dale, and he had changed, perhaps, more than he realized. His eyes now had a dark cast reflecting the torture his soul had suffered ever since his return from France in 1920. Those who knew him had attempted to break his self-imposed isolation, to no avail.

Dale insisted he was just fine. He performed his work as a forester in the Great Northern Paper Company lands with great intensity, frequently remaining in the wilderness for days, even weeks, at a time. The social scene had never been his favorite pastime. The forest had helped to maintain his sanity, and was instrumental in his deliverance from a prolonged depression. Those ideals and people that he had believed in had betrayed him. Now, he was a much more cautious individual than he used to be.

His first true love, Lenore, had left him when he was the most in need of support. It didn't kill him, but it left him in a more vulnerable state of mind. The death of his parents only compounded his anguish. The third event was the most destructive. Iowaka had withdrawn from his life when the love he nurtured for her was at its peak. She simply disappeared just as if she had never been a meaningful part of his life at all. The three losses in such rapid succession: Lenore, his parents, and Iowaka were more than he could bear alone. They had almost destroyed him. He was a much more fragile human being than he had imagined. The pain had not turned him bitter or sullen as it would have many. Instead, he simply retreated to a world where he was able to avoid people as much as possible. People were the cause of his heartaches!

Placing the *Observer* down on the table beside his chair on the newly constructed deck that surrounded the log cabin, Dale picked through the balance of his mail. He had lived full-time at the cabin for the past four years since he had sold the old homestead in Monson. The cabin was his world when he was not in the forest or honoring his obligations in the National Guard. He had used the money received from the sale of the Monson home to upgrade the cabin. Electric lights and a septic system had been installed so that he could build a bathroom in the house and have the pleasure of a shower. It was the one modern convenience he enjoyed more than anything else.

Dale had also added two rooms on the northerly side of the cabin. The improvements provided room for guests whenever they showed up. Rachel and her husband, Gregory Nelson, were annual guests in the summertime, and Ed Blake and his family were also frequent visitors, especially during the summer months.

The Nelsons always enjoyed their relaxing vacations at the cabin. The Indian boy they had adopted was growing into a fine young man with a serious demeanor. They named him after her father, Charles Kemp. Young Charles called Dale "Uncle" and was fascinated with the fact that he was a forester. Gregg and Rachel were devoted to their son and spent a lot of time and energy developing a sense of pride and purpose in his Cree heritage. Children were naturally drawn to Dale who accepted them without reservations.

Ed Blake and his wife Tasha also had kept in touch with Dale throughout the years. Dale was glad that he had cemented his friendship with Ed in the north before Iowaka had dropped out of his life. Ed knew what had happened to his cousin, but he refused to divulge any significant information to Dale, since Iowaka had sworn him to secrecy. All that Ed would say was that Iowaka had gone to London to live with some of her father's family. Dale cried out for more information, but he knew his questions would be futile. Ed would never break a promise to his cousin. These days Ed rarely mentioned Iowaka's name in Dale's presence.

He anguished in silence, and spent sleepless nights thinking about her. Visions of her were everywhere in the cabin. Afraid, disheveled and hungry, Iowaka had been transformed in the short time she had shared the cabin with him. She had responded to him in the same way he had reached out to her. He saw love in her eyes on the banks of the Mistissini River and at her mother's cabin. Suddenly, all that had changed, and she became a hysterical human being that wanted him out of her life.

Dale relived those events every day. Time had eased his despair but the betrayal continued to hurt. He could have understood any reason if Iowaka had been forthcoming with it, but to cast him aside without a word was painful beyond belief. He wasn't sure if he would ever be willing to risk being hurt again.

Later in the day, Dale picked up his mail and returned to the cabin. As he expected, there were letters from Ed Blake, and from Rachel Nelson. He smiled, for both of his friends were planning for their summer excursion to the cabin. He was looking forward to this year's visit more than ever. Dale opened Ed's letter first:

June 20, 1933

Dear Dale,

Another year has passed and we're glad to see the summer finally come. You'll be saddened to learn that Mrs. Huntington, my Aunt, passed away this spring. She was ill for a long time and her passing was a blessing, as she was anxious to be with her husband. I'll miss her gracious presence. She was like a mother to me.

I'm taking several days off from the mill in early July, and I wanted to check to see if you were ready for the gang to invade your privacy once again. We will be coming with a girlfriend of our kids if you don't mind. Tasha and I are looking forward to seeing you.

I have news for you, my friend. Ashley has released me from my vow of silence and I will be able to answer any questions you may have. I hope that this will help put some of your suffering and pain to rest. So, be patient, old friend, until we arrive. You should find comfort in the knowledge that what happened was not your fault in any way. I personally believe that it was a very bad choice on Ashley's part, but I'll leave that judgment to God.

All our love,
Ed and Tasha

The last part of the letter sent Dale's heart pounding. Did it mean that he at last could put to rest all the ugly dreams that have haunted him for years? Perhaps his release from the self-imposed purgatory was just around the corner!

Rachel and Gregg wrote that they, too, would be coming sometime in July. They would call in advance of their departure from New York to let him know the specific dates of their visit. In addition, they wrote that they had established a trust fund for him at their bank in New York. It was his share of the gold found in the cave in Canada. They had set up a similar fund for Ed. Dale folded the letter and smiled. The prospect of seeing old friends was pleasant to look forward to.

The notice in the paper of the class reunion interested him. Dale glanced at the clock. There was still enough time for him to get cleaned up for the reunion. Meeting with old classmates would be good for him.

Dale showered and changed into his Army uniform for the evening. It was the only clothing in his wardrobe suitable for such an occasion. He hadn't seen Lenore for several years, she would probably be present.

The trusty old Studebaker that Dale had purchased thirteen years ago had been upgraded to a bright yellow Model A Ford coupe, which he had purchased after selling his parent's home in Monson. The Ford was a delight to drive and he never regretted the extravagant expenditure. He drove through the center of Monson and parked in the field beside the dance hall. The parking area was half-full of automobiles. The first person Dale recognized upon stepping out of the Ford was Mr. Fred Olman.

"Good evening, Mr. Olman," he warmly greeted the former high school principal. "I was thinking about you and Mrs. Olman on my way here from Greenville. How are you?"

"Hello, Dale, not bad. You look very spiffy in your uniform." Mr. Olman was suffering from Parkinson's Disease, which caused his body and hands to shake mildly most of the time. "It's nice to see you again. So many of my old students have left town. Who can blame them? The slate quarries don't offer very much for young people these days."

"I hope some of them will come back tonight for old-times sake. Lenore and Stanley should be here," added Dale.

Mr. Olman seemed taken aback at the mention of the couple. "You've been out of touch for too long, Dale. They separated a couple of years ago and are divorced now. Lenore has the child. She's a wonderful mother to him. It was destined to never work out for those two." As they walked towards the hall Mr. Olman asked, "Do you mind if I hold your arm? I'm not as sure footed as I used to be, but I wanted to make a show of support for my former students."

Dale immediately offered his arm letting him set the pace. "I'd consider it an honor, Sir. I'm glad you could make it. A reunion wouldn't have been the same without you. Your commitment and devotion to the community are a proud legacy," Dale spoke truthfully. The elderly and fragile teacher was beloved by his students. He never judged, he only gave of himself.

"Mrs. Olman and I have always wondered why you never married, Dale," remarked Mr. Olman. "You had more to offer than most and you never lost that compassion that you inherited from your dear mother and father." When Dale did not immediately reply, he added, "Forgive me for prying, young man, I was just thinking out loud."

"No apology is necessary, Sir," answered Dale, remaining quiet on the subject.

When they stepped inside the hall, a small band of local musicians were playing a string of slow waltzes. Dale escorted Mr. Olman to a table prominently located half way down the hall. "You should be comfortable here, Mr. Olman. May I get you some refreshments?"

"If you could find me a half-filled glass of punch or ginger ale, that would taste good."

"I'll see what I can do," said Dale, slowly making his way to the rear of the hall toward the concession table. He recognized several people along the way and paused to say hello. It was nice to be accepted the way he was in the small town. He asked a young lady at the concession table for a half-filled glass of punch for Mr. Olman. She immediately understood and poured a tall glass partially full.

"I bet he'd rather have a straw to drink it with," commented the lady, passing Dale a straw and a napkin.

"Thanks a lot."

Lenore had spotted Dale from across the room. Before he made it back to Mr. Olman's chair, she approached him and locked her arm firmly in his. "Hi, Dale. I was hoping you would come tonight."

"Hello, Lenore. Be careful, I've got a drink for Mr. Olman."

"Will you dance with me afterwards?" she inquired, her eyes shining.

"Sure, I'll be glad to. You'll have to watch your toes though, I haven't danced in years," he smiled.

"I'll be careful," she answered, letting him go. She sighed as she watched him walk to Mr. Olman's chair. What a fool she had been to give him up for Stanley! She had dressed special for the evening anticipating that Dale would come. Her dark blue dress accented her blonde hair and the crimson bow holding her hair away from her left ear. She was a strikingly statuesque woman and most of the young men in the room followed her about with approving eyes.

Dale delivered the drink to Mr. Olman and came back for Lenore. "I suppose this is as good a time as any for the first dance in years," he said cheerfully. "I'm glad they're playing a slow waltz. By the way, you look lovely tonight, Lenore. Mr. Olman told me about you and Stanley. I'm sorry it didn't work out for you."

She brushed the comment aside. "It was just a terrible mistake, Dale. You look so handsome in your uniform. I remember when you said good-bye on your way to France. God, I hated to see you go!"

Dale smiled sadly. "We've been over that ground before, Lenore. The past is gone and there isn't anything we can do to resurrect it. Nobody tried any harder than I to do that. All we have is now and tomorrow. Why don't we just leave the past to itself."

Lenore looked up at him with her blue eyes glistening. "Dale, is there anything left for me, us, again?" she stuttered "I've never stopped loving you, never!" She laid her head against his chest and held him tight. She was prepared to pay any price to remedy the mistake she had made fourteen years ago, and prayed for one more chance to prove her devotion and fidelity.

"Do you want me to be honest with you?" asked Dale. He knew what was in her heart. It would have been easy to shut out the ugly memories and concentrate on all the good times they had spent together.

"Of course I want the truth," she answered, eager, yet, afraid for his answer.

"You're a lovely desirable woman that anyone in this hall would be glad, even anxious, to claim as his own," Dale spoke slowly and precisely so as to not be misunderstood. "As for me, us, as you delicately put it, I must honestly say that I'm unsure at this time. Now, that's not a yes or a no. It's a maybe, and it means that we've got to have some time. So much has transpired since we were together in school. I couldn't handle another setback, and I'm reluctant to place myself in that position again."

"I understand, Dale, I do." Lenore's face lit up. "I've cried myself to sleep more nights than I like to think about, condemning myself for what I did. When I'm with you I feel whole and secure. If I had another chance I'd make different choices, that's a promise."

"Let's not make any promises for now. Let's just enjoy the moment and let tomorrow take care of itself. I've given up setting itineraries."

"I'll be patient," she said, squeezing him affectionately.

The music stopped and Dale walked Lenore back to her table. "Thanks, Lenore. I'm going to circulate among the crowd for a while, okay? It's good to see so many familiar faces."

"I'm so glad you came, Dale," Lenore replied. "You need to get out more often." She gave him a soft kiss on the cheek and walked away.

Dale chatted a while with some old friends. The music had just started up again when a young boy approached him and asked if he was Dale Cooper.

"Yes I am, young man. What can I do for you?"

"A lady asked me to give this to you. She's at the entrance door."

Dale took the note and thanked the boy. He scanned the entrance foyer for someone he knew, but did not recognize anyone. He opened the note. The light was not very good but he could see well enough to read:

Dear Dale, may I see you outside? Iowaka.

Chapter Seventeen

Dale ran into the foyer of the hall. Iowaka was nowhere in sight. He wondered if someone was playing a cruel joke on him. Then, he stepped outside. In the semi-darkness, near the parking lot, he saw a lone figure standing in front of his car. He cautiously approached it, not even realizing he had been holding his breath, and came face-to-face with Iowaka. She was dressed in a cream-colored suit with white lace around her neck and a maroon beret tilted sharply to the left. Her black hair glistened beneath the street lamps.

"Is it really you, Iowaka?" he asked shakily. "Or am I having another one of my bad dreams?"

"No Dale, I'm real," she answered softly. It was her! He would recognize that voice anywhere.

"I never thought I'd ever see you again," cried Dale. Tears filled his unbelieving eyes. "Now you appear out of nowhere, without warning. My God, what happened to us?"

"That's why I've come. You deserve an explanation, and it would have been cowardly on my part to let Ed do it for me. Please forgive me, Dale. I'm so sorry for what I've done. You didn't deserve to be treated that way," she replied in a clear voice.

Dale leaned against the fender of the Ford. "I can tell you that I'll never be afraid of dying again. It would be a picnic compared to these past years. I've hated and loved you at the same time for so long that I've lost track. I don't know what I feel anymore. I could have forgiven you if I knew the cause of your behavior, but I may never forget how shabbily you treated the love I had for you." Dale's voice faltered and he felt weak.

It was difficult for him to comprehend that she was standing here before him, after thirteen excruciating years of absence... here she was!

Anguish flashed across Iowaka's face. "Is there someplace we could go that would be more private than this?" she pleaded. "Please, just give me a chance to explain."

Dale nodded curtly. "You're right, this is too public for a discussion like this."

"Are you with that girl you were dancing with?" she asked.

"No, we just danced for old times sake."

"She's beautiful. Is that the Lenore you told me about?"

"Yes," answered Dale.

"I watched you two from the door. It's obvious that she loves you..., but that's none of my business."

"You're right Iowaka," he replied. "It's none of your business. How did you get to Monson?"

"I got a lift with a nurse I knew from the Greenville Hospital. We were good friends in school. She's waiting out on the road."

"Why don't you send her back to Greenville. You can ride back with me." Dale dug into his pocket for the car key. "That will give us a chance to talk privately."

"Okay," she answered hesitantly, afraid the wrong response would cause him to change his mind. "I'll tell her to go along then."

"I'll wait for you," Dale told her. Iowaka left the parking lot when Lenore poked her head out the doorway of the hall and saw him standing by the car.

"Are you coming back in, Dale? Is anything wrong?"

"No, Lenore, I'm leaving now and won't be back. Enjoy the rest of the evening."

Lenore was disappointed. "I was hoping to see more of you." Then she saw Iowaka hurrying towards Dale's car. "Oh, now I understand," Lenore exclaimed, darting back inside.

Iowaka looked at Dale. "I'm sorry if I interrupted something."

"It was nothing really. Lenore and I have had the same conversation several times."

Dale opened the car door for Iowaka and helped her get seated. When he climbed into the driver's seat, the subtle aroma of heliotrope filled his nostrils. She had been wearing that same scent the first time he had met her in Mistassini. Memories overwhelmed him. Putting him at a complete loss for words. They rode through the village in silence. Dale was content just to be near her. Her presence was powerful enough to cloud his reasoning.

He had so many questions to ask, yet, he was afraid of loosing the fragile, exquisite moment he was experiencing. He remembered how difficult it had been, and a lump filled his throat. Iowaka took a handkerchief from her pocket and wiped her eyes. She had been crying. He was conscious of the intense emotion they shared. Dale broke the silence.

"Where are you staying in Greenville?"

"At a boarding house near the hospital. I came in on the afternoon train from Montreal. I tried to call you at your cabin but there was no answer. Then I saw the notice in the *Observer* about the reunion celebration in Monson, and took a chance that you might be here. Ed told me what kind of car you drove."

"He wrote me about your mother's passing. I'm sorry to hear that. She was a very gracious lady. I could have loved her as if she was my own."

"I came to settle her affairs, but I was too late for the funeral. She was a good woman. I only wish I were half as strong as she was." said Iowaka, her voice choked.

"I was wondering. Would you mind if we went to the cabin on Three Sorrows? We can drive to it now, and we can talk there undistracted," Dale suggested.

"Yes, let's go to the cabin," she agreed between sobs. "I was going to ask you to take me back where all of this began. It may be a mistake, but I have to revisit that period of my life once more."

Dale reached out and clasped her hand. Her warm fingers sent chills racing through his body. "The cabin looks a little different from how you remember it. I've made a few changes over the years."

"Yes, Ed told me. No matter what you may think, Dale, I never forgot you. From our first encounter at your cabin and through those long years, the thing which sustained me the most, was my memory of your kind and gentle ways. I will never forgive myself for treating you so badly. Life never turns out the way we planned." She squeezed his hand and continued in a tremulous voice. "All it takes is one rash choice and everything changes. You and my people deserved better from me. I failed the ones I cared about the most."

"I'm not judging you, Iowaka," Dale told her, not fully certain of what she was referring to. "I just want to understand." They were passing Spectacle Pond which glowed in the light of the full moon.

"I'm glad it's a pretty night," she remarked. "Somehow it would have been harder to meet with you and explain myself if it had been raining."

"It is nice out isn't it?" Dale answered quietly.

Neither spoke much for the rest of the way. Dale passed Greenville and drove north towards Kokadjo. He could feel the tension in her body increase the moment they left Greenville. By the time they passed Lily Bay, a few miles north, Iowaka was having trouble catching her breath. Dale was worried about her.

"Do you really want me to continue?" he asked, slowing the Ford down.

"Yes, yes, Dale, please go on! If I don't follow through now I'll probably never be able to do it." She nervously grasped his hand.

"The road to the cabin branches off to the left just ahead. If we continue straight we'll go to Kokadjo on First Roach Pond. Which way would you like me to go?"

Iowaka was living in a world all her own, but she heard him and shook her head. "Kokadjo, I want to go to Kokadjo at the dam."

Dale was familiar with the place and drove straight ahead. She knew when they were approaching the dam site, her body tensed. When he pulled the car to the right beside the dam she began to cry, softly at first. Convulsive sobs wracked her body, robbing her of breath, and she fainted, slumping over against his shoulder.

Dale shut off the engine and gently placed her head against the back of the seat. The sudden quiet frightened him. She had collapsed from some sort of emotional trauma, Nature's way of releasing untenable pressure.

Dale understood the pain associated with this place. He checked Iowaka's neck to make sure her clothing was not choking her and reached across her limp body to roll down the window on her door. Her small maroon beret fell in his lap. The cool evening air was laced with the soft scent of spruce and fir. Iowaka started to stir. When she felt Dale's hands on her arm she quickly raised a fist to strike him, but he held her forearms firmly and spoke soothingly.

"Don't be frightened, Iowaka. It's me, Dale," he whispered in her ear. She recognized his voice and relaxed, sitting upright in the seat. "That's better, now breathe the fresh air. Do you want me to continue to the cabin?"

She hesitated. "This is where it happened," she answered in a strained voice. "When I got out of the car I tripped and almost fell against the dam. Then I remember running for a long time in the forest. He followed me for awhile and finally, left. Would you please take me to your cabin?"

Dale responded by starting the car again and turning on the headlights. "The cabin is only a few minutes from here by way of the new road. The route you took through the woods must have been four or five miles," he said trying to remain calm and supportive. He agonized over the ordeal she was forcing herself to relive and appreciated that the trauma was something she probably needed to revisit, on her own terms, in order to put it behind her.

Minutes later, Dale turned the Ford onto a well-packed set of tracks which led to the rocky ledge behind the cabin. The night was spectacular. The moon was bright and the sky was alive with stars. A shaft of moonlight penetrated the opening on the cliffs to the south of the cabin, highlighting the swirling water below. It was always a beautiful sight to Dale, and tonight, he thought it was more exquisite than ever. Almost a tribute to Iowaka's presence, as if the land was welcoming her back from a long absence.

"It's lovely," whispered Iowaka. "More so than I remembered it."

"Come, let's sit on the porch," Dale suggested, coming around the car to open her door.

She took his hand, allowing him to help her out of the car. "I remember coming out of the woods onto the ledge when I saw the cabin. It was a welcome sight. I was hurting all over my body," she recalled. She clung to him and walked unsteadily towards the cabin.

"May I get you something to eat or drink? Coffee, tea, or anything else?" he asked, helping her onto the swinging couch at the center of the porch.

"No, not for me. Thanks for asking," she responded watching him carefully. Dale still had that same easy way about him, always trying to make people comfortable. He was handsome in his uniform. When he removed his service cap, she saw the prematurely silver-gray streaks in his black hair, and she felt guilty, more than ever, at the physical manifestations of the pain she had inflicted on him. It was time for her to release him of the doubts and anxiety that had been his lot for thirteen years.

"Please, sit down, Dale," she requested, taking a deep breath and patting the seat beside her. "Now that I'm here at the scene of our first meeting, I hope that I can answer some of your questions. Let me begin with Kokadjo. I never lied to you about what happened there. The man I was with, Joe Landers, stopped his car at the exact same spot you did tonight by the dam. He started to paw me. The more I resisted the more violent he became. He struck me across the face hard enough that I lost consciousness. When I came too, he was raping me. I was consumed with shame and disgust at what he had done."

"I'll kill him for that," Dale promised.

Iowaka placed a hand on his arm to calm him. "There's more, Dale. You know all that happened after I came to your cabin. It was like an oasis, and you were so kind and thoughtful. I loved you for that, Dale. For a little while I was able to put what happened to me out of my mind. However, the ugly images returned as soon as I left Greenville on the train. They've been with me ever since. I'm as anxious to put those cruel memories to rest as you are for an explanation."

Iowaka paused to catch her breath. "When you came to Canada to work on the land project with Ed and Rachel, I did not deceive you. I truly loved you, Dale. Whatever has taken place since that time, please don't ever doubt what was in my heart." Iowaka again breathed deeply of the fragrant night air. "I honestly believed that we could have been happy together. I felt privileged to be loved by such a fine man. My heart was singing then, and the future was filled with dreams and the promise of great joy."

"I felt that same way too," Dale recalled softly.

"Then an unexpected turn of events changed everything," Iowaka smiled sadly. "Suddenly a crisis of grave consequences confronted me. I shared it with Mother, and she shared it with Ed and Tasha, pledging them to secrecy. My periods were normally erratic, so I did not worry that first month. The second month, I was beside myself with horror and shame. The third month confirmed all my fears. I was pregnant!"

179

Chapter Eighteen

"Why didn't you tell me so that we could have gone to the police?" Dale asked gently, appalled that she had suffered alone.

Tears streamed down her bronze cheeks. "I was too ashamed, besides I was a Canadian national and was scheduled to return to Canada the next day," she told him.

Unable to watch her suffer any longer, he took her into his arms and held her, praying that she would understand all that he could not express in words. She continued to cry, resting her head against him. He caressed her shining black hair. Such a beautiful woman, filled with promise and eager to serve her people, but she was nearly destroyed by a worthless lout. Dale silently vowed that Mr. Landers was going to pay a price!

"Every night for the past thirteen years I've dreamed of holding you like this," he whispered. "If only I had challenged what you were doing! Maybe I could've sheltered you from some of the pain."

"Would my condition have made a difference to you?" she asked hesitantly, looking into his eyes.

"None whatsoever," Dale answered from his heart. When she saw the love in his eyes, she lifted her lips to his. After thirteen years of hurt, confusion, and loneliness, their lips met, and their tears, were, alas, tears of joy.

Two loons called from across the lake to each other. The ancient melancholic cry of the wild reverberated in the cool clear air. The earth was embraced in the solitude of the night.

"I've missed those sounds," she cried, feeling secure in his arms. "Hold me close, Dale. I know how badly you've suffered.

I felt your pain across the miles that separated us and have hated myself for bringing so much misery to everyone's lives. Sometimes I think everyone would have been better off if I'd died in the forest."

"That's not true, Iowaka," interrupted Dale, holding a finger over her lips. "The only question I have is where do we go from here? Is this a new beginning, or is this the beginning of the end? I have to know, Iowaka."

She continued to cling to him not wanting the magic of the moment to be lost. "If I had a free choice, I'd stay in your arms forever if you'd have me."

"You know what my answer would be. From that first day when you came into my life from the forest, nothing else mattered except being with you. Of course I want you. I would have climbed any mountain for you."

"I want you to know everything so that you can make up your mind about me." Her voice held such grief that he wanted to stop her.

Dale began to speak, "You…"

"Please, Dale, allow me to tell the whole story. The last time we saw each other at my Mother's cabin in Canada, I already knew that I was pregnant. The infirmary did not want me on the staff without being married. It was terribly humiliating, and I probably made the wrong decisions, but let me tell you what I did.

"My mother had lived in the outskirts of London with my father's family for several years. They had accepted her and loved her the way most people did who knew her. She suggested that I go to London to be with them, at least until the child was born. I left a few days after seeing you. It was a wretched voyage across the Atlantic. I've never felt so alone in my life as I did on that trip. The Huntingtons made me feel welcome once they knew the circumstances, but they did impose one condition. If I remained with them, I would have to be married."

"Oh, no," cried Dale, physically stung by the statement.

181

Iowaka continued, "I agreed to something suggested by my mother. One of my father's brother's son, my cousin Ronald, was severely wounded in the war and confined to a wheelchair. He's paralyzed from the waist down and requires daily care. It was suggested that for the sake of the family honor and of my baby, announcements be made that Ronald Huntington and I had been married during the war. I agreed to the deception, and agreed to take care of him, so that I would have a place to live with my child. There were never any marriage vows or nuptial certificates for us. If an interested party had wanted to search the public records, they would have found nothing. It was essentially a public relations scheme. My name was already Huntington, so it did not have to be changed. I hasten to add, my dearest Dale, that I am not married, and have not lived with another man as his wife. I agreed to stay until my daughter, Heather, turns sixteen. She's twelve now, and is coming to visit with you this summer."

"I'll look forward to that," said Dale. "What about you, Iowaka?"

"I have to return in a few days," announced Iowaka reluctantly.

"No, not now," he exclaimed. "Why so soon?"

"Yes, it's part of my agreement. If I don't go Ronald will be placed in a veteran's home where he'll very likely die. He's not in good health. I owe the family that." She hesitated before asking him the question she held for him. "So now that you know the whole truth, can you forgive me, Dale? Can you ever love me again?"

"My Lord, I never stopped loving you, Iowaka, not for a second. I'm so proud of the responsible way you conducted your life. After waiting thirteen years to hold you again, four more will be a breeze," he said joyously. "Will you marry me then?"

She lifted her face and kissed him with trembling lips. "Yes, my darling, Dale, I'll marry you. In fact, the last time we were together, you gave me a ring," she smiled, reached into her pocket and held out her hand. In her palm was the same ring he had purchased in Canada and left behind on that painful evening at her mother's cabin.

"You kept it all this time," he exclaimed.

"Yes, I knew that I should have sent it back to you, but my heart would not let it go. It was a symbol of our love and I treasured it for that reason. Oh, Dale, in a few short years, we'll be able to make it a reality."

"Thank you God for hearing our prayers," Dale cried, kissing the top of her head. "Will you stay with me tonight?"

"Yes," she answered simply. "For years I've been uncertain of my ability to be a wife. Now I can start to live again with hope in my heart. I love you, Dale Cooper, for so many reasons, but most of all for your decency and gentle ways. Forgive me for the difficult years."

Dale held her for a long time without speaking. "I forgive you, Iowaka, and I love you so much. The last time I talked with your mother she said that you don't use the name Iowaka much. Which do you prefer me to call you? Iowaka or Ashley?"

"They call me Ashley in England. I use it for mail, banking and most everything else. I'll still use Iowaka if I detect resentment from a person because of my race. It may be childish but I feel better when I do it. You may call me whichever one you like."

"I called you Iowaka when we first met. I'd like to continue that. Speaking of banks, do you have enough money to live comfortably?" Dale asked with concern. "If you don't, let me help you. I sold my parent's house in Monson and most of the money is just sitting in a bank. My salary at Great Northern Paper Company is more than I ever spend."

"Thanks for asking, but I'm getting by," she replied. "Mother had a small insurance policy that will provide for Heather and me until her school is completed."

The mention of her daughter caused Dale to ask, "When Heather comes this summer, what should I have her call me? Does she know anything about what happened to you?"

"All she knows is that the invalid soldier we care for is not her father. I've never told her the whole truth. She's a very perceptive and intelligent girl as you'll soon find out. I must confess, I really don't know the best way to handle the situation. What do you think?"

"My gut feeling is that a child who is loved and nurtured can accept anything if they're told the truth. On the other hand, if she were to search out Landers it could be calamitous for her and for you. I have a suggestion. Why don't you tell her that I'm her father? As long as she's a part of you I can love and cherish her like a father and she'll never know the difference."

"I don't know, Dale. What would we say to her about your absence for all those years?"

Dale brooded for a moment. "You're right, lies beget more lies, and quickly become complicated, besides, living a lie is never comfortable or fair to anyone."

"I think I'll tell her the truth about Landers and you. The truth may hurt her at first but in the end, it's the only way. Maybe we could simply tell her the truth without divulging his name. As long as he remains anonymous, she won't be trying to locate him."

"I think you're right on that. Who else knows his name besides me?" asked Dale.

"No one. I never told my friends at nursing school."

"Then that's it. It'll remain our secret."

"You know," Iowaka continued. "You have a talent for making large problems seem much smaller, Dale Cooper. It makes you easy to love. When I saw you tonight with Lenore, I must confess, I was jealous. She's so beautiful and so desirable. I thought I had missed my chance with you. I wanted to tear her out of your arms and take her place."

He smiled at her. "I detected a hint of displeasure. You have nothing to fear from Lenore. We were finished a long time ago. Yes, she is pretty, but you my dear, have a timeless beauty, greater than anybody I've ever met. I saw that the first time I laid eyes on you. Your inner grace shines through everything you do. Don't sell yourself short, Ashley Huntington."

"Thank you for saying that," she answered shyly.

"Now, when was the last time you had something to eat?" asked Dale.

Iowaka laughed. "I can't remember. My stomach has been tied in knots all the way over on the boat. I was expecting to find you married or angry enough to reject me once and for all. Come to think of it, I'm a little hungry now."

"Me too," said Dale. "I was planning to have a bite to eat at the reunion, but then I got sidetracked by an old friend." They smiled at each other. "Let's see, I've got some fresh water salmon all cleaned and ready for the frying pan. What do you say if I fix us a late evening meal?"

She beamed at him. "It's so wonderful being here with you. I haven't seen the inside of the cabin yet. You'll never know how often I've dreamed of us being together here."

Dale gave her a tour of the renovations. The main portion of the cabin was much as she remembered it. He had wired it for electricity, and had installed a bottled gas cooking range in place of the old dry sink. Iowaka was impressed with the new bathroom and congratulated him on his neat housekeeping. The two new bedrooms were bright and cheerful. The cabin had retained that same relaxing charm that had made her feel welcome so long ago.

The supper that Dale fixed consisted of salmon garnished with sliced pineapple, steamed rice and string beans. The dessert was simple like the last bars of a symphony, fresh coffee and sweet Finnish boulla rolls. Iowaka occupied herself at his desk beside the fireplace looking at photo albums while Dale insisted on doing the meal.

"Come and get it," he announced when everything was ready. "You know how good chefs get angry when their food isn't eaten while it's still hot." He laughed out loud. It was the first time he had done that in a long time.

Iowaka smiled and laughed with him. "You're going to spoil me. It looks delicious, Dale."

They ate everything he prepared and lingered over their coffee. Ashley glanced often at the loft. When they had finished eating she walked over and climbed the ladder to reassure herself that it was the same as she remembered. She sat on the soft feather mattress and continued. "I'll always remember what you said to me that night. 'You are safe here. I pledge my word and my honor as an officer. You are a guest in this cabin, not a captive, and I will protect you from any possible harm.' I can't tell you how comforting those words were to me. I think that's when I started to fall in love with you, Dale Cooper."

Dale climbed into the loft and sat beside her. "I can still picture the way you were with your flashing bright eyes and black hair done up in braids. You were a vision of loveliness, Iowaka. My heart went out to you then, and it's still yours."

"Tonight I've started living again," she said her eyes running over with tears. "The first day of a new future for both of us. Let's celebrate it by being together in the loft."

That night, their love for each other bonded them as one. They were together at last!

Chapter Nineteen

The morning sun cast warm rays through the small window above the loft announcing a new day. Dale held Iowaka in his arms. The sunlight glistened off her black hair. He had been awake since before sunrise listening to her gentle breathing. He moved slightly, and she opened her eyes and smiled.

"Good morning," Dale whispered. "A new day awaits us, my love. I'm so thankful you came to me. Any regrets?"

"Of course not," she answered, touching his lips with her fingers. "I love you so much it almost frightens me."

"None of that now," cautioned Dale, as he started to make his way down from the loft. "How about some hot coffee and boulla rolls for breakfast?"

"That sounds wonderful. I hate to say it, Dale, but I've got to catch the two-thirty train out of Greenville for Montreal. When I leave I'll have beautiful memories to sustain me until we can finally be together permanently."

The day went by quickly. Iowaka's train schedule injected an element of urgency to their remaining time together. Still, they seriously discussed the future and methodically planned what was ahead. They agreed to write frequently and to call on the telephone when possible. She suggested that Dale initiate the phone calls between 7:00 to 8:00 PM, London time, when she could speak privately with him.

Dale took Iowaka to the boarding house where she had left an overnight bag. From there, they headed on to the train station which was close by. Parting, after years of separation, was not going to be easy.

"Train stations can be such sad places," she said, making sure her beret was fitted correctly. Dale was so proud of her. Her soft black hair fell loose about her shoulders complementing her bronze complexion and dark eyes. The rakishly tilted maroon beret gave her a little-girl look.

"I hate good-byes, too," Dale answered.

"You look very nice in your civilian clothes, but you are simply smashing in your uniform, Dale Cooper." Sometimes Iowaka used expressions she had picked up in England, and they brought a smile to his lips.

"Flattery will get you everything," he laughed, squeezing her hand. When they heard the train nearing the station, he leaned close to her and said, "I'll wait for you, dear lady. God has answered our prayers and promised us a future. I'm going to hold Him to that promise. I love you, Iowaka." He kissed her and held her so hard he was afraid of hurting her.

"I love you too, Dale. I don't know what I would have done if I'd found you with someone else. Tell me again that you forgive me," she whispered with trembling lips.

"I forgive you, but in reality, no forgiveness is needed. I'm a lucky man to be loved by a woman like you," he answered, picking up her bag and placing it on the train transom where the conductor carried it inside the car. "I hope you have a nice trip. I'm looking forward to having Heather for a visit. I love you, until next time." Iowaka boarded the train and took a seat next to the window. She continued to wave until the car was out of sight.

There was something he was determined to do that would help alleviate the loneliness that gripped him, and it was better done sooner than later. Dale could not recall seeing Joe Landers since their confrontation at the restaurant years ago. He checked with the owner of one of the local automobile service stations. He needed gasoline anyway and pulled up to the pump. While the owner was filling the tank Dale inquired whether he knew anything about a Joe Landers.

"I remember him," the man replied. "He was a troublemaker in his younger days. I hadn't thought much about him until you asked, Dale, but I did see him at the bar out at the Junction not too long ago. Your Ford still looks like new. Let me know when you want to sell it."

"Not for awhile," grinned Dale, pleased to have a lead to chase down. "I'll be in for a grease job and an oil change next week."

The saloon at Greenville Junction was a popular hangout for local workers. Dale decided to watch the establishment until Landers showed up, regardless of how long it took. He was not anxious to inquire anymore about Landers in case the word got around to him. It was a small town and talk traveled fast. Dale had a sandwich and a cup of soup at a restaurant close to the saloon to kill some time. Chances were good that Landers would not show up until after dark anyway. Dale did not want the yellow Ford to be too conspicuous so he parked it across the street near the entrance to a large veneer turning mill close enough for him to see the people entering the saloon. Then he went inside the bar to check if Landers was already there. He was not, so Dale returned to wait in his car.

Dale's patience was rewarded at about nine o'clock, when Landers showed up with a female escort and went inside the saloon. He checked his watch and waited twenty minutes before entering the tavern. The dark interior made it difficult to identify people, so he lingered at the bar with a glass of beer until his eyes became better adjusted to the limited light. He located Landers at a table with his back to the wall. His companion had her back to the entrance blocking Landers' view of people entering the saloon; consequently, he had not noticed Dale at the bar. The saloon was relatively empty, which suited Dale just fine, and walked directly to Lander's table. He recognized Dale immediately and sneered.

"Mr. Landers, I presume," announced Dale. "I have a proposition for you. You can either call the sheriff and turn yourself in or come outside with me. It's your choice."

"I ain't calling no cops for you or anybody else, you son-of-a-bitch."

Dale stepped into the table and shoved it against Lander's chest pinning him against the wall. "Remember what I told you a long time ago? Send the lady home and step outside, otherwise I'm going to dog your worthless hide every second of every day. If you decide to involve some of your friends then I'll call the police myself. One way or another, it's pay-back time, buddy boy." Landers saw the look in Dale's eyes and knew that he was serious.

"I don't need anybody to help me," boasted Landers. "I'll see you in the parking lot across the street in a few minutes."

"I'll be waiting." Dale turned and walked out of the saloon. He knew that he was taking the law into his own hands and that fact carried some risk, but he was willing to chance it. Justice was long overdue. What he had in mind was just payment for the thirteen years of hell that Landers had inflicted upon Iowaka.

Landers walked across the street with an aggravated swagger and called out to Dale. "I'm over here."

"This is between you and me Landers and we both know what it's all about, so I promise you there will be no quarter given as far as I'm concerned, nor do I expect any different from you."

They walked deeper into the parking lot where it was darker. Dale initiated the first contact by slapping Landers hard across the face with the palm of his hand. Landers, stunned by the ferocity of the blow, was enraged. "I'll get you for that you bastard!"

They danced around each other several times, each looking for an opening. The lights from the nearby buildings offered some illumination but created shadows, making it difficult to distinguish clear images. Dale was the first to strike. He put every ounce of his weight and strength into a hard right to Landers' stomach causing the man to double over in pain. Then Dale solidly positioned himself for a powerful uppercut to

Landers' chin which flung him backwards, momentarily unbalanced. Seizing the moment, Dale grabbed him by the shoulders to hold him upright and delivered a swift knee jerk to Landers' groin, dropping him to his knees like a sack of feed.

Dale backed off and watched Landers. "I've got a message for you, Landers. Do you hear me?" Landers shook his head in acknowledgment. "I'm warning you, leave this area of Maine or I'll kill you with my bare hands. Do you hear me?"

"You son-of-a-bitch," cursed Landers dragging himself to his feet and leaping towards Dale. Dale anticipated the move and blocked it with his shoulder grabbing Landers by the arm, spinning him around and stopping him with a quick karate chop to the throat. While Landers was falling, Dale gave him another powerful knee jab to his groin, intentionally trying to injure him. This time Landers collapsed with a cry of pain.

"Now, let's go through this again tough guy. You clear out or I'll make good on my threat. Do you read me?" Dale asked again in a slow precise voice.

Landers laid on the ground and answered with a single word, "Yes." The voice was filled with rage and hate but Dale felt certain that the coward would comply with the demand.

"Remember, I'll be checking on you to make sure that you're gone," Dale warned. "I'd better not see you around."

Dale started the Ford and drove a block down the street pulling into a side street to park the car in a dark area with shade trees. He walked stealthily to the parking lot, taking care to remain in the shadows. From a distance, he observed that Landers was being helped across the street by his woman friend. She had trouble getting him into the car. Dale turned away, satisfied that what had taken place was not widely advertised. He was not proud of what he had done and derived no pleasure in hurting another human being, but he did feel justified in making certain that Landers paid some retribution for his assault on Ashley.

A week after Ashley left Greenville, Dale returned to the train station. Ed and his wife Tasha and their children were coming for their annual summer visit. Their two children, fourteen-year-old Jon and twelve-year-old Linda were accompanied by Ashley's twelve-year-old daughter, Heather. Dale eagerly watched them file off of the train. Ed always looked the same. His quiet, easy going nature never seemed to change. His wife Tasha was shorter than Ed and a bundle of energy, filled with an enthusiasm and wonder for life. She and Ed perfectly complimented each other.

Jon was a tall lanky young man still in the awkward and uncoordinated stage of adolescence. He was well-behaved and worked enthusiastically with his father. Linda resembled her mother in personality, but physically, she looked more like her father than Jon did. She had a ready smile and was curious about everything. She talked more than the rest of the family members combined. Dale watched Heather step from the train with special interest. She seemed quite shy and uncertain of what to expect. Dale was amazed at how much she resembled Iowaka. She was slightly darker in complexion than her mother but their facial features were very similar. Dale knew instantly that he could love this child!

Dale welcomed Ed and Tasha with warm hugs. Jon was shy about being hugged by another man so Dale shook his hand. Linda, in contrast, leaped eagerly into Dale's arms and gave him a kiss on the cheek. Both children greatly anticipated their annual excursion to his cabin on the lake, and Dale looked forward to it as well. In fact, it served as the highlight of his year, a time when the cabin sprang to life and was filled with laughter and fellowship.

"The third member of the clan is a young lady you haven't met, Dale," Ed announced, holding Heather by her shoulders. "Dale, this is Heather Huntington. Heather, this is your Uncle Dale Cooper. The kids call him Uncle C."

"Hello, Heather," Dale welcomed her warmly. "I'm glad that you'll be spending some time with us at the lake. Is this your first visit to the United States?"

"Yes, Sir," answered Heather, in a clipped English accent. "My mother has told me about you. Linda and Jon said that your cabin was a most beautiful place."

Dale smiled. "Well, I think it is too, but you can determine that for yourself when we get there. Well gang, let's collect your luggage and head for the cabin. I hope we can all fit in the Ford. Who wants to ride in the rumble seat?"

"Maybe I should ride in the rumble seat between Linda and Jon to keep the peace," volunteered Ed, grabbing a couple of the suitcases from the baggage cart.

They strapped the four suitcases onto the rear luggage rack of the Model A and climbed aboard. Tasha and Heather rode inside with Dale. He rolled down the rear window so that the rumble seat passengers could also be part of the conversation.

"Ashley left for England three days ago," Tasha told Dale. "Heather is going to stay with us for the summer. Ashley thought it would be a good idea for her to better understand and appreciate her Cree roots." Tasha placed a loving arm around her niece. "This is her first time away from home and she's feeling a little homesick right now."

"I remember when I left home for school. The first months were terribly difficult," said Dale. "As soon as your mother gets to England you may call her as often as you like, Heather. We have a phone at the cabin. If there's anything you need, just let me know."

"Mother told me the same thing. You're not a Cree Indian are you Mr. C?" asked Heather with interest.

"No, I'm not, Heather. Those who do have Cree blood, like your mother, Aunt Tasha, and Uncle Ed, should hold their heads high and be proud of their rich heritage and legacy of courage and determination that have sustained them for many generations in a harsh but beautiful environment."

"Then why do some people not like us?"

Dale glanced at Tasha to see if she wanted to try and answer the complex question. "You have to understand, Honey," Tasha sighed. "Some people just enjoy being difficult and many don't like themselves very much. People who belittle others of a different race or nationality are simply trying to elevate their own self-esteem because it makes them feel superior. That's what's at the heart of all racism. So when you encounter it, do your best to just turn your back on it, and try to ignore or forget it if you can. There are good and bad people in every race and most people the world over are pretty much the same. British mothers and fathers want the same things for their families that your Uncle Ed and I want, health, happiness, and prosperity."

"I couldn't have said it better, Tasha," Dale quietly agreed, turning the Model A into his long driveway.

It took a while to settle everybody into the cabin. Dale had already prepared a meal for the group, knowing that they would be hungry and weary from the trip, so he had made a large macaroni and cheese casserole that only needed to be reheated. Within a short time, everyone had eaten their fill. Heather and Linda retreated to the loft. Dale had set up three cots on the porch for himself, Jon, and Nakota, Rachel and Gregory's son, who would be arriving in a few days. After the children had settled down for the night, the adults relaxed around the kitchen table and spoke in hushed tones about events of the past year.

"I want to tell you that I knew about Ashley's situation from the very beginning," Ed revealed, hoping that Dale would appreciate the awkwardness of the position he had been placed in. "You'll never know how often I wanted to tell you, but I'd promised Ashley. I apologize for carrying a promise of silence to such an extreme, Dale. I knew that the knowledge I possessed would have given you some hope. I'm sorry my friend."

"Iowaka told me, Ed. I appreciate your apology and admire you for keeping your word. Anyway, what's done is done. On my part I should have demanded more of an explanation. My weakness and foolish pride prevented me from doing so. Iowaka should have been better served by my love. I failed her more than anyone else."

"Now, Dale, it's time to follow your own advice about the past," suggested Tasha, patting his arm affectionately.

Dale nodded and continued in a low voice. "The future does look bright. I can handle the next few years. Did Iowaka tell you about our plans?"

"Yes," admitted Ed. "I've never seen her so happy. She told Heather everything. Only the two of you share the secret in your hearts and that's as it should be. All she could talk about was you. When she first arrived in Canada a few days ago she was determined to see you again. I guess she had prepared herself for the worst and was pleasantly surprised."

"It sounds like a fairy tale," said Tasha. "I went to school with Ashley and have known her all my life. She's one of the world's doers and givers and that makes her special."

"I haven't told you that Gregory and Rachel are driving in from New York sometime this week. It'll be great to have the whole gang together again. I hope the weather is favorable for us, but if we have a rainy spell, we can go to the movies. Greenville recently opened a new theater."

"That sounds like fun," commented Ed. "Incidentally, wasn't it generous of Rachel to share the money with us? Now we'll be able to send Jon and Linda to college if they want to go. We'd have found a way without the money, but it will certainly make things a lot easier."

"Yes, I thought it was very nice of them. If you remember, Rachel wanted to share the gold with us before she left the wilderness tract," Dale responded. However, his thoughts were elsewhere. "Ed, I don't want to pry or have you violate any confidences but do you know how Iowaka gets by financially?"

"I think she has a hard time of it," Ed replied immediately. "Her mother left a little insurance money, and she basically gets room and board for her and Heather in London, in return for taking care of Ronald."

"Even if she was destitute, she'd never let you know," added Tasha.

"You're right Tasha, that would be her way," said Dale, glancing at the clock on the wall. It was near midnight. "What do you say we turn in for the night? You two must be tired."

"Sounds good to me," Ed replied. Tasha's reply was a yawn.

Days went by quickly at the Lake of Three Sorrows. The children spent much of their time swimming or canoeing, and the weather remained warm and sunny for the most part. One day they all crossed the lake and went blueberry and raspberry picking in the old burned area directly across from the cabin, where they collectively picked two ten-quart pails full of raspberries and blueberries. When the children returned to the cabin, they were given a choice: fish or blueberry pancakes for supper. Blueberry pancakes were the unanimous choice.

Tasha made up the batter and tended a large pan of sausage links, while Dale was kept busy flipping pancakes in two large cast iron frying pans. Ed served the ravenous children astounded at the vast amount of food they could consume. Just as he was prepared to cut them off, they declared themselves full and bolted out the door to run off the stored energy. Then, the adults sat down and ate a leisurely meal without being interrupted by the kids.

Linda and Jon included Heather in everything they did. The girls seemed to get along well. Still, Dale noticed that Heather was not joining in the events with the same enthusiasm as the others. One morning the three children returned from a walk around the northern half of the lake and were resting on the porch. The swinging couch was a favorite place to sit and watch the water. Heather sat quietly with her cousins for awhile and then walked off by herself, down to the wooden dock where she sat and dangled her bare feet in the lake.

"Do you mind if I join you, young lady?" Dale asked casually taking off his shoes and slowly placing his feet in the cool water. He realized that she had been crying and was concerned. "Heather, is anything wrong?"

"No," she answered, turning her head away to hide her face from him.

"Do you miss your mother? If so, that's very natural. I can understand why. We haven't had much of a chance to talk since you arrived, but I want you to know that I would do anything to make you feel at home here with us."

"It's not you or the others," explained Heather reluctantly. "All of you have been kind to me. I have never been away from my mother and I miss her, that's all."

"Of course you do. Your mother is a remarkable lady and you must be very proud of her. I am, and I miss her too. Has she told you much about me?"

"She told me that you were going to get married when I turn sixteen."

Dale smiled. "That's right. I love her with all my heart, and I will love you the same way because you're a part of her."

"You're not my father are you?"

"No, I'm not, Heather, but that has nothing to do with my love for you or your mother. Believe me, you are loved by more people than many children. You're not alone in this world." Dale searched for persuasive arguments.

"That doesn't change the fact that I'm a bastard child," she responded forcefully.

"Who told you that?" Dale demanded sharply.

"Since my mother told me what happened to her, I've been wondering who my father is. I've always known that Ronald was not my real father. Sometimes I'm confused about who I am," Heather explained with a sad look on her face.

"Come here, Heather." Dale took her into his strong arms. "Let me help you with who you are my dear girl. Proud Cree blood has been blended with the English blood of your grandfather, a professional engineer, to produce your mother, one of the most beautiful persons that ever lived. You're a product of her womb and have been nurtured by the same values that make her the remarkable woman she is. No child has a legacy any richer than yours. You've been blessed with your mother's beauty, intelligence, and wisdom. I'd say you have a lot to be proud of. So if you're feeling inadequate or inferior to others, then dismiss those bad thoughts. Let the world see what a wonderful person you really are, listen to your heart. You're unique. There's only one Heather Huntington in the world, isn't that a blessed thing?"

"My mother tells me things like that."

"Your mother is right. I know that your mother and I are not married now, but that doesn't mean that I can't love you and be responsible for your safety and happiness. Will you let me be your father in spirit until I marry your mother?"

"Yes!" she whispered embracing him tearfully.

"I pledge that I will always be there for you, whenever you need me, Heather. I've lived alone too long and I look forward to sharing my life with you and your mom. Holding you like this warms my heart. I'm so thankful you came to visit with us. Now, I have a question to ask you young lady."

"What's the question?" she asked curiously, pulling herself free of his embrace. Her eyes were bright and moist, and a smile was poised on her lips.

"I'd like to do something special to celebrate my commitment to you and your mother. Is there anything that I could do to make your visit with me a happier one? If it's in my power, I promise to grant your wish, so think hard about it and let me know."

Heather didn't hesitate. "There is something I would cherish, but I know it's too expensive…"

"Tell me, Heather."

"I'd love to have a piano!"

Chapter Twenty

"A piano," Dale repeated, surprised at her request. "Do you know how to play one?"

"Yes, I've been taking lessons since I was five years old. Ronald has a piano at his house, and I play it a lot. He likes music. Mother has been teaching herself to play and is doing very well, too. I'm sorry, it was selfish of me to ask, a piano is too extravagant. Mother would be angry with me if she knew."

"Let me see your hands," Dale asked, with an amused smile. Her delicate fingers were strong and supple. "Your hands look like those of a piano player. I think it's wonderful. Music enriches our lives and raises our spirits. I'll see what I can do," promised Dale.

"Here come Jon and Linda!" noticed Heather, looking past Dale towards the cabin. The Blake children rapidly trotted out onto the dock.

"Hey, kids" Dale greeted them. "Your father has been digging worms in the garden behind the cabin. How would you like to try your luck at some fishing? I've been getting some big lake trout and whitefish lately."

"Do you have a fishing pole?" asked Jon, scanning the edge of the lake for a shady fishing spot.

"Come on up to the woodshed and we'll see what we can make up for lines. Your father has a can of worms stashed in the shed. Maybe you can catch supper for us," Dale proposed, leading the children to the shed.

Fishing poles and gear were neatly stored on some shelves in the shed. Dale supplied each of them with a pole, fish line, and reels. They then headed for the lake. Jon volunteered to show the girls how it was done. Dale hurried inside the cabin and made a phone call to Mr. Olman in Monson. A few minutes later, he intercepted Tasha.

"Would you mind watching the kids while Ed and I go to town for a few hours?" Dale asked her.

"No, of course not. They look like they're enjoying their fishing right now."

He hurried out to the garden. "Ed," called Dale. "Would you like to run an errand with me?"

"Sure, what's the occasion?" asked Ed.

"I'll tell you later on the road. It's a surprise for everyone, but especially Heather."

"I like surprises. Just let me wash my hands and I'll be right with you."

Dale and Ed drove to Monson and stopped at Mr. Olman's house. A truck was already backed up to the barn door, and three young men were waiting for them. When Dale sold his parent's house in Monson he had retained some family heirlooms, and stored them in the Olman's large barn. One of those items was a piano that his mother used to play. Mrs. Olman told him that it was still in perfect tune.

The three men had positioned sturdy planks from the floor of the barn to the bed of the truck. Within a short time the piano was loaded into the truck body and secured for the trip to the cabin. They also loaded the piano bench which contained a large collection of music books and sheet music.

The movers followed Dale's car back to the cabin. They used the same planks to roll the piano onto the porch. Dale measured the door and found that it was too narrow, so he and Ed removed enough of the jamb to allow the piano to pass through the doorway into the great room.

The children were still fishing, but when they saw the truck backed to the porch they came running wondering what was going on. The piano and bench were padded with heavy blankets so that they could not see what was being carried into the cabin. Dale watched the expression on Heather's face. She knew what it was, and she clapped her hands and jumped up and down like a small child with her first toy.

The men pushed the piano against the wall directly beneath the loft and removed the blankets. The piano was an old one in almost new condition. Dale's mother had meticulously cared for it and polished it often while he was growing up.

"It's so beautiful," exclaimed Heather throwing her arms around Dale's neck. "Thank you, thank you!"

"This piano belonged to my mother and I hereby bequeath it to you, dear girl. All I ask is that you fill this place with music. You'll find an assortment of song books and sheet music in the bench storage space," Dale lifted the top of the bench.

Heather recognized several of the song books and placed a few on the music rack. Dale positioned the bench for her and lifted the keyboard cover. She ran her sensitive fingers over the keyboard and was transformed from a twelve-year-old to a devoted musician. She began with *Chopin's Polonaise* and instantly became a part of what she was playing, feeling the sorrow, pathos, and beauty of the selection. She played with precision and passion, immersing everyone in the music, moving them by her interpretation.

Dale listened with pride and wonder at the child's ability to execute complex passages with apparent ease. He saw happiness, even rapture on her face, and his eyes misted over. Heather looked at him and knew what was in his heart. The power of music had bonded them emotionally and spiritually. It was a special moment in their lives. She stopped playing and reached out to grasp him around the neck, for she too was moved by the experience.

"Thank you for doing this for me," she cried, feeling secure in the strong arms that held her.

"I'm glad that you've come into my life. I promise to love and care for you, Heather. You're never going to be alone as long as I'm around."

For the duration of her stay at the lake, Heather fulfilled Dale's wishes to fill the cabin with music. She loved all types of music including the popular songs of the period, but it was evident that she was most partial to the classics of Rachmaninoff and Mozart, playing them with a skill and sense of timing remarkable for a twelve-year-old. The notes wafted through the sturdy log cabin blending with the wind gently passing through the giant pine trees that surrounded it. Songbirds perched outside offered their replies to the *Whiffinpoof Song, Harbor Lights, Clair de Lune,* and other melodies creating a magical harmony of sound that took on a life of its own.

Two days later, Gregory and Rachel arrived with their fifteen-year-old son Charles, filling the cabin to capacity. Charles promptly announced that he preferred to be called 'Chuck' instead of Charles which, in his opinion, sounded like a butler. Chuck, Jon, and Dale slept on the porch which Dale had partitioned by hanging several colorful Hudson Bay blankets. A festive atmosphere prevailed for the duration of the summer. Activities varied daily, but swimming, fishing, and canoeing were favored events along with softball. Dale had laid out a playing field on the flat area at the top of the knoll behind the cabin where they played part of every day.

The feeding of nine hungry mouths proceeded smoothly. Dale ran the operation as if it were Army quarters. He had prepared a large number of menus and stockpiled enough food to last the duration of the visits. Fresh milk, butter, and eggs were delivered daily to the doorstep. Each day, one of the children was assigned the task of helping in the kitchen and the house with cleaning, laundry, and food preparation. The children alternated so that every fourth day was a chore day as contrasted to a play day. The adults shared their work so that no single person had to do it all.

In addition, they took day trips to various parts of Moosehead Lake and the surrounding areas. The kid's favorite was a trip to the Ripogenus Dam, north of Kokadjo, on land owned by the Great Northern Paper Company. There, they watched thousands of logs hurtling through the sluice gates on their way to Millinocket, thirty miles away, where they would be ground into pulp for papermaking. On several rainy days, they went to the movies. *Little Women* with Katherine Hepburn and David Cooperfield was an acclaimed success with children and adults alike. There was never a problem finding fun and interesting things to do.

Dale's guests planned to leave the first week in August. To his surprise, Heather asked if she could stay with him until it was time for her to return to England the first of September. Dale enthusiastically granted her request. He had already promised to accompany her on the return trip across the Atlantic. On a sunny day in August the Blakes and the Nelsons departed with tearful good-byes and promises to return. That evening, after everybody had gone, the cabin seemed quiet. Heather played the piano while Dale relaxed on the porch listening to the music. His thoughts were of Iowaka so far away and he yearned to hear her voice once again. Checking his watch, Dale called to Heather.

"What do you say if we call your mother? She doesn't know that you're staying with me until you leave on the boat."

"Yes, I'd like to talk to her. It seems like a long time since I've seen her," Heather replied happily.

"Okay then, you place the call and I'll talk with her after you two are done." Dale watched her take a seat at the small phone table.

It amazed him at how mature and alert she was for her age. She had gotten along well with the other children despite never having met them before. Dale also noticed a difference, over the summer, in her attitude toward her Cree heritage. She had observed her three companions of the summer who were comfortable with their backgrounds. That gave her a more secure sense of belonging to something unique. It seemed to satisfy the doubts she had harbored when she first arrived from England, and never mentioned it again.

"The phone is ringing," exclaimed Heather. "Hello, Mother, it's me, Heather." She chatted enthusiastically about the piano and things they had done during the past month, adding that she was staying with Dale a few weeks. "Good-bye Mom, I love you and miss you," she said before passing the phone to Dale.

"Hello, Iowaka," Dale greeted her.

"Hi, Dale. It's so nice to hear your voice. Heather sounds happy and content. Thank you for taking such good care of her."

"She's a precious girl, just like her mother, how could I not love her? By the way, I plan to accompany Heather back to London on the boat. Maybe I can see you for a little while at that time."

"That would be wonderful, Dale. We'll have to be discreet in our meeting, but I do want to see you again. Are you sure it's not too expensive for you to make the trip?"

"It's only money," he replied. "Besides, I wouldn't feel right sending her alone across the Atlantic. We've had such a great time this summer that I'd like to prolong our time together. The music Heather has brought to the cabin has been amazing. She told me that you're learning to play, also."

"I can assure you that her level of competence is far greater than mine. Heather even surprises her music teacher here. It was so generous of you to install a piano for her, Dale. How I wish I were there with you two right now. I'm afraid these four years will be long for me," she sighed. "I do love you, Dale Cooper. When I think of all those wasted years, I get so frustrated at myself."

Dale understood her regrets. "Maybe it was a test the good Lord gave us to measure the depth of our commitment to each other. Anyway, those years are over now and the future holds great things for the three of us. It won't be long before we see you on the boat docks in London. Good-bye. I love you more each day, Iowaka."

"Me too, Dale. Thank you for making my day brighter. Give Heather a big hug for me. I'll be counting the days, good-bye."

Dale hung up the phone and walked onto the porch. The final rays of the setting sun reflected off the water. He was content and a warm satisfying glow filled his heart. For years his life had been filled with torment and mind-numbing repetition without any hope of the next day being different from the one he had already experienced. Now, the future promised to be the happiest time of all.

"You're quiet tonight," observed Heather, taking a seat next to him on the swing. "Are you missing my mother?"

Dale smiled at her. "Yes, and I'm also counting my blessings and thinking about how lucky I am. You're one of my blessings, Heather, and so is your mother. Every time I look at you I see your mother and the proud way she holds her head and looks at the world."

"I know, I miss her too," Heather said in a soft voice. "She sounded a bit tired today. She works hard and asks for very little from the Huntington family. I'm only a child and even I can see that."

Dale frowned. "If I had my way, I'd take her out of that apartment and spend the rest of my life taking care of you and her. A man needs to be able to share his life with the one he loves," Dale confided, putting his arm over her shoulder.

"Do Uncle Gregg and Aunt Rachel know my mother?" Heather asked curiously.

"Your Aunt Rachel does. They became good friends in Canada. Uncle Gregory has never met her but I've talked a lot about her to him."

"Is Uncle Gregg a soldier like you?"

"Yes, he was my commanding officer during the war. We became close friends when we were stationed in France." A thought came to Dale. "Say, I've got an idea. How would you like to visit the National Guard Armory where I'm attached? I could show you our training complex and some of the equipment used by my company."

"That would be exciting," replied Heather. "I've never been to an armory before."

"We could make a day out of it," Dale said, his enthusiasm growing. "I'll also show you around Monson where I grew up. Maybe we'll run into some of my old friends."

"I'd like that," answered Heather in her clipped British accent. Dale squeezed her affectionately.

"Then it's a deal. Hey, you know the water is the warmest at this time of the evening. Do you still have your bathing suit on under the sweatshirt?"

"Yes."

"Then I'll challenge you to a dip. Last one in is a rotten egg!" Dale shouted, untying his shoes and jumping off the porch toward the dock. He started pulling off his sweatshirt on the way and looked back at Heather. She had already shed her sweatshirt and passed him leaping into the water first with a splash. The water was warm but the air was cool as they climbed back on the dock and walked quickly towards the cabin laughing all the way.

"This calls for a cup of hot cocoa. A dip after sunset can be invigorating though," Dale laughed, with his teeth chattering. "I'm not challenging you any more tonight. I've learned my lesson. It's embarrassing to be beaten by a twelve-year-old, you know."

"I'm not just any twelve-year-old," she teased.

"I can't argue with that," Dale grinned, wrapping her in a large thick towel. "I'll go start the cocoa, your Majesty."

They laughed a lot together. Dale assigned her to one of the rooms that their guests had recently vacated and set the teakettle on the gas stove. Minutes later he had steaming mugs of hot cocoa topped with a dollop of marshmallow fluff placed on the table. Heather had changed out of her wet bathing suit into warm flannel pajamas and sat at the table across from Dale.

"Do you remember those cream rolls Aunt Tasha made yesterday?" asked Dale.

"They were yummie. I ate two of them last night."

"Well, I stashed a couple of them in the back of the icebox for some special occasion such as this. Here, we can each have one with our cocoa, compliments of Aunt Tasha." grinned Dale, placing one on a plate in front of Heather.

"These are delicious, aren't they?" she commented with her mouth full of the dessert.

"Would you like to play some songs for me tonight? I have in mind a couple that used to be my favorites, *There's A Gold mine In The Sky* and a wonderful old western song, *Red River Valley.*"

"The melodies are quite easy to play," said Heather recalling the songs. "The lyrics tell a sad story. I like songs that tell a story. I'll play them as soon as I finish the cocoa. Mother warned me to never drink around the piano."

"I think your mom is right!"

Dale sat on the bench beside her and sang the words in a full baritone voice. His family had been enthusiastic singers and he enjoyed it on those songs he was familiar with. Heather accompanied him and joined in on the lyrics while he turned the pages of the song book on the music shelf. They sang both of his requested songs twice.

"One more before we call it a night," explained Dale thumbing through the song book. "Ah, here it is, my all-time favorite: *Londonderry Air.*"

"Ooh, I like that one too. It has a couple of bars in it that give me goose bumps whenever I play them. Mother likes it too. It's a sad story about a soldier going off to war." Heather started on the introduction and paused to ask, "You aren't ever going to be in a war again are you?"

He knew that a pat answer would not satisfy this astute little girl. "We hope not, Heather. Soldiers more than any other people hate war. However, if our country is threatened and our loved ones are in danger, then soldiers like myself are responsible for defending the things we hold dear. But don't worry, young lady, there are no threats on the near horizon."

She did not reply. Dale pointed to the introduction notes on the sheet of music and tapped his finger. Their eyes met, and she smiled just like her mother.

The following week, Heather accompanied Dale to one of his monthly training sessions at the Armory. She watched his company go through intricate marching maneuvers and sat in on some of the instructional classes in tactics and maneuver warfare. She didn't understand everything, and at times she was a little bored, but she was impressed with the seriousness of the training period. On the way home that night she told Dale that if a war were to ever start she wanted to be a nurse like her mother and care for the wounded men.

With that interest in mind, Dale took Heather to Greenville a few days later, to show her the small nurse training school at Greenville Hospital where her mother had studied and became certified. When they left the hospital, Dale drove to Monson. Dale showed her the house where he was born and raised. Then they stopped for a chocolate soda at Hesscock's Drug Store in the center of town. They were talking about going hiking later that day when Lenore walked into the drug store. She noticed Dale right away and stopped at their small table.

"Dale, what a surprise," she announced eyeing Heather with interest.

"Hi, Lenore. I'd like to introduce Miss Heather Huntington. Heather, this is Lenore, a long-time friend of mine. Heather is visiting with me for the summer," he told Lenore. "Her mother is in England."

Lenore smiled. "It's very nice to meet you, Heather. That soda looks good."

"The soda is good. I'm glad to know you too," answered Heather politely, entranced by Lenore's long blonde hair.

"I think I saw your mother at the Monson Academy reunion earlier this summer," pressed Lenore hoping for more information.

"Yes, you did. Heather's mother's name is Iowaka," answered Dale gently. Lenore looked disappointed. "Her mother is the one I spoke to you about, Lenore. We plan to marry and I'd like to hope that I have your blessing."

Lenore's smile was bittersweet. "Of course you do, Dale. To be honest, it hurts to hear those words, but nobody deserves happiness more than you do. No matter what happens, your friendship will always mean a lot to me."

"Thanks. By the way, I saw your son the other day. He looks just like you, and he has that same confident walk that Bernie always had. You've done a good job with him."

"He's been the joy of my life, and he gets along well with Gabe, the man I'm seeing now."

"I'm glad to hear it, Lenore."

"I know you really mean that, Dale, thanks. Heather is a lovely girl and resembles her mother. You tell your mother that she's getting the best of the best in Dale and if she ever fails him in any way, I'll personally scratch her eyes out," Lenore's tone was jovial, but Dale knew there was an element of truth in the statement.

"Yes, I'll tell her," answered Heather, anxious to be courteous, but uncertain about how she should react to the warning.

"Well, I have to run. It was nice seeing you again, Dale. Don't take my words too seriously about your mother, Heather. I'm sure she's a wonderful lady and I sincerely wish her and Dale much happiness, and that goes for you, too."

"Thank you," said Heather, watching Lenore leave the drug store. "She's so pretty! Did she used to be your girl friend?"

"Yes," replied Dale reflectively. "A long time ago. I even thought I would marry her, but it did not work out."

Heather looked apprehensive. "I hope nothing interferes with you and mother. She's been sad and lonely for so long. When she told me about you, I saw a look in her eyes that I had never seen before."

"You don't have to worry, dear girl," Dale was touched by her loyalty to Iowaka. "Your Mom and I have a pact with each other and I certainly plan on keeping it."

The warm days of summer passed quickly for Heather and Dale. By mid-August the air was cooler and the first hint of fall could be seen in the yellow poplar leaves on the old burn across the lake from the cabin. On the last day of August, Heather said good-bye to the cabin and the piano and the Lake of Three Sorrows before climbing into Dale's Model A Ford for the trip to the train station.

They traveled to Montreal where Dale booked passage on the steamship Heather would be taking. They had two private rooms connected by a small lounge area. The rooms were small but comfortable and spotlessly clean. The voyage reminded Dale of the first time he sailed for France as part of the American Expedition Army. Fortunately, this trip was under happier circumstances. It was worth any expense to be with Iowaka, even if only for a few hours.

One evening, half way across the Atlantic, Dale and Heather were eating in the ship's dining room, when a steward delivered a telegram from Iowaka to their table. Dale opened the envelope and read the message aloud to Heather:

London,
September 5, 1933

Dear Dale and Heather,
    This is to inform you that Ronald has passed away suddenly. I am released from my commitment and

plan to return with you on the next available ship. At this time of sadness for the Huntington family, I feel guilty for my own happiness. Now our plans for the future can be implemented as soon as we wish…

All my love to you both,
Iowaka and Mother

Chapter Twenty-One

"I'm sorry that Ronald has died," Dale offered, looking for a reaction from Heather. He was reluctant to rejoice over the death of a brave soldier.

Heather looked grave. "Yes, but he was never well. He told me several times that he wanted to die. His mind wandered a lot and he slept for long periods of time. He was kind and gentle. I'll remember him as a good friend," Heather recalled in a sober tone. "Mother frequently worked and nursed him until she was exhausted. To be frank, it was not a situation that made anyone happy. His death is probably for the best."

Dale marveled at her maturity and insight, and was proud of her. He forced himself to remember that the "marriage" to Ronald allowed Iowaka to raise Heather respectably. Still, the fact that no impediments remained to his and Iowaka's future together filled him with unbridled happiness.

Their ship passed through the North Sea to the English Channel and finally, to the port of London where Iowaka was waiting for them at dockside. She spied Heather first and they embraced ecstatically. Tears of joy trickled down her bronze cheeks. Despite her great happiness, Iowaka looked tired and drained. Dale had held back so that they could have their moment alone. Her eyes brightened when she saw him coming down the gangplank.

"You'll never know how thrilled I am to see you again," she cried, throwing herself into his open arms. "It's been so difficult ever since I returned to London at the beginning of the summer. Thank God you're here now."

"Wild horses couldn't have kept me away," grinned Dale, wiping a tear from her cheek and kissing her tenderly. "Each time I see you you're more beautiful. You're still going to marry me, aren't you?"

"Yes, yes," she exclaimed. They reached out to Heather to include her in their embrace. The three hugged and laughed oblivious to the stares of onlookers.

When they had calmed down, Dale asked, "Are you ready to leave London now?"

"Yes, I've packed all of our things in trunks and had them sent to the port authority for shipment. I haven't made any specific arrangements yet."

"Did you still have some doubts?" Dale asked uneasily.

"I confess I did." Iowaka looked ashamed.

"You bad girl," admonished Dale in a lighter mood, giving her a kiss on the forehead. "We'll have to erase those black clouds for good. Now, let's see about making reservations for returning home. What do you think, Heather, are you ready to go back to the cabin?"

"With Mother there, it will be perfect," she replied, glowing all over.

"Then it's settled. We'll head back on the next ship available."

Luck was with them. The next steamer to Boston was leaving London later that very same day. Dale booked passage for a suite with two bedrooms, one for Dale and one for Heather and Iowaka, and made arrangements for their trunks to be picked up. And so, within six hours of arriving in London, the three of them were standing at the rail of the departing ship watching the London skyline fade from view.

Iowaka was quiet and reflective as she bid farewell to England. It was a bittersweet moment filled with conflicting feelings, yet the promise of a life with Dale gladdened her heart. The wisdom of her choice to leave Canada and have her baby in a foreign land would no longer torment her. Whether or not it had been a wise choice no longer mattered. She was grateful to the Huntingtons for their support, but she had always felt like an intruder, more like an employee than a family member. She had no regrets in leaving London.

"This has been an eventful day for everyone," said Dale, noting Iowaka's exhaustion. "Why don't we retire to the suite and have something to eat sent in? Or we can go to the dining room, whichever you prefer, Iowaka."

"I am tired, Dale," she answered appreciating his concern. "The comfort of the suite will be fine."

"Then just let Heather and me take care of you for a change."

"That's right, Mother," Heather added. "I'm so tickled that we're all together."

Dale escorted them to the suite. Iowaka decided to take a brief nap. Heather helped her mother get comfortable while Dale excused himself. He went directly to the bridge and spoke with the Captain for several minutes. The two parted with a handshake. Dale returned to the suite in an exuberant mood with a smile on his face. Heather opened the door for him and quietly pointed to the bedroom. Iowaka was fast asleep. Dale was all smiles and confided to Heather that he had some news to tell her mother once she awoke from her nap.

To everyone's astonishment, Iowaka slept for ten hours straight. Heather wanted to wake her but Dale restrained her. "She needs the rejuvenation that only sleep can give her."

They spent the evening alone, leisurely walking around the large ship and eating in the dining room. Iowaka was still sleeping when they returned. Dale offered Heather his room so that her mother would not be disturbed. He stretched out on the sofa in the lounge. Dale had barely drifted off to sleep when he felt warm lips kissing his eyes. "What a nice way to wake up," he murmured drowsily. "Did you have a good nap?"

"Yes, I certainly did," she replied. "I woke up a while ago. It's still dark outside but the sun is lighting the horizon. There's nothing like a sunrise at sea is there?"

Dale sat up on the sofa. "Iowaka, I have something to discuss with you. I spoke to the Captain last night, and he can marry us at anytime we want. This is an American ship and he has the authority to marry as long as we're in International waters. If you marry me, that will make you an American citizen. What do you say to that?"

"Oh, Dale." Iowaka's dark eyes widened. "It sounds wonderful. A simple quiet ceremony would be lovely. You've made me so happy I'm going to cry. I spoke to Heather before I fell asleep. She's pleased with the idea of us being together. She cares for you a great deal."

"Yes, we've hit it off very well. Are you comfortable with returning to the cabin on Lake of Three Sorrows for now? Heather can go to school in Greenville. If the cabin turns out to be too remote, we can always consider buying a house somewhere else."

"I can't think of any place I'd rather be than at the cabin with you and Heather. That's where our journey first began. Oh, I've dreamed so often of us being there. For years, that dream was all I had to keep me going," Iowaka's expression turned somber. "Please, don't ever leave me, Dale. I don't think I could survive losing you again."

"Well, you have nothing to fear my love. You're stuck with me, like it or not." She slipped into his open arms.

[Eight years later - Summer 1941]

There was an uneasiness in the air that summer of 1941. Europe and Asia were being torn apart by a struggle for survival against the Japanese Empire and the German Blitzkrieg which was encroaching upon England, France, and Russia. In spite of efforts to remain neutral, the United States was irrevocably being drawn into the conflict. The Americans were woefully unprepared for war. The country had again and again delayed mobilizing its armed forces, in the slight hope that the U.S. would never have to enter the fray. The previous war was supposed to have been the one that ended all wars forever. Instead, it spurned a defeated Germany into a mighty military nation that was successfully and unremittingly toppling and occupying weaker European nations one after another. More ships were being sunk by German submarines than were being built in the United States and England combined. The war of attrition at sea was being lost and the future looked grim.

The gloomy national situation impacted the 1941 summer vacation at the Lake of Three Sorrows. While fellowship and laughter were present, it was overshadowed by events beyond the control of the participants. The traditional annual lake vacation had continued ever since Dale and Iowaka were married on the ship that brought them from England. Iowaka was a generous and considerate hostess. She brought grace and order to the home. The love she and Dale shared permeated everything that took place. She approached her role as homemaker with her usual enthusiasm and hard work. Harmony ruled the household.

Dale had continued to work as a forester for the Great Northern Paper Company, where he quickly rose to the responsible position of Woodland Operations Manager for all of the company's forestland holdings in the State of Maine. Everyone who knew Dale had witnessed a change in him after he and Iowaka were married. His step was lighter and the sad distant look in his face had disappeared. He became the same caring and understanding person he had once been. Now, his life evolved around Iowaka and Heather. He was a family man at heart and the two women in his life gave meaning to everything he did.

It didn't take long for the people in Greenville and Monson to realize that Iowaka and Heather had been responsible for the restoration of the Dale they knew. Iowaka and Heather carried their Cree heritage with dignity, and never allowed narrow-minded people to shake their composure. In fact, most of the community accepted them with open hearts and affection. At first, they were known for their physical beauty, but as time passed, they became better appreciated for their understanding and helpfulness to those in need.

Iowaka returned to the Greenville Hospital to become recertified as a Registered Nurse and worked daily at the hospital out-patient-clinic. After Heather and her cousin, Linda, graduated from high school in 1938, they attended the Nursing School at Greenville together and lived with Dale and Iowaka while school was in session.

One day Dale came home with a set of keys for a well-maintained used automobile for Heather's use in commuting back and forth to school. It was a two-toned blue 1936 Ford rumble seat coupe. Dale thought it was the prettiest automobile on the road. Heather was ecstatic and fell in love with it immediately. The next day, before she drove it to Greenville, Dale seriously informed her that it carried a price tag. When she asked him what the cost would be, he grinned and replied, "I'd say it ought to be worth a couple of hours a week playing the songs I select."

"Oh, Father!" she replied, throwing her arms around his neck. "You know I'll play for you anytime you ask! I'm so proud to call you my Father. I hope that when I fall in love, it's with someone as special as you."

"You will, my dear lady, you will." Dale assured her. "Now, about this little Ford coupe... I'll support you in everything you do except for one situation which you'll have to handle on your own."

"On my own?" questioned Heather, releasing him and looking into his laughing eyes.

"That's right if you get a speeding ticket, you'll have to pay for it out of your own pocket. So drive legally young lady. It'll serve you well financially," he chuckled.

"You're teasing me, Father," Heather replied, kissing him on the cheek.

The carefree atmosphere that had prevailed for years at the Lake of Three Sorrows was tempered by sobering world events.

Canada and Great Britain had already declared war against Germany. Ed had joined the Canadian Merchant Marine when he was refused by the Army on the basis of his age, even though he was probably in better physical condition than many of the new recruits. He and Tasha were cutting their annual visit short because he was scheduled to serve on a freighter leaving Quebec City by the end of July. The cold waters of the North Atlantic were the most valuable piece of real estate in the world that summer of 1941. Potentially, England could be conquered if Germany's submarines were successful in stopping a large portion of the shipping that the island nation needed to survive and defend itself.

That summer, there were also conspicuous absences at the annual gathering. It was the first time since they had started the tradition, that Jon and Linda could not attend. Jon had joined the Canadian Army the first of the year as a young second lieutenant. He had recently graduated from the University of Alberta with a degree in Civil Engineering, a degree that made him very desirable to the Army Engineers. Jon was attending the Army combat engineer school that summer and was unable to attend.

Linda had graduated with Heather from the Greenville Nursing School and had returned to Mistassini to work in the infirmary where Iowaka had originally served. However, the scarcity of nurses in the military services created an opportunity where she felt that she could best serve her country and her people by joining the Army. She was now stationed at an Army base in New Brunswick. In her latest letter to Heather, who was working at the Greenville Hospital as a permanent member of the staff, Linda wrote:

Somewhere in,
New Brunswick
July 2, 1941

Dear Heather,

A few words to share some thoughts with you tonight. I can't tell you when we're moving to England but it's imminent. There's a tremendous feeling of urgency and uncertainty among the Canadian troops stationed here. The war is going badly for the Allies. The losses from German U-boats are frightening and I'm worried sick over Dad's volunteering to sail on the merchant ships. There are hundreds of them in the bay close by waiting to be assembled into convoys to England. I noticed several United States Coast Guard cutters acting as escorting gunships for a recently dispatched convoy. I don't know if the United States has declared war or not, but I do know that the Royal Canadian Navy welcomes every bit of help they can get.

I worry a lot about Dad and Jon. I saw Jon a couple of weeks ago in his uniform and hardly recognized him. He really hasn't changed much, except that he's matured into the serious officer we all knew he would be. There was a grimness and determination in his eyes that frightened me.

I wish this crazy war was over and we could all go swimming in the lake again. It was such a fun place to visit every year. After you came back from England it was more fun than ever. I carry those warm memories close to my heart. I think often of you, Heather. It was wonderful to go to school in Greenville with you. Give your parents a hug and kiss for me and tell them that I'd be there with the rest of the gang if I could.

Give my love to everybody, especially Mother if she has not already left. Take care of yourself, Heather.

Love,
Linda

Tasha was noticeably apprehensive that both of her children were now in the Canadian military beyond her protective wing. Now she also had to face the fact that Ed was joining the fight against the enemy and would leave her alone. She found it difficult to hide her fears. Rachel and Iowaka tried to compensate by showering her with love and support, even though they had sinking feelings that their own families were about to dissolve. It was a time when great uncertainty touched every household in the land.

The stability of the world was at stake. Piece by piece, the free nations of the world were overwhelmed by force, until there were very few left capable of opposing the tyranny that was inundating the globe. Dale and Gregory had been working overtime with their National Guard units. They were certain that the United States would be pulled into the conflict one way or another, and they were feverishly trying to prepare their units and their families for that horrible eventuality.

With Linda and Jon gone, Heather and Chuck were the only representatives of the younger generation at the cabin. They spent a lot of time that summer talking about the future. Chuck had just completed his college studies and was teaching at a small town in northern New York. He confided to Heather that if war was to break out, he intended to join the Army Air Corps. He had taken the Reserve Officer Training Corps classes at college and had seriously considered a career in aviation, but ultimately settled for teaching history in a small high school.

Gregory, Rachel, and Chuck had to shorten their stay at the cabin. They left a few days after Tasha returned to Canada. The cabin seemed especially empty after everyone had departed. Dale and Iowaka sat on the porch and were silent for a long time. The gathering at the Lake of Three Sorrows during the summer of 1941 would be remembered primarily for its brevity and for those who were absent. Dale kept a lot of worries to himself, but, as usual, Iowaka knew what he was thinking.

"If there's a war involving the United States, how soon will you be ordered to active status?" she asked directly. "I know that you're thinking about those things and I don't want you to shelter me from what's really going on, Dale. If I had my choice, I'd take you and our friends into the wilderness where nobody could ever find us. I know it's a wild fantasy dream and a very selfish one, yet, I've thought about it. I don't want to be an emotional burden to you, Dale. I can handle whatever comes, and I want to share your fears and concern about the responsibilities ahead of you. You have enough on your mind without pampering me, so please just tell me the truth."

"Well, the truth is, I could be ordered to active status at any hour. My experience in the last war and with the Guard since that time, make me a likely candidate for an early call to duty." Dale paused and looked at Iowaka. "You know that Heather intends to join the Army Nurse Corps, don't you? I didn't try to discourage her when she told me. It wasn't exactly a surprise. Even so, it makes me sick when I think of her serving in a combat zone. I know that we need people like her, but…." His voice wavered and he shut his eyes holding back the tears.

Iowaka embraced him. "Now, my darling husband, you know how we feel about you." A mist formed over her eyes. The harmonious world she had experienced for the past eight years was beginning to crumble. Those she loved more than life itself, were threatened and she was powerless to do anything to stop it.

Chapter Twenty-Two

December 7, 1941 was a sad day for the people of the United States. When the Japanese bombed Pearl Harbor they celebrated their success with abandon. In time, it would prove to be a hollow victory for them. Out of the ashes of death and despair a mighty nation collectively resolved to repay the cowardly act, and a deep sense of retribution and unity of purpose prevailed across the land. As America geared itself for war, the rest of the world was astonished at the country's manufacturing capacity to produce tools and materials needed to defend the concept of liberty. Every family in the country worked toward a common goal, united in their effort to never submit to the tyranny that had spread over much of Asia and Europe. The last hope for the free world was the moral and physical strength of the United States of America, but the costs were high!

That winter, the lonely cabin at the Lake of Three Sorrows sat buried in a sea of snow. The winter of 1941-42 was long and severe, the wind howled across the landscape more intensely than Iowaka had experienced. War had been declared against Germany and Japan, and every American household settled in for the long painful cycle of waiting, hoping, and praying. Long lists of casualties were issued daily by the War Department.

After the bombing of Pearl Harbor, Iowaka sat up all that night making a flag large enough to cover the top half of the cabin's front window. The flag was snow white with a three-inch red border. Iowaka made seven stars, each six inches in diameter from a dark blue piece of felt, and stitched them to the white field of the flag. Each of the blue stars represented one of the members of the armed forces from their small group of family and friends. Each person's name and rank was embroidered in white thread on their star:

> Seaman Edward Blake, Canadian Merchant Marine
> Lieutenant Jon Blake, Canadian Army Engineers
> Lieutenant Linda Blake, Canadian Army Nurse Corps
> Brigadier General Gregory Nelson, U.S. Army
> Lieutenant Charles Nelson, U.S. Army Air Corps
> Major Dale Cooper, U.S. Army
> Lieutenant Heather Cooper, U.S. Army Nurse Corps

Immediately after Dale left for Fort Benning, Georgia, Iowaka accepted a black Labrador retriever puppy, called *Shadow*, from a hospital acquaintance in Greenville. He kept her company and offered some protection against unknown intruders. She spent a lot of time training him to obey voice and arm commands. *Shadow* made her feel more secure, and his companionship was especially welcome on those long winter nights at the cabin's remote location. She was determined to maintain the home exactly as Dale and Heather had left it.

Upon completing a refresher course on infantry tactics at Fort Benning, Dale was promoted to the rank of major and ordered to a regiment as its Executive Officer. To Dale's surprise and pleasure, he learned that Gregory Nelson had been promoted to the rank of brigadier general and was assigned as Assistant Division Commander to the same division. They were a part of the gigantic build-up of infantry divisions from scratch. With the exception of a small nucleus of experienced veterans, these new divisions were filled with raw replacements fresh from the training depots. It was a tribute to their leadership and to the troop's determination and courage that they took on two of the world's most militant nations and defeated them on the field of battle. The American citizen-soldier was a formidable foe in combat and a compassionate caring defender of the rights of oppressed people the world over.

Iowaka received her first letter from Dale a month after the Pearl Harbor bombing.

January 10, 1942

My Darling Wife,

A few lines tonight to let you know that I'm fine and miss you and Heather so very much. I can't tell you where I am or what I'm doing. We had discussed that possibility before I left so it doesn't come as any surprise. Even though you have not heard from me, I've been receiving your letters regularly. They are like a breath of fresh air to my hectic days. I saw Gregg the other day, and though security won't let me give much detail, rest assured that we are training one of the best divisions in the United States Army.

I'm so glad that you have a puppy for companionship at the cabin. I feel better knowing that he is with you. You should have enough firewood to last this heating season. The Great Northern will be short of men in the woods while the war is on, but the plant manager promised me that he would personally see to it that you received a fresh supply of seasoned wood each year. I understand that some of the mills in Canada are placing German and Italian prisoners of war to work in the forests cutting firewood and pulpwood. Perhaps we'll do the same thing as the war continues.

My heart is with you every hour of the day and I miss your soft warm presence more than words can say. I was blessed the day I married you. I'm so glad we waited for each other all those years. I send my love to you by way of the stars tonight. I am taking good care of myself.

Love,
Dale

Iowaka reread the letter two more times so as to not miss anything. Letters were a precious link with loved ones in the armed forces. She wrote to Dale every day, without exception.

The war dragged on month after month and then, year after year. 1942 passed to 1943, and there was still no end in sight. Italy had surrendered to the Allies and on October 13, 1943, she declared war against her former ally, Germany. That, however, did not lessen the fighting in Italy. In fact, the conflict increased in intensity as the Germans reinforced their lines of resistance and refused even more stubbornly to give up ground. In January of 1944, American and British troops landed behind the German lines at Anzio, Italy. The assault was only the beginning of a long and vicious struggle for the Italian peninsula.

Heather was assigned to an Army medical aid battalion that was the first stop for wounded men from the front lines. Her unit operated as close as possible to the combat zone. She was part of a surgical team that operated on the most seriously injured men. Heather's battalion had set up their tents one day after the assault troops had cleared the beaches. She had been on duty in the operating tent for the first twenty-four hours at that location. On the second day ashore, the chief surgeon ordered her to get some rest. She retired to her tent and immediately fell asleep on the folding cot. In her fitful sleep she dreamed of all the unspeakable things that hot jagged metal could do to human flesh. A few hours later, she started a letter to her mother.

Somewhere in Italy
January 28, 1944

Dear Mom,
I hope you'll be able to read my scribbling. I have a few hours to myself before I go back on duty in the operating tent. I have a sinking feeling that this war will never end. You would not believe what some of these young men have had to endure. When I first saw

225

their horrible wounds I wept for hours at a time. I no longer cry for them. There are no more tears left to shed! Most of the soldiers are younger than I am and no matter how badly they are injured, they still ask about their buddies out on the front lines. I am so thankful to be able to make a difference with some of them.

Home seems a long way off right now. How different a world it was when we were all together at the cabin. You'll be glad to learn that for the past couple of days I've been able to see and talk with Linda. She's with a Canadian medic battalion that has set up operations beside our tents. There are a lot of Canadian and British troops fighting on this front with the Americans. Linda looks tired and exhausted like the rest of us, but she was in good spirits. We laughed about some of the good times we had in school together. It was such a pleasant surprise to see her this close to the combat zone. She is terribly worried about her father because she has not heard from him for months.

I received a letter from Dad last week. I don't know where he finds the time to write. The men under his command are fortunate to have him as a leader. He was such a kind and loving father to me, that it's difficult to imagine him as a warrior. I understand now that the strong silent type like him, are the most formidable foe. I pray every night for him to be safe.

No one here at the active end of the battle campaign can ever be sure of what tomorrow will bring. We live from day to day. I don't want you to worry about me. I'm doing what I want to do and when this war is over I'll be anxious to come back home to absorb some of the peace and serenity of our lovely home on the lake. I want you and Father to know that no child could ever be more proud of her parents than I am of the two of you. Thank you, Mother for your courage and dedication to me for all those years in England. I appreciate now how difficult it must have been for you. The love you share with Father has been a wonderful thing to witness. I only hope that I'm blessed with a similar love for a man as worthy as Dad. Until next time, I love you, Mom.

Heather

A few hours after Heather had posted the letter, she was working once again under the bright lights of the operating tent when a heavy German artillery barrage could be heard in the distance. It increased in intensity, drawing closer and closer to the medical compound. Suddenly, the operating tent took a direct hit, instantly killing everyone inside. The nearby Canadian facility was also hit several times and sustained hundreds of casualties. One of the casualties was Lieutenant Linda Blake who died at the side of a seriously wounded soldier. She was patiently feeding soup to him when the shells struck their tent.

Back in Maine, Iowaka had just left the Greenville Hospital. It was just after noon on a bright sunny day. She had been on duty for the past twenty hours and was exhausted. She stopped by the Post Office and checked the box, elated to see letters from Dale, Heather, Tasha and Rachel. Ignoring her impulse to read them immediately she first drove to the cabin where she could sit in front of the fire and take her time to read them in private. Dale's letter was brief and Iowaka was relieved to learn that he was not in combat at that time. He had fought in all of the campaigns through North Africa and Sicily. Now, he was in England, rebuilding and equipping his regiment. "At least he's safe for the time being," she thought thankfully.

Heather's letter gave Iowaka an uneasy feeling. Despite the uncomplaining tone, it unnerved her enough that Iowaka's hands shook as she read it a second time. She placed Heather's letter aside and opened one from Rachel. Upon reading the opening lines, Iowaka became physically ill.

"I am filled with so much pain that I'm not sure I can handle it without going out of my mind. I just received word that Chuck's plane was shot down during a bombing raid over Germany. Those who saw the plane crash claim that no one could have survived it. There were no parachutes visible from the plane as it fell out of formation. He's presumed dead…"

Iowaka's stomach retched. "No, not young Charles," she wept, burying her face in her hands. She remembered the quiet, sensitive young man with the good manners, and mourned that the promise everyone saw in him was lost to the world forever.

Hours later, Iowaka was not sure how long she cried, a strained Iowaka tore open the letter from Tasha praying that it was not bad news. Jon had been wounded in Burma and was on his way back to Canada to recuperate from his wounds. Ed had been ill on his last voyage across the Atlantic and had returned home to Tasha, to spend the duration of the war at her side. Iowaka sighed in relief. Thank God dear Ed and his son Jon had been spared. She continued to read. The words leaped from the page to stab her like a knife to the heart: "Our beloved Linda has been killed in action in Italy…"

Stunned by the news, Iowaka stared out the window at the snow-covered landscape, unable to cry or move. The only relief from the pain came when darkness surrounded her, and she slumped to the floor unconscious.

The next thing Iowaka knew, she was lying on the couch with her head resting on a pillow. As if in a dream, she saw two figures standing over her. One was wearing an Army uniform, and the other she recognized as a young nurse acquaintance from the hospital.

"We found you on the floor," explained the nurse, taking Iowaka's hand to check her pulse. "Are you all right, Mrs. Cooper? You frightened us."

"I feel better now," replied Iowaka, sitting up on the couch and staring boldly at the young soldier.

"I'm Captain Turner, Mrs. Cooper," he introduced himself. "I inquired at the hospital for your address and Miss Hansen agreed to show me where you live."

"What do you want with me?" asked Iowaka. She felt dangerously close to hysteria.

The officer's face was grim. "I have the sad duty of informing you that your daughter, Lieutenant Heather Cooper, has been killed in action in Italy."

It took a second for the words to register. Then a long high pitched wail poured from Iowaka's lips, originating in the deepest recess of her being, filling the cabin with all the pain only a mother was capable of feeling. The product of her womb, a beloved daughter, was lost to her forever, without a chance to say good-bye, or hold her in her arms one last time. News of the tragic loss was beyond her ability to accept. "No, no you've got to be wrong. Not my Heather... It can't be my Heather..."

"I'm so sorry Mrs. Cooper, there's no mistake," said Captain Turner, his voice was sympathetic but firm.

"It isn't fair! It isn't fair" she kept repeating over and over. Shaking off any attempts to console her, Iowaka finally lapsed into complete shock. Nurse Hansen had brought along a mild sedative in case of such a reaction, and administered it to the distraught mother. Captain Turner and Miss Hansen made her as comfortable as possible on the couch.

Iowaka lapsed in and out of consciousness every few hours. Captain Turner had departed, but Miss Hansen remained to spend the night with her. Later, when Iowaka awoke enough to recall what had happened, she began weeping again, uncontrollably, and was shuddering as if she was cold. Miss Hansen administered another dose of the sedative, and Iowaka dropped off to unconsciousness again.

It was a day so filled with sadness that the Heavens masked the sun with dark menacing clouds and the earth became still and silent. Soft flakes of snow started to fall from the sky, as if weeping in sorrow.

Several hours later, the second sedative had worn off. Iowaka saw her young friend asleep in a chair beside the warm stove. The snow was still falling, and as she looked out the window, Iowaka recalled the words Heather had written in her recent letter. "…there are no more tears left to shed…". Iowaka continued to stare out the window even though it was dark. Suddenly, she could see the faces of Heather, Linda, and Chuck smiling and looking back at her. A soft light shone around the images illuminating their faces. They radiated contentment and joy. Iowaka cried out in disbelief and fainted again, consumed with pain.

Chapter Twenty-Three

The letter Iowaka wrote to Dale informing him of Heather's death, and that of Linda and Chuck, was the hardest thing she had ever done. There was no way to be gentle or ease the pain attached to the message. She knew how devastated he would be upon receiving the news, and hated herself for having to inform him.

Depression became a part of Iowaka's life the minute she was notified that Heather would never be coming home. The piano against the wall next to the ladder to the loft was a constant reminder of her loss. Never again would Heather sit at the piano, expressing her joys and sorrows through the music she played. The melodies ran through Iowaka's head day and night, at times so loudly that she turned to see if Heather was sitting there playing. The empty bench eventually became a source of disappointment and torment, until she took it away and placed it in a closet, out of sight.

Iowaka rarely went to work at the hospital. The small staff was concerned, and her coworkers made a habit of checking in on her daily to make sure that she was all right. One of the things that helped her begin to come to terms with the tragedies was the alterations she made to the large flag in the kitchen window. She removed the blue stars for Heather, Linda, and Chuck, substituting them with gold stars edged in black.

Dale and Gregory were relieved of their commands as soon as their division took up a holding position within Germany. Neither of them had been home since the war started and much to their surprise, the Army rapidly rotated them homeward on a priority basis. In April of 1945 Dale called Iowaka from the Dow Air Base in Bangor, and asked her to drive down to pick him up.

The suddenness of Dale's homecoming filled Iowaka with great relief. She needed him now more than ever, and the two hour trip to Bangor seemed an eternity. She thought of the night twelve years ago when she met Dale in Monson after thirteen years of being apart. Ever since then Dale and Heather had been her world. Heather was gone now, and his absence during the war had created an empty void that only he could fill.

The security guard at the Air Base instructed her to park their 1941 Studebaker Champion coupe beside the gate. Shortly, an Army Air Corps sedan pulled up beside her. The driver opened the back door, and a tall uniformed man stepped out of the car. It was Dale! Words failed both of them. Iowaka ran into his outstretched arms with tears flowing down her cheeks. They held each other for a long time. She continued to cry uncontrollably from sadness and from relief that her beloved husband was home, safe from the ravages of war.

"I was afraid I'd never see you again," she cried between sobs. "I need you so much, don't ever leave me."

"You look wonderful, Iowaka," Dale cried, wiping the mist from his eyes. "I won't leave you alone again, I promise. When I think of Heather I almost lose my mind. I never dreamed it could hurt so much and last so long. I loved that girl. I'm so sorry that I was not with you when the bad news came. It must have been hell to face it alone." They continued to cling to each other, their tears intermingling.

At last, Iowaka pulled free of Dale's embrace to look at him. It had been three and a half years since they had seen each other, and Dale had aged. His hair was now totally gray and his face was gaunt and tense. Yet, the most frightening were his eyes. Their deep recesses reflected the horrors he had witnessed. On his shoulders Dale wore two silver eagles, the rank of full colonel, and his chest was covered with ribbons. The one he was most proud of was the Combat Infantryman's Badge at the top of his campaign ribbons. It was a rectangular badge with a blue field and a Kentucky long rifle embossed on the front in silver.

They returned home to the cabin. It was a sad period of adjustment that didn't seem to be working. As glad as they were to be safe and together, their pain continued showing no signs of healing. In desperation Dale suggested that they invite their old friends back to the Lake of Three Sorrows for a memorial reunion. Hopefully, as they acknowledged their mutual losses, treasured memories, and precious echoes from the past, the pain and grief that was crippling them would subside. So Dale and Iowaka sent word to Gregory, Rachel, Ed, Tasha, and Jon that they were reinstating the old tradition of gathering at the cabin on the Lake of Three Sorrows.

The gathering took place on August 14, 1945, the same day that Japan surrendered to the Allies. The symbolism was not lost on anyone. A group of friends from Monson and Greenville had prepared a banquet in honor of this first day of their gathering. The day was warm with a slight breeze, perfect for an outdoor get-together.

Everyone had arrived and soon the banquet was in full swing. Gregory, Dale, and Jon wore their uniforms for the occasion. Dale volunteered to give the first toast. He stood up from his chair, acknowledged the friends around the table, and thanked them for coming. Dale then lifted his eyes to the East across the lake. In the distance, a loon called and its mate offered her melancholy reply. Dale cleared his throat and spoke in a clear resonant voice:

"My dearest friends and most precious wife. We are gathered here to give thanks to the victory the world is now celebrating, and also to remember the empty chairs that grace our table." His eyes overflowed and a tear ran down over his firm jaw falling on the Combat Infantryman's Badge on his chest. Iowaka clasped his hand and squeezed it tight. He continued in a wavering voice with measured words. "Three young lieutenants have given us the best years of their lives. All proud Crees, two of them served the world as nurses comforting the sick and injured. The third was a teacher, with a desire to cultivate young minds. They will remain forever young, and their spirits will always be in our hearts. This blessed victory over tyranny was won with the blood of young people like our beloved trio. Perhaps the price was too high, but who am I to judge the Almighty?"

Dale's tears flowed more freely but his voice remained strong. "I know that I speak for all of you when I ask our Lord to ease the pain in our hearts. We all loved Linda and Chuck and Heather. My love for Heather was special because she filled an empty void in my soul the first time I met her twelve years ago. I'll remember her with an emptiness in my heart whenever I hear a song like Danny Boy being played on a piano. I'll remember her sitting on the dock with her feet dangling in the water as she watched a sunrise with a soft breeze caressing her coal black hair. I see her and hear her and feel her, everywhere. When I listen to the heartbeat of the earth I know her spirit is with us. She is the gentle autumn rain, and the quiet hush of the morning when the dew glistens in the sun. She is the brightest star that shines at night and the quiet calm of a new dawn. She is gone, yet she lives forever in my heart."

The gathered friends lifted their glasses and toasted one another through tear-dimmed eyes, giving thanks for their blessings and for their memories. They gave tribute to the past and honored their dead. All that was left was to embrace the future.

The solemn silence of the heartfelt offering was interrupted by three mournful cries that rose from the dark depths of the lake and echoed across the water....

The End

OTHER BOOKS

BY

Clifton LaBree

Fading Shadows

Fading Shadows is the saga of Glenn Hastings, a severely wounded Medal of Honor recipient in World War II, and his long, tortuous search for fulfillment and happiness.......

Flickering Flame *(Colonial Series Book One)*

A historical novel, about the Cullen family who settled in Portsmouth, New Hampshire, and their participation in events prior to the French and Indian War. Freedom and opportunity were on the march, but it extracted a heavy price. Frontier settlers were ruthlessly killed and butchered by rampaging Indians lead by French officers and Jesuit priests who frequently incited them to greater levels of inhumanity. A peaceful future was in jeopardy and fear gripped the land. A story of love, family and heroism on the colonial frontier.

Raising the Torch - *(Colonial Series Book Two)*

A continuation of the saga from Flickering Flame, Colonial Series book one, of the Cullen family in Colonial Portsmouth, New Hampshire. This is a moving story of love and sacrifice when a small colony had the audacity to fight for independence from their motherland...

NON-Fiction Books

By

Clifton LaBree

NEW HAMPSHIRE'S GENERAL JOHN STARK, LIVE FREE OR DIE: DEATH IS NOT THE GREATEST OF EVILS

A fresh look at one of America's staunchest defenders of liberty and freedom. John Stark was a courageous New Hampshire citizen-soldier who fought in both, the French and Indian War, and the Revolutionary War. His pursuit of leadership excellence on the battlefield distinguished him as one of the most successful combat commanders of the war, and one of the least appreciated.

His selflessness, modest life style, and devotion to the cause of freedom are an inspiration that time has not diminished. He remains today the embodiment of the frugal, independent, and cantankerous New Hampshire Yankee.

GENTLE WARRIOR, GENERAL OLIVER PRINCE SMITH, USMC.

Published by - Kent State University Press. Kent, Ohio, 2001

The Story of one of the United States Marine Corps best General Officers. His flawless performance in Korea is a story that needed to be told.

www.ingramcontent.com/pod-product-compliance
Lightning Source LLC
Chambersburg PA
CBHW072224170626
46813CB00003B/1076